The Luminosity Prize

The Luminosity Prize

Liz Paice

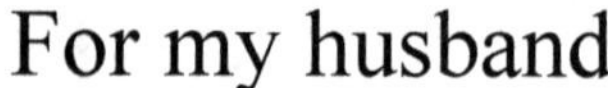

For my husband

Chapter 1

2nd April 2018

What had this badger eaten for supper? Jennie Cliffe needed more natural light in order to be able to tell. She raised the blackout blinds fitted to the laboratory's windows. Sunshine streamed in and glinted off the barrel of the gun lying in front of her on the lab bench. That's better. She lowered her head and peered through the microscope's eyepiece at a slide smeared with a slither of musky-smelling excrement. She adjusted the focus. The remains of several earthworms could now be clearly seen. Her phone pinged. She couldn't resist picking it up. It was the email she had been waiting for.

West Country Universities
(prizes@westcountryuniversities.ac.uk)
Submissions are now open for the Luminosity Prize
awarded annually to the outstanding ecological doctorate
of the year. Closing date 31st March 2019.

Jennie knew that winning the prize would enhance her chances of landing her dream job in wildlife conservation. Her thesis should be finished by the closing date but currently was far from outstanding. A ripple of determination filled her eyes. Somehow, she would find a way to improve it. Her reverie was disturbed by a young dark haired woman dumping a cardboard box next to her. A card was pulled from the pocket of her white lab coat and thrust at Jennie.

'Happy Birthday,' she said.

'Thanks, Sana,' replied Jennie. She opened the envelope and smiled at the cute drawing of a badger on the front but winced at the number twenty-three in large numerals.

'You've personalised it.'

Sana ripped off the Sellotape securing the cardboard box. 'Moonpig,' she said as she lifted out an assortment of tranquillizer darts, ear tags and animal collars.

Jennie picked up one of the animal collars, which had a tiny GPS tracker embedded in it, and fastened the buckle with a click. 'This will be brilliant for mapping the badgers' movements.'

'What did David give you?' asked Sana.

Jennie beamed and angled her head to show off the pair of gold earrings that he had presented her with that morning.

'They're gorgeous,' said Sana, 'he always gives you something nice.' She opened a box of silver labels proclaiming: Property of University of Oakfield - Do not Remove. She started sticking them on to the collars.

Jennie turned back to her microscope. 'They match a necklace he gave me for Christmas. What about the new darts? How long will I have before the tranquiliser wears off?'

'Thirty minutes.'

'Enough time to take a blood sample,' she said. 'Has Dylan proposed yet?'

Sana grimaced. 'He's still saying that he is happy as we are,' she answered. 'But I want to get married. Don't you?'

'Not yet,' said Jennie turning back to her microscope and adjusting the focus again. Her concentration was disturbed by Dr Amina Ahmed, the Head of the Department of Ecology, coming into the lab. In her late thirties, she was dressed in a smart trouser suit and a black headscarf. She stood inside the door and pulled herself up to her full height, which was barely five foot two inches.

'Good morning,' she said.

Jennie and the other researchers paused what they were doing and looked up at her.

'All staff and postgrads are to meet in the common room in ten minutes. I have an announcement to make,' she said turning on her heel.

'What on earth can be so important?' said Jennie. She got off the stool, stored her gun away and took off her lab coat. As usual she was wearing blue jeans and a woollen jumper, her fair hair tied back in a ponytail. She picked up a bottle of sanitiser from the window sill and squeezed some onto her hands.

Sana shrugged. 'She never usually calls meetings.'

Jennie gazed around for David. She spotted him at the far end of the lab wearing a white lab coat using a pestle and mortar to grind some leaves from a tropical plant. His wiry weather-beaten appearance always reminded her of a desert nomad.

'Are you coming?' she asked as she approached him.

'I just need to finish this,' he said. She waited patiently.

Together they entered the small packed room and found a place to stand at the back. Amina swept in. 'Thank you for coming at such short notice. This morning I have been in a meeting with the senior team and the governors about an unprecedented situation,' she said, looking directly at the assembled crowd of young academics. 'The university is on the verge of bankruptcy and the Vice Chancellor has been suspended with immediate effect.' A gasp of disbelief flew around the room.

'Professor Lowry? But he's been here for ages,' said a lanky youth at the front.

'Exactly,' said Amina. 'Consultants have been called in to recommend how costs can be cut.' She paused for effect. Jennie tried to guess what she would say next.

'I'm afraid that this department's budget has been slashed to almost nothing,' she said with a calm face. There was an audible communal intake of breath.

'But what does that mean for us?' said a raised voice.

'There will have to be redundancies and funding for research projects will be cut in half.'

'That can't be right,' protested someone, 'our budgets have already been approved.'

Jennie heard several people muttering about Tory cuts. Amina held up her hand, 'I would like to make it clear that the situation is as a result of decisions taken by the university and not by national government.'

A shout came from the back. 'But the impact on us is just the same whoever is responsible.'

The implications of the situation dawned on Jennie. She looked at David who was standing immobile at her side, his eyes fixed on Amina. Did he understand what this meant?

Amina's eyes swept over the concerned faces in front of her. 'I acknowledge your concerns.'

'But what are our choices now?' asked Jennie.

'You can continue if you can finance yourself, or you can defer for a year.'

'You are kidding,' said an angry voice. 'So if we are rich we can carry on but if we are not we have to give up? That's like a scenario from the nineteenth century!'

'I am sorry but that's the situation,' said Amina her face set firm. 'I need to know your decisions by noon tomorrow.'

Jennie observed David to gauge his reaction but his face remained expressionless. She was surprised – she already knew what she was going to do. She listened attentively to the answers that Amina gave to the many questions that were fired at her. At the end she turned to David but his face was still unreadable.

'We will discuss this later,' he said as they returned to the lab. For the rest of the day she wondered what he meant - surely he felt the same as she did.

At five o'clock they cycled back together into the town centre of Oakfield passing a fine mix of residential and commercial buildings on the way. Jennie opened the door of the flat they had shared for the last eighteen months in a converted four-storey house. On the walls were David's prints of faraway places including the Sahara Desert, the Alps and the Arctic. Several birthday cards lay on the doormat. She picked them up, opened them and smiled at the cheerful pictures and messages. She placed them next to David's on the mantelpiece.

'Happy Birthday my intrepid darling,' he said coming up behind her and kissing her with an urgency she was accustomed to. He led her into their bedroom and tugged off her jeans and knickers. They fell on to the double bed, their limbs entwined and their lips seeking each other's.

'Love you,' he muttered into her hair.

She smiled into his eyes. Their love making was sweet and satisfying. Afterwards she snuggled up to him.

'That was a quite a bombshell today. How are we going to manage?' she said expecting him to discuss ways of finding enough money.

'I'm not going to,' David said as he reached for his pack of cigarettes on the bedside table piled high with Lonely Planet guides.

She raised herself on her elbow and searched his face expecting him to declare that he had just being kidding.

'You can't mean that.'

'I'm not even going to try to self-fund,' he said as he lit up.

'So what are we going to do? Find sponsors?' she asked with a look of puzzlement on her face. He blew some smoke into the air. 'Take a gap year.' Surely he wasn't being serious.

She rolled off the bed in exasperation. 'Is that a joke?'

'We've always wanted to see the world and now here is our chance.'

'But after we have finished studying – not in the middle,' she said. She couldn't believe what she was hearing.

He fell silent for several minutes. 'For some time I have known that my research was leading up a blind alley. Amina has discovered some major mistakes I've made and told me to repeat several experiments,' he explained.

She knew that he would have hated hearing that. 'You didn't tell me – I could have helped you,' she said coming over to him and rubbing his shoulders.

'I am starting to think that I'm not suited to research,' he said as he shook her off. He left the bedroom and headed straight for the fridge in the L-shaped kitchen area of the living room. His words had taken her by surprise. She gazed through the door. Her assumption that he was content was plainly wrong. How could she have been so blind?

'So this has happened at an opportune moment? So that you can drop out with a legitimate reason?' she said following him. He kept his head in the fridge. She knew that she had hit on the truth.

He turned round to face her. 'The rug has been pulled from under our feet. I don't want to carry on if it means scrimping and saving or trying to beg, borrow or steal from somewhere. We can just defer the whole thing – take a year off and start again when hopefully the funding is back in place,' he said. He flipped off the top of a beer bottle.

'I can't,' she said. 'I want to win the Luminosity Prize.'

'You won't win that,' he scoffed, 'there will be entries from all the top ecologists in the country.'

Jennie blinked. Normally he was so supportive of her. He was right though, there would be a lot of competition for the prize, but that would make it more of a challenge.

'Besides which, we always said we would go to Colombia and on to Machu Picchu.' He was right again: on numerous occasions they had discussed their fantasy round-the-world trip. His arms encircled her waist and he kissed the nape of her neck.

'Jennie, I need to know – whether you are going to come with me or not.' His touch made her tingle but she couldn't face him. Her mind was made up.

'I'm sorry,' she said. 'I need to do this now. The opportunity may not be there next year.'

She moved to the window. Dark clouds covered the sky. Her eyes flew over the rooftops to the countryside beyond. The places where the badgers lived were under threat. She turned and looked straight at him.

'Don't go – I need you to help me collect my data.'

'Is that the only reason you want me to stay?' he said with a note of disappointment in his voice.

'Oh course not.'

An icy silence descended between them. He paced up and down the room with his hands in his pockets.

'Come with me – we could have so much fun – there is a whole world out there.'

'You know it's impossible.'

'But what if we grow apart whilst I'm away?'

'We won't if we love each other enough,' she said.

'You're right,' he said. He picked up his phone from the table. 'I'm going to go. I'll email Amina and tell her that I am deferring for a year.'

'It's just not the right time for me,' she said. 'My future is dependent on winning that prize.'

'Sleep on it – you may feel differently in the morning.'

It was on the tip of Jennie's tongue to retort that she wasn't going to be the one who changed their mind, but seeing the expression of stubbornness on his face she refrained. David finished writing his email and pressed Send.

'Right that's done,' he said, 'now we are going to celebrate your birthday. Shall we go out? To the tapas restaurant?'

Jennie shook her head. She switched on her laptop and clicked on the West Country Universities website. 'I'll order in a take away pizza,' she said.

He opened the fridge. 'Prosecco?'

She downloaded the application form for the Luminosity Prize. 'Definitely not.'

He huffed and pulled out another beer.

*

3rd April

The next morning Jennie cycled to the university's campus which was built on a greenfield site on the edge of the town. She chained her bicycle to one of the cycle racks just inside the gates. Pink blossom blew from cherry trees as she made her way across the central courtyard, past the greenhouses full of growing plants, dodging groups of self-absorbed students as she went. Her security pass opened the automatic doors of the red-brick building housing the

Department of Ecology. She made her way up the stairs to the postgraduate office, one of the many rooms along a wide corridor on the first floor. It was much quieter than usual.

Her desk was piled high with textbooks and papers. She switched on her laptop and read through what she had written so far for the literature review section of her thesis. There was still a lot to add. Her thoughts strayed to her finances. With David moving out, she could advertise for another flatmate but she hated the thought of sharing with a stranger. The only alternative was to move back home, even though her father was annoyed with her for carrying on studying. He had wanted her to start working on the farm. But economies had to be made if she was to make up the shortfall in her funding. Decisively, she typed an email to their landlord, giving notice to quit. When complete, she pressed Send.

At eleven, she went along the corridor and knocked on Dr Ahmed's door. She entered a large office, which was furnished with functional furniture bought from a catalogue. Two large cheeseplants adorned the window sill. Amina was staring at a computer screen but she turned and smiled a welcome.

'Come in Jennie and take a seat,' she said. 'I assume that you are going to carry on?'

Jennie nodded and was rewarded with a beam of approval. Amina shuffled some papers in front of her.

'Because of the cuts, I am going to take over as your PhD supervisor.'

This was totally unexpected news. Jennie knew that sometimes staff changes meant that this happened but it would mean building up a new working relationship with someone who could be quite intimidating at times. It was pointless to protest and on the plus side, Amina was a leading expert in the field of ecology.

'Have you thought about your funding?' said Amina.

'I'll find the money somehow.'

Amina took off her designer glasses. 'My feelers are out to see if we can attract some new donors.' She pulled a white tissue from a box and cleaned her lenses. 'Now bring me up to speed regarding your thesis. Start with your aim and objectives.'

'My aim is to achieve a sustainable future for the badgers of Liltford. I am locating their setts and mapping the different habitats so that I can estimate badger numbers and the biodiversity. I am collecting data on their characteristics – their age, sex, size, weight and health and looking at how they interact with their environment.'

'Your hypotheses?'

'The lower the biodiversity of a habitat, the further badgers roam to search for food and the more likely they are to catch diseases.'

'How far have you got with your data collection?'

'Midway,' she replied. She took her laptop out of her bag and turned it on. 'I am aiming for a large sample size so that my results are statistically significant.'

'Good,' remarked Amina, 'remind me of your study area.'

'Liltford is south of Oakfield and covers approximately one thousand hectares. There are three farms - Green Meadow, Hightree and Beesnest and I have permission from the owners, who include my parents, to access their land.'

'Your methodology?'

'Observation, measurement and statistical modelling. And some experiments.'

'Are you using quadrats?'

Jennie nodded. 'It's time consuming counting all the different species.'

Amina tapped her biro.

'Jennie, your dissertation is too dull. You need to ramp it up. Make it more distinctive.'

The criticism hurt but Jennie knew that it was justified. Her thesis did need something extra. Amina's phone pinged. Her attention distracted, she brought the meeting came to an abrupt end.

'I want your ideas on how to do that by the end of the day,' she said.

Jennie made her way downstairs to the laboratory, where she found Sana washing petri dishes in the big stainless steel sink.

Sana paused, mid task. 'Well?'

Jennie put on her lab coat. 'David is going to take a gap year.'

'You didn't want to go with him?'

'This is more important,' she said switching on her laptop. 'You're not at risk of redundancy are you?'

Sana scrubbed hard at a congealed mass. 'I hope not,' she said. 'How do you think Professor Lowry managed to lose the Uni's money?'

At the mention of that name, an unpleasant memory came to Jennie. In her first year as an undergraduate she had been in a lift in the Admin block. It was so crowded that everyone was squashed up against each other. At first she ignored the male body that was pressed too close to her, but when a hand groped her she stamped on his foot. He had stifled a cry and jabbed his elbow into her ribs. She never wore such a short skirt again. A few days later at a Freshers event, she discovered that the hand belonged to Professor Lowry. After that she took care to avoid him.

'I've no idea,' said Jennie. 'But I wouldn't put anything past that man.'

Banishing the painful recollection to the back of her mind, she sat at the lab bench thinking about how to improve her dissertation. She pulled her laptop towards her and searched for ideas on the internet. To no avail. Usually she wasn't short of inspiration.

Sana brought her a mug of hot tea. 'You're working late.'

'Amina wants me to jazz up my premise,' said Jennie.

'What about proving that the badgers don't have bovine TB?'

Her words rang in Jennie's ears. That was it. It was a topical issue. As far as she knew no other PhD student was looking at that. It was perfect. She leapt up and hugged her.

'You are brilliant, thank you Sana.'

*

6th April

Two weeks later David was ready to depart. As Jennie walked along the High Street with him he chatted incessantly about what he was hoping to see and do, in Columbia. At Oakfield coach station the Heathrow Express was waiting to depart. The driver loaded his suitcase into the boot. Clutching his ticket David turned to her.

'I love you,' he said. 'Promise you'll wait for me?'

'I promise,' she said as they kissed.

He climbed into the coach without a backward glance. The coach pulled away and Jennie stood and waved until it had disappeared from sight. Had she made the right decision? If he had really loved her he would have stayed. He knew how important her research was to her.

That afternoon, her father Giles arrived at the flat in his Range Rover.

'Are you ready?' he asked when Jennie opened the door.

'Almost,' she said as he came in.

'Your mother has your old room ready,' he said. 'She says you can live rent free.'

'I'll help out on the farm,' she said, 'when I can.'

It took several trips to carry her books and files to the car. Her clothes fitted into just one suitcase. With her laptop and phone she had all she needed. Arriving back home at Green Meadow Farm her spirits were revived by the fresh smell of the countryside and by the enthusiastic welcome she received from her springer spaniel Bramble.

*

7th April

Jennie was woken by the sound of mooing cows. Black and white Friesians were sauntering in a single file behind their leader Zoe Mudmaker from the milking parlour, through the cluttered farmyard into their lush green meadow.

Dressed in a long sleeved tee-shirt, a fleece, indigo jeans and a pair of black riding boots she went downstairs to the kitchen. Her mother Nancy was busy at the cooker frying bacon and eggs. In front of the large bay window overlooking the garden was an easel on which stood an unfinished canvas. Nancy's hobby, when she wasn't cheese making and running the household, was painting pictures of chickens in bright bold colours. Jennie fondled the silky ears of Bramble, who was lolling in her basket. The back door burst open. Giles and her brother Ian came in smelling of manure.

'I'm hungry,' said Giles. He went over to the sink and scrubbed his hands. Ian slipped off his boots and started to clean them with a horsehair brush.

'Zoe Mudmaker is definitely below par today,' he said.

Giles's face reddened. 'She's perfectly well. She just doesn't like the swarms of flies that have sprung up from nowhere.'

'I think you should call the vet,' said Ian. He sat at the kitchen table.

Giles scraped his chair on the tiled floor. 'I've told you – there's nothing wrong with her.'

'What makes you so sure that there is something amiss?' said Nancy as she plated up the eggs and bacon.

'She is getting thinner and has a nasty cough,' said Ian. An alarm bell rang in Jennie's head. 'Those are the symptoms of bovine TB. If she has the disease it would be a disaster for the farm and my research,' she said.

'If she's sick then it is probably something to do with those bloody badgers,' said Giles.

Jennie looked indignant. 'The badgers around here are perfectly healthy.'

Ian wiped a piece of buttered bread around his plate soaking up the remaining egg. 'You are kidding yourself, Sis. You must know that the badgers are riddled with TB.'

'They are not,' she insisted, 'and I am going to prove it – that's why I am doing this PhD.'

'Enough,' said Giles, 'the vet is coming on Monday to do the annual tests – we will find out then if anything is wrong.'

Ian scowled.

'I have heard that the new vet is very good,' said Nancy.

Giles huffed. 'Phil Oldman is my man – he knows my cows.'

Her breakfast finished, Jennie stood up and headed for the door.

'Oh Jennie - I have a cake for Mrs Sitwell if you are going past Hightree this morning,' said

Nancy. She stood up and went over to the cake tin sitting on the side.

Jennie readily acquiesced and adjusted the route of her morning ride in her head. She put the foil wrapped cake into her rucksack. Holding her riding hat she ambled towards the stables. Sukey, her brown horse with a white stripe down the middle of her face, greeted her with a neigh. After brushing her down and mucking out the stable she swung into the saddle. The fresh air brought colour to her cheeks, oxygen to her lungs and clarity to her mind. Around her the countryside was springing into life with new leaves on the trees and green shoots in the fields.

She cantered south east along a bridleway to Hightree the dairy farm where Douglas Sitwell, her father's best friend, lived with his elderly mother. There had been an outbreak of bovine TB on the farm late the previous year and the Sitwells' had lost their entire herd. Jennie had been living in Oakfield at the time, but she had heard all about how devastating it had been for them when their Jerseys had been condemned and taken to the abattoir.

Arriving at the farmhouse she tethered Sukey to the fence and looked around. The last time she had been here was over a year ago and then the farm was full of life with the cows in the fields and chickens in their coop. Now it was still and quiet. She knocked on the door, waited and knocked again. After several minutes the door slowly opened and a small woman peered out.

'Good morning Mrs Sitwell. My mother has baked you a lemon drizzle cake,' said Jennie.

The door opened wider.

'Ah Jennie, come on in.'

In the kitchen a black cat was dozing in old armchair and a rugged middle aged man was sitting on a sofa reading The Racing News.

'Douglas, Jennie has brought us one of Nancy's cakes,' said Mrs Sitwell. 'I'll put the kettle on. You will stay for a cup of tea, won't you?'

Douglas grunted a greeting.

'Not for me thank you. I left my horse outside,' said Jennie. 'How are you?'

Mrs Sitwell sighed. 'My chest is playing up. But Douglas has had good news.'

Jennie raised her eyebrows.

'The compensation for losing our cows has just come through,' he explained.

'You'll be able to restock the farm,' said Jennie.

There was a silence as mother and son regarded each other.

'I'm too old to start again. Farming isn't easy,' said Mrs Sitwell. 'If I'd known that in the first place I probably wouldn't have married a farmer. Douglas has done his best since his father died, but it's been a struggle at times. The outbreak of bovine TB was the nail in the coffin. It's a wicked disease.' Tears welled up in her eyes.

Jennie stretched out and squeezed the old lady's hand. She knew that she wouldn't be able to bear it if the herd at Green Meadow Farm suffered a similar fate. 'That's why I'm researching ways of preventing its spread,' she said.

'Badgers are wretched creatures,' continued Mrs Sitwell her voice rising in pitch, 'it's them that have caused all this trouble.'

Douglas nodded in agreement. 'They should be shot, every last one of them.'

Jennie swallowed hard, taken aback by their vehemence. People's opinion of badgers clearly differed from hers. She stood up. 'I have to get on,' she said with an apologetic smile.

Outside she mounted Sukey and headed further south towards a small copse. On arrival she slowed her mare down by pulling on the bridle and squeezing her thighs. Dismounting she went over to a round hollow surrounded by loose soil and soft squidgy deposits. Badger droppings. She put on a pair of disposable gloves to pick up the faeces, which she placed into a plastic container. Securing the lid tightly, she wrote the date and time onto the label and put it into her rucksack.

It was late afternoon when she returned to Green Meadow. She checked her phone to see if David had been in contact. He hadn't. His battery must be low.

Jennie
Did you arrive safely? Miss you xxx
After a short delay she was pleased to receive a reply.
David
In Bogota missing you x

Chapter 2

20th April

As Jennie crossed the farmyard, which smelt of a mixture of diesel and manure, a sharp cry rang from the milking parlour. Alarmed, she went inside and heard a sting of rude expletives being shouted above the rhythmical sound of the milking machines. She saw Ian at the far end standing behind a cow, nursing his left leg. He had a hurt expression on his face which he tried, unsuccessfully, to hide from his sister. Blood was staining his trousers.

'Are you alright? What happened?' she asked.

'It's nothing. It was an accident,' he said. 'You won't tell Dad, will you?'

She gave her assurance, but added, 'As long as you are OK? Did that cow kick you?' His silence confirmed her suspicion. A strange thought entered her mind: was Ian frightened of the cows? Did they sense that?

'That cut needs attending to,' she said. She opened a small cupboard attached to a wall and lifted out the first aid box. She rolled up Ian's trouser leg and cleaned the gash with antiseptic lotion and cotton wool.

He started to fidget.

'Keep still,' she commanded. Deftly she applied a thick dressing and a bandage. Finally she finished.

'Thank you, Jen,' he said.

'Anytime,' she replied as she returned the first aid box to the cupboard.

He pulled himself up. 'You know I said that there's something wrong with the cows? Well, I have the data to prove it.' He pulled out a sheet of paper from his pocket and thrust it at her. Jennie gave it a quick glance. It was a graph showing the farm's milk output over the last six months.

'Dad says that it's normal for the yields to fluctuate,' she said.

'When I was at uni, I discovered that a lot of things that Dad says are outdated and sometimes just plain wrong,' he retorted.

'Explain the graph to him,' suggested Jennie anxious to start her evening's data collection. She left Ian to resume his chores and headed outside. Wearing a navy gilet with many pockets, she followed a footpath which led west from Green Meadow through the fields. The conditions that late spring evening were perfect for catching sight of her favourite badger family. A warmish breeze rustled the trees. A grass snake slithered across her path and the cows grazed contentedly on clover occasionally swotting flies from their behinds.

After thirty minutes, she reached the isolated far side of the farm. She strolled along a sunken track, which followed the course of Bramley Brook, until she arrived at a steep south-facing bank. Pitted by half a dozen or so dark burrows and sheltered by an ancient oak, this sett was home to her secret cete of badgers.

Agilely she climbed up the tree to a wooden platform which she had built when she had discovered that badgers rarely looked upwards. From her rucksack she pulled a black balaclava and cushion. Aware that badgers possess a hyper-sensitive sense of smell, she checked that her scent was being blown downwind.

It was still light: in that magical time just before dusk. Finding a comfortable sitting position, she put on her night vision goggles. She sat as still as possible. It would be an hour or so before the nocturnal animals felt that it was safe enough to emerge from their underground home. A tawny owl hooted in the distance, but otherwise the silence of the night reigned.

Eventually her patience was rewarded. She heard a strange grunting noise and detected a flash of movement. Out of the biggest burrow came a sleek black and white snout which keenly sniffed the air. A second later, having established that all was clear, a large badger with a distinctive scar above his left eye emerged. He started to scratch around for lobworms, his favourite supper. It was Bullitt, the adult male patriarch of the colony.

Jennie logged the time in her field book and jotted down some observations about his appearance. He was a mature boar – stocky with well-developed muscles and a broad backside. His head was cream and rectangular. Two black stripes ran from his button-shaped black nose through his eyes to his pointy ears. When he turned round to face her, she could see that predators would be frightened by his fierce appearance and strong stance. He paused to squat. He lifted his short white tail and rubbed the glands underneath along the leaf-covered ground. The musky smell he left behind would signal his presence to other creatures.

Presently, he was joined by Pocahontas, who had a narrower head and a leaner body. She went over to Bullitt and scratched his back, receiving a squirt of scent as a reward. Shortly after, three cubs, about ten weeks old, appeared out of the safety and warmth of the den. They started to play a game of chase. The largest cub took the lead but the smallest one, with the palest coat, hesitated before joining in.

From the pockets of her gilet, Jennie pulled out five test tubes each containing a tranquilizer dart. The darts were filled with ketamine which she had chosen because it was considered to be the safest anaesthetic for badgers. She loaded her gun. She aimed and silently fired at Bullitt's back thigh. Before Pocahontas had time to realise what was going on, Jennie shot her and then in rapid succession the three cubs. Immobilized they all fell to the ground.

After a few minutes, Jennie put on her gloves and climbed down. In torch light, she carefully monitored the vital signs of each badger before taking the darts out. Skilfully she fitted them all with ear tags and took blood samples. GPS collars were clicked around the necks of the adults.

She climbed back up into the oak. After a while, the tranquiliser wore off and the badgers staggered to their feet. Pocahontas plodded off, with the three youngsters scampering to keep up with her. Bullitt continued to sniff and dig until he too set off for a stroll. Jennie remained in position fighting off boredom and cramp.

Eventually Pocahontas returned, accompanied by two of her cubs. Jennie waited to see if the third cub would appear, but it didn't. The breeze strengthened. Deciding that it was time to head back, she slung her rucksack over her shoulders and switched on her most powerful torch. She marched back along the shady track.

Further along, at the junction with a modern road, the glare from headlights momentarily dazzled her. A vehicle sped past forcing her to step on to the verge. A thump rang out. She looked to see what it was and spotted something lying in the gutter. Getting closer, she realized that it was a badger cub. The one missing from Pocahontas's litter.

Without hesitation she approached it and tentatively examined it. Still and scared, it was alive but its hind leg lay at an awkward angle. She put on her gloves and bent down. The cub snarled, scratched and tried to bite her. She picked it up. It weighed the same as a puppy. Holding it in her arms she started walking.

Large rain drops started to fall. She stumbled over a root and lightly sprained her ankle. She hobbled along, anxious to reach the sanctuary of the farmhouse. The badger struggled in her arms and tried to nip her. She began to worry that she wouldn't make it home that night.

Her arms started to ache. To her relief she saw the outdoor light of the farmyard. The back door of the red roofed farmhouse was shut – it was normally kept ajar. She gently laid the badger down on the wet ground and frantically searched for her keys. Just as she was getting desperate, she found them in one of her deep jacket pockets and she opened the door.

She picked up the cub and let herself into the warm kitchen. It was late and the rest of the family were in bed. Bramble woke up from her slumbers and came over to greet her, waging her tail. Smelling the injured badger, she jumped up and tried to sniff the animal in Jennie's arms.

With some difficulty, Jennie managed to shut the dog in the front room. She laid the terrified badger onto the tiled floor and found a cardboard box. After lining it with newspaper, she placed the cub in it. She closed the lid and put the box in the utility room, closing the door softly behind her. In the morning she would decide what to do with it. After releasing Bramble, she climbed the stairs to bed.

She checked all her devices to see if there was any communications from David but there were none. There was no missed call, no voicemail, no text and not even a post on Facebook or Instagram. She had anticipated that they would be in frequent contact. He must be enjoying himself. Disappointed, she turned out the light. Maybe she should have gone with him after all. If only he had stayed. If only he had understood how important her research was to her.

*

21st April
She was awakened by a shriek.

'What's a badger doing in here?' yelled her mother up the stairs.

Jennie rubbed her eyes. 'Has it survived the night?' she shouted. Quickly she slipped on denim jeans, a blue shirt, and a khaki jacket and went downstairs. She went straight to the utility room. Her mother was standing at the door. The cardboard box was open and the badger cub was stirring.

'It was run over. I found it on the way back home last night,' Jennie said. She picked the box up and took it into the kitchen.

Nancy followed her. 'What are you going to do with it?'

'I'll take it to the vet's in town this morning,' replied Jennie putting the box on the sideboard away from Bramble's reach. Her father and Ian entered the kitchen hungry for their breakfast.

'Vet?' asked Giles.

Nancy nodded in the direction of the cardboard box. 'She brought back an injured badger cub last night.'

'Damned badgers,' snarled Giles who had been up early milking the cows. 'I hate them. Spreaders of disease. Killers of calves. I hope you are going to have it put down. One less badger on this farm is good news in my eyes.'

'I think it may have broken its leg, but if it can be treated, then it should be,' said Jennie giving her father a warm

23

smile. She knew that his rumbling stomach was making him grumpy.

'Do what you want, but I'm not paying the bill,' he barked.

Jennie kept a calm face. 'I wouldn't expect you to.'

'Remember that you promised to help me on the market stall today,' said Nancy.

Jennie reassured her. 'The vet's visit won't take long.'

Ian went over to the cardboard box and peered at the young badger. 'It's alive, alright, but I agree with Dad, we don't want them on our farm – they're a menace.'

'This has been the badgers' home for thousands of years and they have the right to be here,' said Jennie.

'You ought to become an animal activist if you feel that strongly,' said Ian.

She cast him a defiant look. 'Maybe I will.'

After breakfast, she made an appointment with the vet and offered the cub some milk and dog food. The badger welcomed this nourishment and settled down for a snooze. She helped her mother load up the Range Rover with fresh eggs, cheese, and paintings to sell on the stall. A pet carrier containing the baby badger was safely stored in the boot. Jennie got into the passenger seat and Nancy started the engine. The three mile drive through the rolling countryside to Oakfield passed without incident.

The market was held every Saturday on a cobbled square in the shadow of the medieval cathedral. It was early when they arrived but a few people were already browsing. The smell of fresh bread, fruit and vegetables attracted shoppers from near and far.

Nancy parked the car behind their stall and they unloaded all their produce. Together they put it on display. To the top of the stall, Jennie attached a banner, proclaiming 'Green Meadow Farm –free range eggs, farmhouse cheeses and folk art'. To the front she pinned a garland of spring flowers. Nancy hung her paintings of chickens on to hooks at the back. When they had finished, Jennie opened the car boot and took out the pet carrier holding the badger cub.

'Maybe you will meet the new vet,' said Nancy.

'So?'

'I thought that you had broken up with David,' said Nancy.

'Absolutely not,' said Jennie, 'he has just gone travelling.' She was reluctant to discuss her love life with her mother. She picked up the pet carrier and headed off down the High Street.

It took less time than she expected to reach the Oakfield Veterinary Clinic which occupied the whole of an Edwardian house. On the ground floor was the reception, two consulting rooms, an operating theatre, an animal ward and a laboratory. The staff kitchen and common room, offices and self-contained accommodation for Phil Oldman the senior vet and owner of the practice were on the next floor. The top floor boasted another flat.

Jennie noticed that the whole building was in need of maintenance and restoration. The paint was peeling off the window frames and the brickwork needed repointing. A bell rang when she pushed open the door to the poorly lit reception. She went up to the counter which was cluttered with piles of Manila envelope files.

'Good morning,' said the dark haired receptionist.

'I'm early,' Jennie said putting the carrier down on to the floor.

'Let me take your details.'

'Jennie Cliffe, Green Meadow Farm, Liltford.'

'Fine, take a seat.'

She sat on the red padded bench seat, which ran round two of the walls. A pile of well-thumbed magazines lay on a table in the middle. There was a noticeboard full of posters advertising dog grooming, vaccination and doggy day care.

On the opposite wall she spotted one of her mother's paintings of a Leghorn chicken with a red comb and white feathers. She examined the painting again. She knew little about art, even though she had grown up with a mother who was always sketching or drawing. Now she realised that although at first glance the painting seemed rather rudimentary, the expressions on the birds' faces and their poses were actually decidedly meaningful as well as being well observed and skilfully painted.

While she waited, she scrolled through her mobile phone. Maybe she had missed David's call? She texted him again, wrote him a long email and left a voice message. In between all of which she checked on the badger, which was sleeping soundly.

The clinic's doorbell rang. A pretty young woman wearing a stylish coat and leading an appealing cockapoo puppy entered. She spoke to the receptionist and sat down next to Jennie. The puppy jumped up at her eager to make a new friend.

Jennie smiled and stroked its head. 'You have a lovely dog.'

'She's causing me no end of trouble, but owning her means I can see the new vet regularly,' she said. The puppy transferred its attention to the pet carrier which it sniffed and barked at with great excitement. The alarmed badger started to squeak.

'What on earth have you got in there?' She spoke with a soft country lilt.

'A badger cub,' said Jennie.

The woman shied away. 'Ugh! They have fleas and diseases.'

Jennie wanted to reassure her but she couldn't deny the truth of her statement. Fortunately before she could reply, the receptionist said in a loud clear voice, 'Freya Dennis, you can take Lola through now.'

The puppy was led out of the room and along a corridor to a consulting room. A door closed behind them and remained firmly shut for what seemed like a very long time. Jennie consulted her watch more than once. Eventually Freya, carrying her coat and her short curly hair in disarray, reappeared with Lola straining at the leash. She went up to the counter and paid.

'Goodbye,' she said.

'Jennie Cliffe, the vet will see you now,' said the receptionist.

Carrying the pet carrier, Jennie went down a long corridor to the consulting room.

Inside was a tall handsome man with broad shoulders who stood up to greet her.

'Edward Hollyer,' he said with a firm handshake. 'How can I help you?' His intelligent blue eyes and mane of dark hair momentarily disarmed her.

'I've an injured badger cub.' She put the pet carrier onto the floor beside her.

'Well, let's have a look at it.' He put on his blue disposable gloves and gently lifted the quivering animal out of the container and onto the consulting table. The cub snarled and bared its teeth. He muttered soothing words as he tenderly and thoroughly checked it over. Jennie stood at his side finding comfort in his concern for the defenceless animal.

'She's been ear tagged,' he said.

'Yes,' she admitted. 'I'm researching the local badgers for my thesis.'

'Ah,' he said continuing his examination.

She looked closely at the cub and noticed that it had a complicated pattern of fur. The outer hair of its coat was white for much of its length but had a darker tip. Beneath this top coat lay a dense white under fur. The head and neck were snowy-white except for the dark stripes stretching from its snout, to its eyes and ears.

'Well, first the good news, she only has a broken leg. Something that can heal reasonably quickly and easily,' he said with an irresistible smile.

'And the bad news?'

'She has a slight cough. It could be something serious I'm afraid,' he said putting the badger back into the carrier.

'Can you help her?' said Jennie with a look of concern.

'I will keep her here at the clinic overnight for treatment. If she responds well, I'll contact the wildlife rescue centre – they are experts in hand rearing cubs of this age,' he said turning to his computer and typing in some notes.

'Can she eventually return to the wild?'

'If she tests negative for bovine TB.'

Jennie sighed with relief. 'She is such a gorgeous creature, I would hate for her to be put down.'

'If you check back with me in a couple of weeks' time, I will let you know what has happened to her,' said Edward. 'Does she have a name?'

'Survivor,' she replied, making it up on the spur of the moment.

Edward smiled. 'Well let's hope that she does – survive I mean.'

Jennie stood up to go. 'By the way, I am pleased to see that you have one of my mother's paintings in your waiting room.'

He appeared puzzled for a second until a recollection dawned. 'Oh yes, I bought it at Oakfield Market. It cheers everyone up and is a talking point. So thank your mother – it was worth every penny.'

The consultation over, Jennie smiled her thanks. She walked back to the market place carrying the empty carrier, relieved that Survivor was going to be alright and thinking about Edward. He had been knowledgeable as well as kind and reassuring.

At the stall, Nancy was doing a brisk trade. Jennie put the empty carrier under the table and started tidying up the cheese display of cheese that was becoming higgledy-piggledy.

'I see they kept the badger,' said Nancy.

'Until she goes to the rehabilitation centre.'

'Did you meet the new vet?'

'One of your paintings is hanging in the waiting room.'

'Really?'

'Don't you think you might sell more if you lowered the prices, Mum?' said Jennie straightening up one of them.

Nancy flicked her hair back. 'I sell more than you think.'

Giles rushed up to the stall, panting and red in the face.

'What's the matter?' asked Nancy.

'Douglas hasn't turned up. He was supposed to meet me in the pub. I spoke to him yesterday. We arranged to meet today to celebrate his compensation coming through,' he said. 'His mobile is switched off. He never usually turns off his phone.'

'Maybe he is stuck in traffic,' said Nancy.

He dismissed this suggestion with a wave of his hand. 'I have spoken to his mother and she said he left Highfield Farm this morning. But no one knows where he is now.' He sounded worried.

'You should report his disappearance,' said Nancy.

Giles shook his head.

'It is too early to do that.'

He huffed and stomped off. Jennie gazed after him. She knew how much Douglas meant to him. Nancy looked at her watch, reapplied her lipstick and wrapped a silk scarf around her neck.

'Right,' she said, 'I am taking my lunch break now. Jennie, would you mind manning the stall for a while?'

'Don't be too long,' Jennie shouted after Nancy as she disappeared into the crowd, looking much younger than her fifty-four years.

Jennie turned her attention to a middle aged couple who wanted six large eggs and some farmhouse cheese. Just as they turned away with their purchases, her phone rang. She rushed to pull it out of her bag.

'David?' she said. 'Is that you? Where are you?'

'Bogota – it's quite thrilling. You should have come.'

'Where are you staying?'

'In a hotel – it's clean and friendly,' he replied. 'I went to the Museo del Oros yesterday – it was full of treasure – lots of gold. Just fantastic.'

'Any idea when you are coming home?'

'No,' he said, 'my adventure has only just started.'

Just as she was about to ask more questions the line cut out and he was gone. She put her phone away happy to have heard his voice.

Chapter 3

23rd April

QQA rook twisted and dived high in the sky and a solitary blackbird belted out its full-throated song. Many badger setts were well hidden in inaccessible places and Jennie needed Bramble to help find them for her. Heavy dew dampened her trainers as she made her way across the grass towards a spacious shed which she knew to be empty. In her right hand she held a soft toy shaped like a carrot. Bramble, who possessed an excellent sense of smell, ran behind her, eager to start her training session. Inside the shed, Jennie squeezed the toy until it squeaked and then threw it about ten metres ahead of her.

'Fetch,' she shouted.

With a bound, the dog ran after it and picked it up in its mouth. Wagging her tail she returned it to Jennie and was rewarded with a chocolate drop. The game was repeated for another ten minutes until she was satisfied that Bramble had learnt to retrieve.

'Sit,' she commanded.

Bramble obediently sat and was immediately given another treat. Jennie placed the stuffed toy about five metres away.

'Seek.'

The dog ran to the toy and brought it back, dropping it at Jennie's feet. She placed a cardboard box over it and repeated the commands until Bramble had mastered the skill of finding a hidden object. Out of her pocket she pulled a plastic bag. She unfastened it and took out a rag covered in badger scent which she threw instead of the toy. Again the exercise was practised until she felt confident that Bramble would be able to track a badger and sniff out its hiding place.

Finishing the lesson, Jennie lavished praise and more rewards on Bramble. Outside, she saw Giles leading his favourite cow into the cow shed. Zoe Mudmaker was endowed with a handsome head, a straight back and a wide mouth surrounded with white whiskers. A v-shaped pale patch of hair lay between her ears and on the top of her head was a black tuft. She was still a fine specimen, but to Jennie's eyes she seemed to have lost weight and to lack her old sparkle.

Jennie followed them in. The cow shed was a light and airy building with corrugated-iron walls and roof. Down the centre was a space, wide enough for a tractor, which separated the indoor stalls.

'How is she?' asked Jennie.

'Just fine,' Giles replied. He filled the feeding trough with a mixture of silage, hay and molasses. Without warning Ian burst into the shed and waved a computer printout at them both.

'The milk yields are down again – they have gone below five thousand litres,' he said.

Giles took the sheet from him and screwed it up.

'That computer is rubbish – it just spews out nonsense,' he said, his face turning puce with irritation.

Ian argued. 'But our income will fall if we have less milk to sell. Our margins are tight enough already what with the fall in wholesale prices.'

Giles looked unconvinced.

'The vet is due soon. Let's see what Phil thinks.'

Jennie was unsure what to think. If Ian was right and the declining yields were a permanent feature then that would be of concern to them all. If milk output was down because some of the cows were ill then again that was a serious situation. She heard a car arrive and with the others she went to see who it was.

Edward wound down his car window. 'Good morning, Mr Cliffe have you any biosecurity measures that I should use?'

'No, we haven't,' said Giles quite gruffly, 'I was expecting Phil, isn't he coming?'

'He's cutting down his hours. I'm taking over some of his case load,' Edward replied.

Giles stood with his legs apart and his arms folded. 'Well, I am not happy at all about this. In fact I am bloody furious.'

'I can go, if you don't want me,' said Edward unperturbed by his confrontational tone.

Giles hesitated and pursed his lips. 'You are here now, my lad, but make sure you do a good job.'

Jennie sighed with relief. Precious time could be lost if there was any delay in examining the herd. She followed as they went into the cow shed.

'What's the problem?' Edward asked.

Giles pointed at Zoe Mudmaker who standing listlessly. 'This cow has lost her appetite.'

'Let's have a look.'

Jennie and Ian both hovered anxiously whilst Edward took his time examining the cow, taking her temperature and feeling her body for any lumps or bruises. His expression became more serious.

'There's something wrong, isn't there? ' asked Ian.

'Let him get on with the job, son,' said Giles.

Finally, Edward indicated that he had finished.

'Well,' said Giles, 'what do you think?'

'I am not going to beat about the bush, I think that she might have an infection,' he said making some notes on his iPad.

'She is just under the weather,' protested Giles. 'She isn't ill.'

Edward replied, 'I disagree, but to be sure of my diagnosis, I need your permission to give her a skin test.'

Giles stomped his foot but slowly nodded his consent. Edward opened his veterinary bag and took out a pair of clippers. He trimmed Zoe Mudmaker's hair at two different sites on her neck and with a pair of callipers he measured the thickness of her skin at both places. In his record book he wrote down the number on her ear tag and her measurements. He then injected avian tuberculin into the skin on the top site and the lower site received some bovine tuberculin.

'Now we have to wait and see what the reaction is,' he said.

Giles scowled. 'She is fine. Just you wait and see. Zoe Mudmaker has never let me down and she isn't about to start now.'

Ian stuffed his hands into his pockets.

'But what if she is sick?'

'Until we have the results of the test we won't know,' said Edward starting to pack his equipment away. 'Wasn't there was an outbreak of bovine TB on your neighbour's farm a few months ago?'

'At Hightree,' said Jennie.

Giles clenched his fist. 'But we have been disease free here.'

'To stay that way, make sure that you clean and disinfect the whole farm and adopt a biosecurity protocol. I will be back in three days,' said Edward getting into his car and driving off.

Jennie caught the look of denial on her father's face. He was in no mood to start making any changes to the farm. Ian sloped off, unable to disguise his disgust.

*

26th April

Seventy two hours later Edward returned to the farm. Jennie heard his car arrive and went out to hear his verdict. Giles and Ian appeared from the milking parlour.

'Good morning Mr Cliffe,' he said getting out of his car and looking around. 'Are there still no biosecurity measures in place?'

'Not yet, my lad, not yet,' said Giles.

Edward seemed displeased but held back a remonstration. Zoe Mudmaker was in the cow shed lying on some straw. He checked her ear tag to make sure that it was the right cow and looked to see if there were any swellings at either of the places where he had injected the tuberculin. At both sites there were small lumps, but one lump was slightly larger than the other. Edward cleared his throat. 'The test result is inconclusive, I am afraid.'

'What does that mean?' asked Giles.

'Well the tuberculin skin test doesn't show anything definite – she may have the infection but then again she may not,' he said opening a notebook and jotting down some figures.

'What infection are we talking about?' asked Ian.

35

'Bovine TB, I'm afraid - the test I used detects and measures her immune response to Mycobacterium bovis,' said Edward looking first at him and then at Giles.

Jennie absorbed this news in silence. His diagnosis could spell months of stress and uncertainty for the farm. The badgers could be unfairly blamed for infecting the cows.

Giles stuffed his hands into trouser pockets. 'What happens now?' he asked.

'As Zoe Mudmaker is an inconclusive reactor, she must be put into isolation straight away. Her milk has to be kept separate and not used to make cheese. You should also try to find out the source of the infection,' said Edward.

'Will I lose my whole herd?' said Giles, his face a mixture of anger and anxiety.

'Not necessarily. For the time being, your herd has lost its official TB free status. The Animal Health Agency will tell you what restrictions will be put on the farm so that the virus is contained.'

'How can we stop it spreading?'

'There are many ways that an animal or indeed a person can catch TB. Finding out how a cow became infected can be very challenging,' said Edward.

'So, Zoe Mudmaker may have caught it from another cow?' asked Jennie.

'Indeed. It may be that she was infected when she was grazing in the fields or it could be that a new cow brought the infection on to the farm,' said Edward.

'I would never buy a sick animal,' protested Giles.

'It's not easy to tell whether a cow has bovine tuberculosis or not. Affected animals can appear healthy for some time after becoming infected, during which time they are contagious. Close surveillance of your healthy animals therefore plays a key role in halting the spread of the disease.'

'I knew that there was something wrong with her,' exclaimed Ian after listening closely to the whole exchange.

'One more thing, Zoe Mudmaker and the whole herd will have to be tested again in sixty days,' said Edward.

'Sixty days? That's too long. It is like having a death sentence over our heads,' said Giles.

'That's the situation, I am afraid. In the meantime, there are things you need to do,' he said looking around. Jennie knew that he had noticed that nothing had been cleaned since his previous visit. 'Good hygiene is essential. Do you have badgers here on the farm?'

'Those damned badgers – I knew that they would be the root cause of this,' said Giles giving Jennie an accusatory look.

'There is talk about extending the badger culling area to Liltford,' said Edward.

'A jolly good idea,' said Giles, 'about time too.'

'Oh Dad, surely you can't be serious? It would be dreadful if our badgers were killed,' said Jennie, her strength of feeling shining through.

'I am deadly serious,' he said firmly, 'bovine TB is costing too many livelihoods.'

'The badgers can coexist safely with your cows. There are some tips I can give you,' said Edward.

'Tell Jennie. She can let us know what to do,' said Giles. He stomped off.

'I can inspect the farm now to see if we can identify the source of the TB breakdown if you like,' said Edward turning to her.

'Ok. Follow me,' said Jennie. She led him across the farm yard past the red brick outhouses to the dairy where Nancy made cheese. It was an airy white room with lots of stainless steel.

'This is a fairly new addition to the farm – it's only about twenty years old. The cow's milk comes here directly from the milking parlour. It is cooled before bacteria and rennet is added to make the milk solidify. The curd is then separated from the whey before the cheese is put into containers and sent to the ageing room where it develops over time,' said Jennie as they walked around.

Edward checked the building to see if any animals could get in and noticed a large gap under the door where they could squeeze through. She took him next to the chicken house which was made from high quality timber and surrounded by a large run bordered by a heavy wire fence dug into the soil to prevent foxes digging a tunnel underneath. About twenty chickens were running around foraging for food.

He inspected it thoroughly. 'This all looks very secure.'

Jennie laughed. 'My mother values her chickens too much to let them be attacked.'

They moved on to the nearest cow shed where he peered at some gaps in the walls.

'Look,' he said, 'they can get in there and head straight for the animal feed for a midnight feast. If they mix with the cows they could pass on infection to them.'

'I don't think it has ever occurred to my father that this could have been happening,' she sighed as they walked out to the paddock. Sukey ambled over to greet them. Jennie pulled a carrot out of her pocket for her.

'The badgers can easily get to the feeding troughs in this field,' said Edward pointing to the open fence.

'I see what you mean,' said Jennie. 'Should we change the type of fencing?'

He nodded. 'It's expensive but you can have a rolling programme.'

'I don't think my father will be rushing to make a start,' she said crossing over a stile into a field where the cows were munching the grass. The air was filled with the scent from the spring flowers. She stooped down to pick a meadow buttercup.

'When did you first come here?' asked Edward.

He walked alongside her on the path around the field's perimeter.

'My great-grandparents bought the dairy farm in the early 1920s. My great-grandfather would drive a pony and trap around the lanes, stopping to ladle out the milk to his customers from a churn in the back.'

He gazed around the large field. 'How large is the farm today?'

'We have 250 hectares of prime pastureland for our herd of around 350 Holstein Friesians.'

'Your neighbours?'

'To the south is Beesnest Farm, where Mr and Mrs Nelson live. In the east is Hightree Farm which is owned by the Sitwell family.'

'Look there is quite a large gap in this hedge,' said Edward pointing it out.

'Big enough for cows to squeeze through. I will tell Dad,' she said. She looked sideways at him.

'Do you like being a vet?' she asked.

'Every day is different. I never know whether it will be guinea pigs, cats, sheep or cattle.'

'That's quite a mixture.'

'I didn't want to have an urban practice – just pets and their anxious owners.'

The field was full of cow pats buzzing with flies but the heads of soft yellow cowslips were nodding in the air. Jennie started to gather a bunch of wild flowers.

'I have heard that Phil Oldman is retiring,' she said.

'He is procrastinating. But there is a lot to sort out before he goes – the practice is still in the pre computer age.'

'Don't you miss your friends and family?'

'Sometimes, but I want to make a success of this. My father wanted me to go into business.'

Jennie crossed over a stile leading into the next field. Edward followed.

'My parents wanted me to become a dairy farmer, but I had other ideas,' she said.

'So who will take over the farm?' asked Edward. 'I mean eventually – when the time comes.'

'Oh my brother Ian – he graduated from agricultural college recently and he is already working on the farm full-time – fortunately for me!'

They carried on searching for places where the cows could stray onto the land of neighbouring farmers or mix with wildlife. After half an hour they returned to the farmyard.

'So what should we do to improve the farm's biosecurity?' asked Jennie already having some good ideas of her own.

'Repair all the holes in the fences and walls. Or put up electric fencing. Store all animal feed in a secure dry area and wash all the farm equipment with disinfectant,' said Edward heading towards his car.

'That sounds like common sense,' said Jennie. 'Hopefully Dad will take it all on-board. By the way, do you know how Survivor is getting on?'

'The rescue centre report that her broken leg has healed and she is growing fast,' he said. He opened his car boot and rummaged around.

'What about her chest?'

'It was clear of mycobacterium. If she stays clear, she will be paired up with another cub,' he said. 'Provided that she keeps testing negative, she will be put into a release group before being returned to the wild.' He handed her a wodge of leaflets on biosecurity. 'Give these to your father.'

'All the badgers around here are healthy,' she said adamantly.

He opened his car door.

'It isn't easy to diagnose TB in badgers. Often there are no visible signs. Sometimes though, there are lesions on their necks and they look emaciated but only an autopsy can determine whether they have the disease or not,' he said.

'The government has to control bovine TB – I understand that, but badgers don't spread the disease,' she said.

His eyebrows shot up. 'It is a generally held belief that they do,' he said.

She shook her head. 'I am not convinced and I am hoping that my research will find evidence of that. But I am worried about our cows – it would kill my father if he lost our herd,' she admitted.

'It doesn't need to happen,' he reassured her. 'If you follow the practical precautions, then the outbreak can be controlled. Hey – why don't we talk about this some more? Would you like to go out for a drink?'

His question took her off guard and she hesitated. He was good company and quite charming but she had promised David that she would wait for him.

'I have a boyfriend – he is away travelling at the moment.'

His neck reddened and a look of disappointment flashed across his face.

'Oh,' he said, 'I didn't know. Anyway, see you around.'

With that he was away. She gazed after him trying not to feel regret.

*

27th April
The next morning Jennie awoke early. A bright blue sky welcomed her when she drew back her curtains.

'How is Zoe Mudmaker?' she asked Giles at the breakfast table.

'She hates being isolated from the rest of the herd. She feels like a pariah,' he said a picture of gloom.

'Is there nothing we can do?' asked Jennie. She knew that Giles was aware of what needed to be done but that he also hated to be nagged.

'It costs money to repair boundaries and to spruce up things – money we haven't got. The price of milk is falling. Our yields are declining. Our income is down but our costs are rising. Also we have the continued expense of your studies and we have only just finished paying off the money that it cost to put Ian through college. It all adds up you know,' he said.

Jennie coloured. 'I would pay rent if I could,' she said.

'If you want to earn some money, come and work on the stall,' offered Nancy.

'Seriously?'

Nancy inclined her head. Jennie did a quick calculation in her head – it wouldn't be a lot of extra cash but it would help.

'Ok then – when do I start?' she said. She loaded the dishwasher.

'This Saturday,' said Nancy. 'It's the Spring Show.'

Jennie smiled and thanked her mother. It would mean a whole day away from her studies but she needed the money. She finished in the kitchen and went back up to her room to carry on with some reading until just before dusk Sana arrived ready to help in the field. Jennie divided the equipment between them. When their rucksacks were full, they set off across the fields in an easterly direction.

'What's up?' asked Sana immediately sensing that Jennie was preoccupied.

Jennie kicked some stones along the well-trodden path. 'One of our cows is ill,' she said. 'I hope the government doesn't think that the badgers are responsible for spreading bovine TB.'

'You will just have to prove otherwise,' said Sana.

'I will try,' said Jennie, 'but it is easier said than done and I am worried about the possibility of the badger cull area being extended.'

'I hadn't thought of that – but of course – you will just have to collect as much data as you can - in case,' said Sana. She strode at Jennie's side through the fields in which the crops were responding to the warmer temperatures and longer days. The brambles were spreading their tendrils, the wildflowers were having a growth spurt and the pollinators were unfurling their wings.

Jennie pointed to a track along the hedgerow. 'Look over there,' she said. Sana looked across but could see nothing.

'It's an animal track,' said Jennie. 'It is marked on an OS map from the eighteenth century. It connects this field to the wood we are going to and the river. Generations of deer, badgers and foxes have used that path.'

'That's extraordinary,' said Sana. 'What else can you tell me about badgers?'

'Just that they omnivorous, social and territorial animals,' replied Jennie. She moved on briskly and Sana panted to keep up. They entered a small wood not far from the River Fogle, which flowed westwards through the northern part of Highfield Farm. Jennie signalled to Sana that they had arrived at a sett located at the side of a path and surrounded by nettles and shrubs. Only a keen observer would realise that it was there. Jennie knew from the webcam she had trained on the entrance that it was home to a male and two females.

Jennie scouted around for a surveillance spot. She found a suitable position and beckoned Sana over. She took out her gun from her rucksack and loaded it with the tranquilizer darts, which were a type of ballistic syringe. The light faded and it gradually became darker but the moonlight cast odd shadows across the wood. Jennie remained alert.

After a patient wait, two adult badgers appeared. Silently, Jennie aimed for their strong thighs and fired the darts at them. The feathered projectiles moved slowly through the air like shuttlecocks. Upon impact the badgers were injected with a sedative causing them to slump to the ground and fall asleep. After a few minutes Jennie went over to them and monitored their vital signs.

She signalled to Sana that all was satisfactory. 'The tranquilliser has knocked them out but be careful. Handle them with care as they are large and strong and have a dangerous bite and sharp claws.'

Over the course of the next half hour, Jennie and Sana quickly fitted the GPS tracking collars and tags to the badgers. Their skins were pricked with a lancet and test tubes filled with their blood.

'I'll process these samples in the morning,' said Sana.

'The data I get from their blood enables me to build a health profile of each badger plus their DNA. It's a treasure trove,' said Jennie as she weighed a young sedated badger using a handheld scale.

'The thing I like the most is that the GPS collars start transmitting data as soon as we fit them,' said Sana.

'What I didn't know before was that the badgers are like us – creatures of habit – walking the same track in a circular route. They go out on patrol each night, walking several kilometres – visiting their favourite watering holes and feeding grounds and meeting other badgers,' said Jennie.

She lifted her camera and took several photographs of them and their surroundings.

'Eyeing up the local talent,' said Sana with a chuckle.

'Too right – they definitely don't pass up any opportunities for a quickie if it comes their way,' agreed Jennie with a smile as she measured the length of each badger.

'Life in the wild isn't always tough,' observed Sana.

'Especially for opportunists and scavengers such as badgers,' added Jennie. 'They are always on the lookout for any scraps of food left out for farm animals or pets. They have a symbiotic relationship with us.'

'They look very healthy though,' said Sana.

'Exactly – their glossy coats and bright eyes show no evidence of disease,' agreed Jennie. 'Right that's it I think we are done.'

They packed up their gear and tiptoed away leaving the badgers to come round from the tranquilizer none the wiser about the intrusions upon their persons. They arrived back at Green Meadow and Sana got into her car and sped off.

Jennie's phone pinged. She took it out of her pocket hoping that it was a message from David. She hadn't heard from him for several days. It was only an alert from her bank warning her that her balance was low. She sent him a text anyway.

Jennie

How's it going? Missing you xxx

To her surprise a reply came straight back.

David

Started learning Spanish - taking the coach to Quito in Ecuador tomorrow xx

Jennie

Enjoy! Text me when you get there xxx

She went up to her bedroom and started to write up her notes and observations. Even when a troupe of grey moths began dancing around the pendant light hanging from the ceiling, she kept on working. Finally, she finished the section she was on to her satisfaction and she flopped, exhausted into her single bed.

*

30th April

It had been over a week since Douglas disappeared. A police car drew up outside Green Meadow and two policemen got out. The doorbell rang. Jennie opened the door.

'Good evening I am Police Sergeant Miller and this is Police Constable Allen,' said the older officer. 'May we come in? We are making door-to door enquiries.'

Jennie led them in to the kitchen where the rest of the family were relaxing after their meal.

'Sorry to interrupt your evening, but we are investigating the whereabouts of Mr Douglas Sitwell, your neighbour. I believe that a Mr Cliffe reported him missing?' said PS Miller.

'Yes that was me,' said Giles. 'He was due to meet me for lunch in an Oakfield pub but he never showed up. He hasn't been in contact since. Which is very unlike him. Normally he's on WhatsApp all the time. Have you any idea where he is?'

'We are following up all the usual leads but so far we have drawn a blank,' said PC Allen.

'We would like you all to recall the last time you saw him and any details that you think might help us track him down,' said Miller.

Giles scowled. 'What about searching the fields? He might be in a ditch somewhere.'

'So far, no body has been found,' said Miller.

'Do you think he might be dead?' exclaimed Nancy as if the idea had only just occurred to her.

'We have to consider all possibilities in a missing person case,' said Allen.

'Right let's get started, if we can see you individually to get your statements?' said Miller.

Jennie waited until her turn but she had very little to tell them apart from the fact that she had been at Hightree Farm a few days before Douglas went missing and that he and his mother were undecided about the future of the farm. At the end, the police officers left, thanking them for their cooperation.

Chapter 4

5th May

The Oakfield Spring Show was traditionally held on the first Saturday in May. Volunteers from the local Community Association always erected a large marquee in the middle of the municipal park. Around the marquee the market traders set up their stalls selling food and drink, clothing and shoes, agricultural machinery, seeds, gardening and dog paraphernalia.

That day, the cumulus clouds were moving steadily across the sky sometimes obscuring the sun but at other times allowing its warm rays to stream through. Jennie helped her mother unload their car and to set up Green Meadow's stall with their usual range of cheese, eggs and Nancy's paintings. As soon as the gates opened, visitors from all over the locality flocked in to admire the flower displays, restock their cupboards, renew acquaintances, and to watch the dog show. Children ran around laughing and playing as colourful bunting fluttered in the breeze. On the 1930s bandstand a live folk group played.

Jennie knew that a long day lay ahead. Her mother was paying her by the hour – not a great deal but enough to make it worthwhile. It was hard living on a low income. She had a small student loan and a few hundred pounds in savings but even so it was difficult to live within her means – a constant juggling act. She read a short email from David describing all the fun he was having. His communications were becoming more infrequent as time went by. And then there was Edward – she couldn't deny that she found him attractive. Maybe she should have gone out with him after all. She was deep in thought when she heard his voice.

'Hello Jennie.'

'Edward,' she said with a blush as she remembered their last meeting. Next to him was Freya, who was stylishly dressed in a cotton floral outfit and high heeled sandals, holding Lola on a lead.

'I think you met Freya and Lola when you brought the injured cub in,' he said. Jennie nodded. The memory of that morning was still fresh.

'Lola would have eaten that badger alive given half a chance,' said Freya.

Jennie smiled. 'Fortunately she is now in Edward's excellent care.'

'You're the new vet?' asked Nancy.

Edward smiled.

'I hear that you have one of my paintings in your waiting room,' said Nancy.

'It's certainly a talking point,' he replied, his eyes twinkling. 'You are?'

'I'm Nancy Cliffe – Jennie's mother.'

Freya pointed at one of Nancy's vivid portrayals of a white and speckled Sussex Light chicken. 'I like that one,' she said, 'what paint have you used?'

'Acrylic – I find that works well on canvas,' answered Nancy.

'My father loves your paintings – he has one at home,' said Freya.

'I buy his beer,' said Nancy. 'All the stall holders here support each other.'

'That's where we are heading now,' said Edward. He and Freya moved away towards a beer stall near the entrance with Jennie's eyes following them.

'So Edward is dating Freya Dennis,' said Nancy.

'Do you know her?' asked Jennie, a note of surprise in her voice.

'I know her father Colin Dennis. It's been tough for them both since her mother walked out. Colin has done his best as a single dad but money is always short.'

'Oh,' said Jennie. From Freya's appearance she had assumed that she was rich.

The morning passed quickly as trade was brisk. Jennie hardly paused for breath. When Ian joined them on the stall, Nancy grabbed her handbag.

'I'm off now for lunch,' she said. 'Try to sell another painting, won't you?'

Jennie gave her a doubtful look but seeing her mother's face, she softened and smiled her agreement. Nancy hurried off and Ian took his place behind the stall and helped serve the constant stream of customers. Finally there was a lull and the market scene was so picturesque that Jennie whipped out her smartphone and started to shoot a video. Drumbeats rose above the normal sounds of the market.

'What on earth is going on?' remarked Ian craning his neck.

Into their view marched a group of people led by a stocky man in his early thirties with a dark complexion. They were all dressed in black fleeces with an embroidered logo of a purple dragonfly. Some of the activists were holding large placards proclaiming 'Stop the Cull', 'Fauna Protection' and 'Save our Wildlife.' A couple were banging drums and several were shaking plastic buckets into which the onlookers were throwing money. Bringing up the rear was a tall young man with straggly hair. As they paraded past the Green Meadow stall their leader gave Jennie such a fierce look that she stopped filming. He thrust a leaflet into her hand.

'Why not join us? ' he said.

Behind him came a pale young woman with a nose stud and short spiky hair. Ill-fitting clothes hung off her thin frame and on her feet were a pair of Dr.Martens. She stopped in front of the stall and viewed the cheeses on display. Her eyes were a deep blue and her eyelashes were long and lush even without any mascara. Ian stared at her, clearly struck with her elfin looks. She shook a bucket at Jennie who chucked in a pound coin.

'Have you any vegan cheese?' the protester asked.

Jennie shook her head. 'All our cheeses are made with cow's milk.'

The expression on the woman's face changed to one of annoyance. She pointed her finger. 'I might have known – this is such a bloody backwater here - it's about time people like you started to realize that the world has changed,' she said angrily.

A flabbergasted Ian stepped back and Jennie opened her mouth but before she could answer, the woman stormed off. Jennie and Ian both gazed after her.

'What was that all about?' wondered Ian.

Jennie shrugged. 'Who knows? That's animal activists for you.'

Nancy returned and Jennie shot off for her break. She made a beeline for the pet stall where she bought a squeaky toy for Bramble, and the second hand bookstall where she rummaged around for natural history books. She checked her phone again to see if David had replied to her last text. He hadn't. He must be very busy.

The sound of drumming intruded again. She looked up and saw members of Fauna Protection still parading around the show ground. A remark of Ian's reverberated in her brain: 'You ought to become an animal activist if you feel that strongly.' She agreed that the badger cull was wrong and

51

pointless. One of the protestors shook another bucket in front of her. This time she tossed in another pound coin.

When she returned, Ian wandered off to meet his friends. The rest of the day was quieter and it was late afternoon when they packed up and headed back to the farm. Jennie recalled former Saturday evenings when she and David went to the pub, or ordered in a takeaway and watched a movie together.

Later, when alone in her room, she pulled the Fauna Protection leaflet out of her bag. She typed their website address into the Google search engine of her laptop. The website was of a professional standard with emotive stories and images featured alongside their slogan and dragonfly logo. She clicked on their promotional video. It featured a green field with a badger gambolling about. In a serious tone a voice proclaimed: "Recent research has shown that badger culling doesn't work. Bovine TB spreads from cattle to cattle. We must stop the wanton killing of badgers. Support our cause by donating today."

She then followed the link to the section entitled 'About Us'.

"Founded in 2001, Fauna Protection aims to work with landowners, universities and the general public to keep our wildlife safe; to protect our indigenous species from harm; and to defend all wildlife from attacks by unscrupulous people."

There was a drop down menu where one could select their local area so Jennie scrolled down and clicked on Oakfield. She was directed to another page where there was information on an introductory meeting on Monday evening at Oakfield Town Hall for those interested in joining the organisation. She jotted down the details and completed the online enquiry form which included her name, address, date of birth and current occupation.

7th May

The meeting was scheduled for 7pm Monday. Jennie drove herself there in her father's Range Rover, determined to try and stop the extension to the badger cull area. She wasn't sure whether joining a protest organisation was the best way of achieving this but it was something practical that she could do.

After parking at the rear of the Victorian gothic-style building Jennie was directed to a large meeting room. At the door she was greeted by the same young woman who had wanted to buy some vegan cheese from their stall. On registration she was given a name badge to pin on her jacket and a brown paper carrier bag full of leaflets and other things.

'Welcome,' said the woman sticking a round green spot onto her lapel, 'I hope you join us.'

'Hello Sophie – I remember you from the Spring Show.' said Jennie reading the woman's name badge. 'What does the green spot mean?'

'That you are credit worthy,' said Sophie, 'you have to be - if you want to become a member.'

'Oh,' said Jennie with a nod. She found a seat in the room, which was already full of people dressed in colourful garb and sitting quietly with their heads bowed. Other members of Fauna Protection, all wearing black fleeces with the purple dragonfly logo were busy acting as stewards.

Promptly at seven, the man who had given her the leaflet entered the room. His black hair was cut short at the back and sides, and left longer on the top. Everyone stood up as he walked to the front.

'Welcome everyone. Thank you for coming this evening and for your interest in our organisation. I'm Jeremy Boyle and I have worked for Fauna Protection for over ten years.

We welcome new members but this is a fight that requires you to make enduring and irreversible commitments,' he said. 'Tonight we are going to show you the work we are doing and then we will commence the enrolment process.'

The lights were dimmed and Jennie settled down to watch, interested to hear what they had to say about what they were doing to restore habitats and to protect endangered species. The first video featured the stories of people fighting for justice after being evicted from their homes in some unspecified city. The second film focused on something called transformational change, which was needed to address inequality, climate change and poverty. It claimed that the root of many problems lay in the inequalities of land ownership in the United Kingdom with over half the land being owned by just a handful of wealthy individuals. Jennie felt drawn in by the narratives and the images of distress and desperation but she wondered why there were few practical solutions being suggested – just a lot of rhetoric.

The lights went on. Boyle sat facing the blank wall at the front. He put his hands together with his fingers pointing upwards and started to repeat the Buddhist chant *Nam myoho renge kyo*. Everyone, including Jennie joined in. The repetition of the words formed a pattern of sound. It was like being hypnotised.

'Through peaceful means we are working together to achieve our aims. Amongst the many benefits of joining our organisation are our wrap around care and commitment to you whilst you are engaged in our work. If you are feeling lost: follow us. If you are looking for brotherhood: find a place to belong,' he said as the audience soaked up his message. When he had finished, a round of thunderous applause broke out.

The tall young man with untidy hair that Jennie recognised from the marketplace came onto the stage. 'We will now take questions,' he said.

A hand shot up at the front.

'It says in your blurb that there is a membership fee – could you elaborate more on that?' asked a clean-shaven man.

Jennie leant forward to hear the answer.

'Our organisation needs funds to function so we require our activists to make an upfront payment and a monthly donation,' said Boyle with a reassuring smile.

'But what if I can't afford the payments?' persisted the man.

'We will advise you on how to take out a loan. Don't worry – our members are waiting to help you to start your new life so that you can make a real difference,' said Boyle holding out his arms as though to encompass his flock and sounding straightforward and reasonable. Jennie watched as people formed queues in front of the tables at the front. She opened the bag that she had been given and pulled out a souvenir t-shirt and several leaflets and forms plus a biro emblazoned with the purple dragonfly. One of the leaflets contained thumbnail pictures of Boyle, Sophie and many other members.

Wanting to join, Jennie started to fill in the application form but something made her stop and read the small print at the end. One section was particularly incomprehensible. She read it several times before realizing that becoming a member was conditional on being able to devote at least fifteen hours a week to the organisation and to paying what she considered an extortionate amount each month. She immediately understood that she would be unable to meet both these conditions. She stood up to leave. An activist noticed, came over and blocked her exit.

'I am sorry,' said Jennie, 'but I have to go.'

'Stay,' he said in a friendly manner, 'someone will speak to you soon – they will help you fill in the form and set up the direct debit.'

'But I need to leave,' she said sounding firm.

He glanced around. 'You won't have to wait long,' he said. He beckoned the man with straggly hair over. He came immediately and read Jennie's name badge.

'Hello Jennie, nice to meet you,' he said with a smile that escaped his eyes. 'Let me help you.'

'No I am sorry, but I really have to go,' she insisted.

The expression on his face changed into one that was unmistakably threatening. He stood in front of her. It was like being trapped in a spider's web. She looked to see if there was a way out. Seeing an opportunity, she pushed past him, ran for the door and exited the building without looking back. Out in the fresh air, still holding her goody bag, she bolted down the High Street and then cut down a side road until she stopped to catch her breath and to check that she wasn't being followed. She'd had a lucky escape.

*

25th May

Jennie cycled along the winding road into Oakfield, admiring the surrounding countryside as she went. Arriving at the university, she secured her bike and headed up to the department's postgraduate office. She said hello to a couple of other research students, who were too engrossed in their work to reply.

She entered her password and logged on to one of the computers. Her personal files were securely saved in a series of folders, although she also kept backups on a USB. University protocol decreed that her research remained secret until its official publication. The only person who was allowed to read her work in progress was her supervisor Amina.

An interactive digital map of Liltford loaded onto the screen. She was using a geographic information system to map the location of the badger setts, annexes, subsidiaries and outliers that she had discovered so far. Badgers were as fond of second homes, summer houses and granny flats as people. Privacy and hygiene were also as important to them: their latrines were located some distance downwind of their setts.

Currently she estimated that there were about three-hundred badgers living in the district, the population having been swollen after the birth of cubs from February onwards. She brought up another map which showed the distribution of recent outbreaks of bovine TB in the neighbouring counties. She ran a statistical test which showed that there was a positive correlation between the outbreaks of bovine TB and the number of badgers.

Her attention turned to data entry. Painstakingly she typed in the results of her field observations. Her supplies of tranquiliser darts and GPS collars were running low. The department's budget was exhausted and she was going to have to fund the next order herself. She reminded herself that this was what she had chosen to do. She could have been exploring the Andes but instead she was glued to a computer screen.

The day passed quickly by. It was late afternoon when the door opened and Amina came in. She surveyed the room and when she has ascertained that Jennie was on her own she said, 'Ah, Jennie, I am glad I've caught you. I have some news.'

Jennie looked up wondering what she was going to say.

'The department has a new donor. They are going to sponsor us for twelve months,' said Amina.

Jennie's face lightened. 'Great.'

'They wish to remain anonymous but they are donating enough money to be able us to keep on our laboratory staff and to buy some new equipment.'

'Is that usual? I mean to remain anonymous?'

'There are conditions attached.'

Jennie raised her eyebrows.

'They would like regular updates on your research,' said Amina.

'But I thought that my thesis was confidential?'

'It is. Just a brief summary is all that is required.'

'Oh,' said Jennie internalising this information. She wondered if all the other PhD students were required to do this but the look on Amina's face discouraged any further questions.

*

9th June

On Saturday evening Jennie turned on the television and slumped onto the old sofa in the farmhouse's front room. Bramble jumped up beside her and wedged her hot body close to her. She put her phone onto the sofa's arm and settled down to watch a movie. Her phone rang and she picked it up. It was David.

'Jennie?' he said.

'Yes,' she replied straining to hear his voice as the line faded in and out. 'How are you?'

'I'm in Lima. There are loads of great museums full of ceramics, gold and textiles. You would love it,' he said.

'You sound as if you're having a great time,' she said. 'It's been difficult here – the herd might have bovine TB.'

'I'm going to Machu Picchu tomorrow. Got to go now. Bye. Love you,' he said as the phone went dead.

'Love you too,' she replied although only Bramble heard.

*

22nd June

Sixty days after Zoe Mudmaker's inconclusive test, on one of the first hot days of the summer, Jennie was in the farmyard when Edward returned to Green Meadow Farm to carry out the follow-up tests on the rest of the herd. Giles handed him the records of the cattle's movements and treatments.

'Are these accurate and up to date?' asked Edward.

'Everything is ready for your inspection, my lad,' said Giles with a look which implied that it was insult to suggest otherwise. 'The cattle are this way.'

Giles led the way to a modern shed, which was open on both sides. Inside there were six large pens with straw covered floors where the cows were munching away, blithely unaware that they were just about to be tested. In the middle was a handling unit with guillotine gates. Jennie watched as Edward opened his bag, pulled out a clipboard and pinned the farm's paperwork to it. He checked the entire herd's ear tags one by one before Giles and Ian manoeuvred the first cow into the central unit so that he could carry out the test.

Jennie needed to get on with some work so she left and went back up to her bedroom. Later she returned to hear Edward telling Giles that he had finished testing the herd and now needed to do Zoe Mudmaker. She followed them to the isolation shed which had been the stricken cow's home for the last two months and watched as Edward carried out the test. When he had finished he wiped the perspiration from his brow.

'The clinic can process these samples quickly so I will be back in a couple of days with the results,' he said.

'It'll be an anxious few days for us,' said Jennie.

'A bloody nightmare more like,' said Giles. With his feet weighed down, he walked off in a different direction. Jennie's eyes followed him.

'There are support organisations that can give advice,' said Edward.

Jennie sighed. 'That's just not Dad's thing. Until it happens to your farm, you don't realise what a dreadful thing this disease is.'

*

26th June

Four days later Edward's car crunched up the gravel drive. Jennie accompanied her family out into the farmyard. Giles's face was full of dread and foreboding. Edward got out of his car in a way which encouraged no optimism.

Giles approached him. 'Well, my lad, have you got the results?'

Edward indicated that he had. He handed over a brown envelope.

'Unfortunately the results were positive – that means that your cows reacted to the test,' he said in a serious tone.

'Oh no,' cried Nancy her face full of consternation. Jennie and Ian both remained silent.

Giles sought clarification. 'So?'

'That means they could have bovine TB,' said Edward in a soft voice.

'Fuck,' said Giles. He kicked an empty metal bucket across the yard, 'all of them?'

'All.'

Ian looked exasperated. 'You said, could be infected – don't the tests show for sure?'

Edward was apologetic. 'Unfortunately not – the science is too imprecise at the moment.'

Giles mopped his brow. 'What happens now?'

'I am afraid that the herd has to be slaughtered.'

Nancy saw the tears starting to well up in her husband's eyes. 'Surely not? That's dreadful.'

'No! This herd is my life's work. They are my children as well as my livelihood. I have some lovely heifers – gorgeous animals – they are too young to die!' said Giles. He held his stomach as if in pain. 'I have nurtured this herd for over thirty years.'

Behind him, his family stood still and silent – to all of them the cows were more than just animals - they were family. Some of the best members of the dairy herd were over ten years old and they had been on the farm all their lives.

'But there is no other way. I am sorry,' said Edward with a look of genuine sympathy.

'I don't believe this is happening. You must have got it wrong,' said Giles his voice rising in pitch.

'I'm afraid not. The test results mean that your cows are likely to have bovine TB. You will now need to clean and disinfect the entire farm and prepare for their slaughter,' said Edward. He turned towards his car.

Later on, the whole family met for a conference in the farmhouse kitchen. A feeling of huge sadness hung in the air. Giles was a shrunken, more shrivelled version of himself.

Nancy put the kettle on.

'Let's all have a cup of tea – that will make us feel better,' she said as everyone sat around the kitchen table. She cut a freshly baked Victorian sponge and handed it around.

'Not for me,' said Jennie who had suddenly lost her appetite.

Ian bit into his slice of cake. 'We can replace the cows – surely?'

'It isn't that easy,' said Giles, 'you must know that?'

'The badgers will be blamed, I know,' said Jennie her eyes full of gloom.

'Rightly so,' said Giles, 'I hope to shoot the bloody lot of them!'

'That's not fair – you don't know that they caught the disease from the badgers – you are merely guessing – they could have caught it from cows on neighbouring farms,' said Jennie. 'You have never bothered with biosecurity.'

'Dad, she's right,' said Ian.

Giles huffed and turned red. He couldn't bring himself to acknowledge that the old lackadaisical practices might have let down the cows and the farm.

'What will happen to my cheese production?' asked Nancy.

'If there are no cows, then you won't able to make any cheese –isn't that obvious?' snapped Giles.

'Then I will have to sell something else instead – to make up for the lost income,' said Nancy.

Jennie got up and left the kitchen. She needed some fresh air.

*

1st July

Giles didn't have to wait long to hear about what was to happen next. The following day he received an email from the Animal Health Agency authorizing him to go ahead with the slaughter of his herd. He retreated to his study. He was like a bear with a sore head. Jennie and the rest of the family tiptoed around, hardly daring to raise their voices or to make any comment, question or statement in case they were shouted down. It was agony for everyone – a mixture of sadness, regret and anger.

*

3rd July

It was so hot that Jennie put on shorts, a tee-shirt, sunglasses and a baseball cap. Over the hedge the cows were grazing, oblivious to their imminent fate. Edward arrived in his car followed by three dark-grey trucks. She greeted him along with Giles and Ian.

'All set to go?' asked Edward.

Giles nodded and handed him several forms. The first truck driver got out of his cab, opened up the back and lowered the ramp. Ian unfastened the gate and tempted the herd out with some fresh hay.

'Come on girls,' cried Giles. He walked alongside them as they moved forward into the back of the trailer. A few stopped dead in their tracks as if sensing their destiny and had to be pushed in. The last to be loaded was Zoe Mudmaker, who looked up at him with trusting eyes as Giles led her from her stall to the trailer. A tear ran unchecked down his cheek. Jennie pulled out a tissue to wipe her eyes. Ian lowered his head and bit his lip.

'I just need to do something,' he said. He disappeared into a shed and remained there until the last of the trailers had been secured.

'Right, that's done,' said Edward. He handed Giles a leaflet. 'You will get compensation for each animal, as long as it has the correct ear tag and passport when it's slaughtered.'

'Compensation?' asked Giles.

'If I send in my report today, you should hear soon from the Animal Health Agency, confirming that you will get payment for each one. More testing may have to be done here and on your neighbouring farms. An official letter will confirm that Green Meadow has lost its official TB free status and that you won't be able to restock until they have renewed your licence,' said Edward closing his document bag.

'What's the point?' asked Giles with some bitterness in his voice, 'I'm not going to go to all the trouble of building up a new herd only for the same thing to happen again – whilst those bloody badgers are here they could re-infect the cows. Anyway, money is nothing – what is money?'

'If it is on offer then you might as well apply for it,' said Ian. He booted a stone across the yard. Giles grimaced, folded the leaflet in half and put it into his pocket.

'Are you coming to the abattoir?' asked Edward. Without waiting for a reply he got into his car and followed the trucks down the drive.

'Might as well, I have nothing else to do,' said Giles reaching in his other pocket for his keys, 'anyone coming with me?'

'I will,' said Jennie. She climbed into the Range Rover alongside him.

At the slaughterhouse, the cows were reluctant to be unloaded. There was a smell of blood in the air which made them confused and unhappy. The staff from the abattoir took over and Jennie was left standing outside with Giles and Edward. She struggled to keep back her tears.

Edward regarded her. 'It's very hard but there's no other choice.

'What happens next?' she said.

'The abattoir vet will carry out post mortems on the cows. Carcasses with any lesions or areas possibly damaged by TB are incinerated, to stop the infection spreading to other animals. The inspectors take no chances. They will do culture tests as well – you will get the results in about six weeks,' he said.

A butcher came out of the abattoir with some papers for Giles to sign. That done, Jennie retuned to Green Meadow with him. She went up into her bedroom and looked out on to the empty fields. To take her mind off the situation she immersed herself in her work.

Later she went down stairs and found her mother at her easel, painting yet another canvas.

'The farm doesn't feel the same without the cows,' said Jennie.

'It's very strange – too quiet for my liking,' said Nancy just as Giles came into the kitchen.

'The tests were wrong – I don't believe that the cows had the blasted infection at all,' he said. He opened the fridge for a beer.

'It's too late now and anyway no farm is viable with diseased stock,' said Nancy daubing bright red paint onto her painting.

Giles huffed, switched on the television and slumped on to the sofa.

*

4th July

Without the cows, the farm was just a house surrounded by fields. The chickens clucked away oblivious to what had happened, but Bramble and Sukey both moped around missing the smells and noises from the dairy herd. Jennie resorted to her research as keeping busy kept her mind off the situation. After supper she went upstairs to her bedroom to read. Her peace was interrupted by Giles shouting for her to come to his study. She found him staring at his monitor.

'This compensation form is so complicated that I can't make head or tail of it,' he said without turning around.

She leant over his shoulder and peered at the screen.

'It should be straightforward,' she said.

He scowled. 'That would be too easy, wouldn't it? They want to make it so difficult people don't bother to make a claim.'

She pulled up a chair. 'Let me have a look,' she said. The first page was full of instructions. The age and role of each cow in the herd had to be entered. A young heifer was worth only about £300, but if they had calved and were a good milker, they could be valued at over £1,200. It would make a difference.

'How far have you got?' she asked.

'I've only just started.'

'Have you got the information?'

'Yes, Ian printed it all out,' he said picking up a sheaf of papers.

She sighed. It would take hours to do all the entries but she knew her father's expertise lay elsewhere. She looked at her watch. The evening was still young and she had time to spare and this needed to be done.

'I'll do it, if you want,' she said as the door opened and Bramble came in.

An expression of relief flooded Giles's face. 'I'll leave you to it,' he said. He got up and made his escape.

To lessen the boredom, Jennie navigated to an online music station and clicked Play. Bramble found her way under the table and lay near her feet. She entered the information on each cow and then calculated the total amount of compensation they were claiming just as Giles returned.

'Wow it comes to £250,000. That's a lot of money, isn't?' she said as he put down a mug of tea on the desk in front of her.

'It has taken me years to build up my herd – it isn't just a case of buying in any old cow and milking her – I have nurtured all my cows since they were born. The money doesn't compensate us for all that time and attention. Besides which, the famous Green Meadow cheese depends on the milk from them,' he said.

'Will you buy some new cows when you get the money?'
she asked picking the mug up and having a sip.

'I don't know. Bovine TB is a dreadful thing – no wonder
many dairy farmers are throwing in their hats. The world is
against us – maybe I should just grow cereals instead.'

'But the rainfall is too high and the summers too cool here
for arable farming,' said Jennie with a soft smile.

'So, no choice – but to be a dairy farmer.'

'Do you know how much Douglas Sitwell received in
compensation? His herd was roughly the same size as ours,'
she said turning her eyes back to the screen.

'No, all I know is that he complained about how
complicated the forms were.'

'Have you heard anything from him yet?'

'Not a dickey bird.'

'Do you think he is still alive?'

'He must be, they haven't found a body.'

'Right, I think that's almost it. I'll just type in Oakfield
Veterinary Clinic, High Street, Oakfield,' she said, 'they
want details of our vet.' She saved the form and submitted
it to the Animal Health Agency. Immediately an
acknowledgment appeared in the inbox.

*DO NOT REPLY Animal Health
Agency(compensation@animalhealthagency.gov.uk)
Your form has been received and is being processed.*

Giles yawned. 'Thank you, Jennie.'

She got up and stretched. Bramble uncurled and came out
from under the desk. She inspected her phone. There was a
message.

David
Catching the overnight bus to Santiago in Chile
Jennie

Hope you get some sleep xx

Chapter 5

5th July

The smell of frying bacon filled the farmhouse kitchen when Jennie bounded in for breakfast. She headed straight to the coffee maker and loaded it with a capsule. Beside it lay some unopened mail. She leafed through hoping for a letter or postcard from David. There was nothing. It had been weeks since he had been in touch.

'These are all for you, Dad,' she said to Giles who was sitting at the table eating a big bowl of cornflakes. Radio 4 was on in the background. The seven o'clock pips sounded, and the broadcaster read the news:

'The government has announced an extension of the badger culling area in the West Country to include the districts of Bovington, Gemingly and Liltford. This decision has been taken because of the recent rise in the number of bovine tuberculosis cases in dairy cattle. Badgers are known to harbour bovine TB and to be strongly linked to previous epidemics. Recent studies have shown that a reduction in the number of badgers leads to fewer outbreaks.'

Jennie's face went pale. 'That's awful. I've always feared that the badger cull would come to Liltford.'

Giles looked up. 'It should have happened before - those badgers have to go –they are threatening our livelihood. The farm is more important than them, I'm afraid.'

'I agree,' said Nancy to Jennie's consternation. Usually her mother sympathised with her.

'Me too,' said Ian sipping a mug of tea, 'badgers are riddled with disease.

'They're not,' said Jennie vehemently. 'They are perfectly healthy. Besides which, they have the same right to live here as we do, and they are a protected species.'

'You are just worried that your research will be affected,' he retorted.

Indignation rose in her breast. 'It jolly well will be, if all the badgers around here are killed.'

'Surely they won't kill all of them?' said Nancy bringing plates of bacon and eggs to the table.

'How can they?' said Giles. 'There are miles of underground tunnels for them to hide in.'

'Anyway there is no evidence to show that cows catch TB from badgers – they are just as likely to get it from other cows,' said Jennie.

Ian scoffed. 'You are talking rubbish. At college, we were taught that the most frequent route of infection is from badger to cattle.'

Not to be defeated, Jennie battled on. 'Killing wild animals is brutal – I would never in a million years commit such a barbaric act.' Abruptly, she rose from the table and took her plate to the sink.

'Sometimes hard choices have to be made,' said Giles. He reached for his mail. One particular letter caught his attention. He opened and read it.

'The Animal Health Agency,' he said, 'have sent us an invitation to attend a public meeting about the badger cull.'

'When is it?' asked Ian.

'Next week at the Town Hall. Who wants to come?'

Ian straightaway indicated his interest but Jennie declared emphatically that she didn't want anything to do with it.

'It might be useful for your research,' said Nancy.

Jennie considered this. 'Possibly. For that reason, and that reason only, I'll go.' She headed for the back door with Bramble close on her heels. She needed some fresh air.

*

11th July

The following week, still in two minds as to whether it was the right thing to do, Jennie accompanied Giles and Ian to the meeting. The large hall was filling up quickly with a mixture of local farmers and Oakfield residents of all ages. The atmosphere was buzzing with excitement as everyone anticipated a lively discussion. They found seats near the front. Before she sat down, Jennie picked up the programme from the chair. Her eyes lit up as she browsed through it.

'Look,' she said, pointing to the list of speakers, 'my supervisor Dr Ahmed is speaking.'

From the back of the hall came the sound of drumming. Jennie turned around and saw Edward and Freya taking their seats and members of Fauna Protection marching through the door. In the lead was Jeremy Boyle followed by his sidekick, the tall young man with unkempt hair. Two of the activists were banging drums. Others, including Sophie, were carrying placards proclaiming: 'Badgers are Innocent' and chanting 'Stop the Cull'. They congregated at the back blocking an aisle until a steward ushered them to one side. A man wearing a grey suit came onto the stage and tapped the microphone, which sprung into life.

'Good evening everyone,' he said. He waited until quiet had descended.

'Welcome. Thank you all for coming tonight. I'm Councillor Thomson, Leader of Oakfield Town Council,' he said. 'As you know we are all here to find out more about the proposed extension to the badger culling area. This is an

71

issue that divides local opinion. Farmers fear losing their livelihoods to bovine TB and want their livestock protected. Conservationists are against killing a wild animal.'

In the audience heckling broke out. Cllr Thomson paused with his lips set in a firm line until the noise had subsided.

'Tonight all sides will have an opportunity to express their views,' he said as more shouting erupted. He made eye contact with members of the audience as he waited again. 'In the last three years, many farms in this area have been affected by bovine tuberculosis. Thousands of cows have had to be slaughtered, and millions have been paid out in compensation at great cost to the public purse. The government is determined to stamp out this disease which is causing so much distress and misery. Badger culling has been shown to be the most effective weapon in the battle against it. I will now hand over to Dr Amina Ahmed from Oakfield University to explain more.'

Amina came to the podium holding her notes and put on her reading glasses.

'Bovine TB is a nasty, infectious bacterial disease which kills both farm animals and wildlife. The bacteria can be transmitted from cow to cow when they touch noses or come into contact with saliva, urine, faeces and milk,' she began.

'Can it be transmitted from cows to people?' An audience member interrupted. Cllr Thomson rose to his feet.

'Questions will be taken at the end,' he said.

'Yes, anyone can catch bovine TB if they come into close contact with an infected animal. That it is why it is so dangerous,' said Amina nodding in his direction. 'So what are the ways of eradicating this disease? Firstly the government could do nothing and let the disease rip through the dairy industry.' She paused.

Someone shouted, 'That would be a total disaster. It is heart breaking when your herd is affected, as I know all too well.'

'So option one can be ruled out. Option two is to manage the disease by improving farm biosecurity and by confining it to known areas which are then closely monitored. Any farm animal that tests positive is slaughtered.'

'That is being tried already,' someone else yelled, 'but it doesn't always work.'

'So we need to go one step further and cull the badgers,' she said.

In response, voices rose and placards were waved. Cllr Thomson rose to his feet again, 'Put your hand up if you would like to ask a question and wait until the roving mic comes your way,' he said in a strict tone.

A tall bearded man stood up and asked, 'Wouldn't vaccination be better?'

Amina smiled and took a deep breath. 'A very good question. Thank you. There isn't an effective badger vaccine at present. Even if there was, badgers difficult to vaccinate as they are so elusive. A cull is the only way to delay the spread of bovine TB across the country.'

Jennie raised her hand. Cllr Thomson pointed to her and a young man brought her the microphone. She stood up and cleared her throat.

'What about a vaccine for cows?' she asked.

'Unfortunately at present we cannot differentiate between a vaccinated cow and one with TB,' answered Amina looking directly at her with a smile of recognition. 'The government's research scientists are working on a solution.'

'Aren't there any effective treatments?' said a middle aged lady at the front.

'Not at the moment,' said Amina.

'So are you saying that the only option is a badger cull?' asked Sophie from the back.

Amina shuffled her papers, 'What I am saying is that there are limited ways of reducing the impacts of the disease. The government has decided to go ahead with a cull in this area.'

More noise broke out and Boyle stormed to the front of the hall followed by half a dozen of his supporters. A security guard rushed to stand between them and the stage.

'It's cruel to kill wild animals and this cull should be stopped before it starts,' he roared. A cacophony broke out as people stood up and made their feelings known.

Cllr Thomson strode onto the stage and spoke clearly into the mic. 'Can everyone return to their seats?'

Boyle took his time but complied and the noise died down. Further questions were taken and at the end, Cllr Thomson concluded the evening by saying, 'Thank you to everyone who has made contributions tonight. The cull will be starting this summer and we welcome online applications from anyone wanting to be involved. The closing date is a week today. Good night.'

At that, the activists starting shouting and banging their drums. They blocked the exits. The audience milled around unable to leave. Jennie waited with Giles and Ian.

Ian glanced around. 'The Fauna Protection mob is making itself heard,' he said.

'Nasty people,' said Giles with a glare.

'Most of them have good intentions and want to protest peacefully,' said Jennie.

'Rubbish,' said Giles, 'they will resort to any means they can.'

'Surely not violence?' asked Ian.

'I am going to apply to be a marksman,' said Giles. 'I'm a good shot. What about you two? You both have the necessary skills – you have been shooting since you were tiny tots.'

Jennie laughed. 'That's true – before we even went to school you taught us how to ride, shoot and hunt.'

'But surely it involves a lot of extra work and effort?' asked Ian with a slight cough and a hesitant tone to his voice.

'Needs must,' said Giles, 'someone has to do it and it might as well be us.'

'I would never kill any badgers. It is too horrible to even think about,' she said adamantly.

'Hi, Jennie,' cried Amina rushing up to them. 'Have you a minute? In private?'

'Yes,' said Jennie wondering what she had to say as they moved to the side of the hall which had started to empty.

'Jennie, I hope you don't mind but I have recommended you to the Animal Health Agency as an ecologist who knows about the local badger population and who is researching bovine TB. They need an expert to help run the training courses for the new badger culling team.'

Jennie looked surprised and she hesitated. 'I wouldn't say that I am an expert.'

Amina's expression became more forceful. 'I have said that you will do it,' she insisted, her tone of voice betraying her annoyance at Jennie's reluctance. 'They pay well. Look, I have to dash. Let me know when you have decided.' She spotted an exit out of which people were starting to file and headed that way leaving Jennie on her own.

The mention of money made Jennie stop and think. Her bank balance remained stubbornly low – finding the payment for her increased fees every month was a struggle.

'Decided what?' asked Edward as he and Freya came up beside her.

'Amina has recommended that I help train the cullers. I know that it is wrong to kill badgers – they are a protected species after all. So I'm not sure that I can….,' her voice trailed off.

'Anyone getting involved in the cull will have to run the gauntlet of those protesters,' said Freya. She cast an eye over the activists beating their percussion instruments.

'Both badgers and livestock all deserve a healthy future without TB. My maternal grandmother died prematurely from the disease not that long ago. It has almost been eradicated in people and it is important that it is wiped out in animals as well,' said Edward.

'I know why the cull is needed but I am not sure if I should get involved,' said Jennie.

'You know more than anyone else about the local badgers, if you don't help then who will?' he said with a persuasive look.

She paused.

'What about you? Are you going to volunteer?' asked Jennie fully expecting a negative answer.

'I am seriously considering it,' said Edward. 'I want to make sure that the whole thing is done as humanely as possible.'

Both Jennie and Freya opened their mouths in surprise.

'Oh,' said Freya, 'if you are going to sign up, then so shall I.'

Jennie tensed her shoulders and raised her eyebrows.

'There will be selection tests,' she said.

'Hopefully we will all pass,' said Edward. He moved towards the door with Freya right behind him. Jennie gazed after them as her father and brother caught up with her.

'You had better get your applications in quickly if you want to join the team – I expect that there are lots of people who are interested,' she said as they left the hall together.

Amina's offer (or was it an order?) had taken her by surprise. On the one hand, Bullitt and his family needed her protection plus knowledge gained from participating in the cull could maybe help her win the Luminosity Prize. Her research currently lacked a certain element of originality. Plus the extra money would come in handy. On the other though, was the fact that she had vowed not to harm any badgers and she could ill afford the time that it would involve. She took out her phone and wrote a text to Amina:

'What is the pay rate?'

She replied straight away with an amount that was too large to turn down.

Jennie's mind was made up. She texted her acceptance of the job to Amina.

'Brilliant,' came the reply, 'I will let them know.'

*

25th July

When Giles mentioned that his and Ian's applications to become badger cullers had been successful, Jennie wondered about hers. She didn't have to wait long as that morning an email pinged into her inbox.

Animal Health Agency
(backgroundchecks@animalhealthagency.gov.uk)
Dear Miss Cliffe, We are pleased to be able to inform you that the checks into your criminal record and mental health have been performed and no issues identified. You have been cleared to take up the position you have been offered as Ecological Advisor to the badger cull team.

Shortly after, another email arrived, this time from Joe Friend, an Environmental Officer working for the council who wanted to meet with her to plan the training course. With interest she read all the information. She liked something new to do and this was certainly different. She reassured herself that she was only taking part to ensure that the badger killing, if it had to be done at all, was carried out as humanely as possible.

*

1st August

Jennie went with Giles and Ian along to Oakfield Shooting School. It had been established in 1898 and was located on the outskirts of the town down a narrow tree lined lane. The school boasted state-of-the-art facilities including both an indoor and an outdoor shooting range. Jennie led the way into the large training room located at the front of the building. The room smelt of stale ammunition and was decorated with framed pictures of guns. A dozen or so wooden chairs were arranged in a rough half circle in front of a table. Many were already occupied. Jennie recognised Edward and Freya. She picked up a set of course notes and took a seat.

Joe Friend was setting up a PowerPoint on his laptop. When everyone was present, the session started.

'Right. Good evening everyone,' he said. 'First of all housekeeping.' He pointed out the fire escapes and toilets. 'Thank you for coming to our first training session on badger culling. A digital form of the course will be available online afterwards. Can you introduce yourselves? Shall we start at one end of the row and work along?'

Edward stood up. 'My name is Edward Hollyer. I'm a vet in Oakfield. I am looking forward to working with the team.'

Next Freya rose to her feet and looked around at everyone. Her hair and makeup were immaculate as usual. 'I am Freya Dennis. I'm interested in using my skills.'

Jennie heard someone whisper, 'I wonder what skills she's referring to?'

A good-looking man in his early thirties, wearing a Ralph Lauren polo shirt and leather brogues, introduced himself next.

'Tony McKensie. I'm in property development but shooting is one of my hobbies.'

He was followed by a shorter man of a similar age with a darker complexion.

'Hi, I'm Ibrahim Khan and a solicitor working in Oakfield. I'm a friend of Tony's,' he said with a wide smile that exhibited his even white teeth.

'We're local dairy farmers,' said Ian, coughing slightly and indicating his father. 'So we want to prevent more outbreaks of bovine TB.'

Jennie stood up. 'I'm Jennie Cliffe – your ecological adviser. Giles is my father and Ian's my brother.'

'A family affair,' muttered Ibrahim.

'Thank you everyone. Right, let's get started,' said Joe. He switched off the main light, turned on the projector and started the PowerPoint. 'Firstly, I am going to give you some background information to the current situation. Many farmers are convinced badgers are responsible for spreading bovine tuberculosis among their cattle.'

'It's a fact,' said Giles folding his arms, 'how else would the cattle be infected?'

'There's evidence that the higher the number of badgers, the higher the incidents of bovine TB,' said Ibrahim leaning forward.

'The evidence isn't that clear,' said Jennie, 'many believe that badgers aren't spreading disease.'

'To find the truth of the matter and to evaluate the effectiveness of badger culling, in the last five years the government has been funding a large-scale field trial,' said Joe moving the slide show onto a map of Somerset and Gloucestershire.

Tony stretched his long legs out in front of him. 'How did they do that?'

'They divided the area into three zones. In the first zone, seventy percent of the badgers were killed; in the second one hundred percent, and in the third, none,' said Joe pointing to the map.

'What did the trial find?' asked Edward.

'They found that going for one hundred percent was best,' said Joe.

'That's extermination,' said Tony.

'Exactly,' said Joe. 'Now let's look at how to kill badgers.' He moved on to the next slide which showed two photographs – one of a wire cage with a badger inside and the other of a badger running across a field. 'There are only two approved methods – they can be trapped first and then shot with a rifle or a shotgun, or they can be shot in the field. Poisoning and baiting with dogs are forbidden. Whether we use trapping or free shooting it should be done as humanely as possible. Therefore we aim to train every one of you to the highest standard so that you know what you are doing and that you do it effectively. What is important is that the animals suffer no unnecessary pain or harm.'

'Aren't badgers a protected species?' asked Ibrahim. 'I don't want to get into trouble with the law.'

'Unless you have a licence, it is illegal to kill or injure badgers in England. If you pass the assessment at the end of your training you will be licensed. Even then there are strict conditions you will have to observe,' said Joe.

'What are they?' asked Tony.

Joe answered with a firm expression on his face. 'You can only operate within the cull period; only use certain types of firearm; and only kill the permitted number of badgers. No wounded badgers are to be left in the field – you should make sure they are dead and then remove their carcasses. Finally, you should keep and provide accurate up-to-date records of all your activities.'

'How do we know how many badgers there are?' asked Ian.

'Our local expert – Jennie Cliffe - has estimated the total,' he answered. 'The health and safety of you – the licensed operators – and the public is our highest priority. At least two people are needed when night shooting. In the event of an emergency such as an injury you should know the measures to take and use a communication device to inform others. You should follow all necessary hygiene and biosecurity precautions. It is also essential that you have a good understanding of badger ecology, so that you can trap or kill badgers without harming any other animals. Now I am going to hand you over to Jennie.' He finished speaking and sat down.

Jennie got up and cleared her throat. She navigated to her presentation and clicked on the title page. 'Good evening everyone,' she said, 'First of all I want to say that badgers are an important British native species – they play an essential role in food chains. They deserve to be treated with respect. Tonight I'll show you how to identify their setts, runs, tracks and latrines and how to differentiate between signs of badgers and other animals, such as foxes. Plus I will go through with you the characteristics of badger behaviour, how these differ from other animals and how they can be used to maximise the success of the cull. I will cover the social structure of badgers; their foraging and ranging behaviours; their senses and, in particular, their behaviour in response to smell, noise and light. Remember also that badgers are nocturnal creatures.'

There were one or two soft groans from those seated in front of her. A look of boredom spread over Freya's face.

She must only have come to be with Edward, thought Jennie rather uncharitably.

She brought up the first slide which showed a typical badger sett – a hole about ten inches wide surrounded with soil dug up from underground. 'There can be up to thirty metres of tunnels under each sett and each sett can have up to twenty badgers.' She changed the slide to show a family of badgers out at dusk. 'Badgers are opportunist animals – they are always on the lookout for food, water and other badgers.'

'How do they forage?' asked Tony.

'With their noses – they have a very well developed sense of smell and they will eat anything but they particularly love peanut butter sandwiches.'

'How fast can they run?' asked Ibrahim.

'Up to twenty miles per hour - they are very agile,' said Jennie as she moved on to a slide of a badger flying through the air like a fox in flight.

At the end of the slide show Jennie thanked everyone for their attention and she returned to her seat to a short round of applause.

'Thank you Jennie - I think that is enough information for one evening,' said Joe. He got up and turned on the light.

'I didn't know much about badgers before today, but I have to admit that listening to all that, I now have a grudging admiration for them.' said Tony.

'You wouldn't say that if your herd was threatened,' said Giles with a grunt.

'Probably not,' said Tony.

'How easy is it to find the badgers?' asked Ibrahim.

Joe switched off his laptop. 'Difficult – they can be very shy.'

'Don't worry – Edward will be able to – he is very clever,' said Freya. She gave Edward's hand a squeeze.

Edward had the grace to look embarrassed. 'I expect we shall all receive the proper level of training,' he said.

'Next week we will be talking about firearms,' said Joe. 'Bring the firearm you will be using to the session. If you don't own a gun – don't worry we will provide you with one. Just a word of warning – do not talk about this very important work to anyone. We have to be as discrete as possible. Thank you all for coming. Oh Jennie – a word, please.'

She waited to hear what he had to say.

'I want you to train as a marksman – just in case,' said Joe as he picked up his bag.

'But I am just the expert on badgers,' she protested.

'I know, but if you do the training alongside everyone else you will be able to give your insights to the team,' he said as they walked to the door together. It made sense.

'You will be paid an extra rate,' he said. She hesitated. Her bank balance could do with a boost.

'Alright,' she said, 'I will.

*

8th August

Jennie knew that the family's rifles were locked in the gun cabinet located in the farm office, which was at the front of the farmhouse. The cabinet was made from sheet steel and secured with a hardened padlock. Ammunition was stored in a separate lockable container. That evening Giles took out three guns from the cabinet and put them in the boot of the Range Rover. He drove Jennie and Ian to Oakfield Shooting School. In the car park, he opened the boot and lifted out the rifles.

'Here is yours, Jennie,' he said handing her a rifle. She took it and held it carefully. Since she had been a teenager she had been learning how to shoot. Her father had encouraged such skills arguing that country folk needed them. All the necessary firearms certificates had been kept up-to-date.

She signed the visitors' book left on a table in the small lobby and went into the training room followed by Giles and Ian. Tony and Ibrahim were already there and Edward and Freya arrived soon after and took their seats in front of Joe. He was standing at the front next to a table on which was his laptop. Jennie noticed that Freya was looking very pretty with her blonde hair contained by a thick hair band. Joe welcomed them all. He switched on the projector and started the slide show.

'We have a number of traps stored here at the shooting school which we will place outside the setts and bait with peanuts, which is their favourite food. When we find a trapped badger we will shoot them with a gunshot to the head which is relatively quick and painless,' said Joe clicking on a short video taken to illustrate the technique. Jennie watched in silence. It looked brutal. When the badger slumped down inside the cage she lowered her eyes.

'Is that considered humane?' asked Freya. She twiddled with her rings.

'The point is we all need to be skilled enough to shoot the badgers dead with the first shot so that they don't suffer needlessly,' said Edward.

Joe nodded in agreement. He picked up a ruler.

'Whether you are shooting from the ground, or from an elevated position, you need to aim straight at the heart and lung area of the badger, which is located behind their large muscular shoulders,' he said indicating the correct place on the badger pictured on the slide. Jennie craned her neck to see the exact spot she should aim for.

'If they are moving, it can be hard to hit that area. You need to practise until you are skilful enough to kill as rapidly and humanely as possible. You will also be going out at different times of the day – sometimes there will be moonlight, other times it will be pitch black. The weather will also play a big part in how accurate your aim is – for instance if it is very windy, your bullet may be blown off course,' Joe said.

'What should we do, if there are several badgers at one time, around a bait point?' asked Jennie, knowing that she had frequently observed whole family groups feeding simultaneously.

'In those situations, there is a greater risk of wounding rather than killing a badger, so what I recommend is that you go out as a small group and that you agree beforehand which animal each of you is going to target,' said Joe.

'What should one do with an injured badger?' asked Freya with a look of concern.

'It will obviously depend on how injured the animal is. If it is unable to move, that is easier but if it has escaped, that is more problematic - different badgers react differently to being shot, just like humans. If a wounded badger runs away, you should follow it and try to deal with it,' answered Joe pacing across the room.

'My dog has been trained to find badgers,' said Jennie volunteering the services of Bramble. She was absorbing all the information the best she could, but she also realized that she would have to wait until she was in an actual situation before knowing how she would react for real.

'You can certainly use dogs to help, but you must be confident that you can control them,' said Joe. 'Right, I would like to introduce you to your shooting instructor, Bob Smith.'

Jennie looked across to the doorway where a middle aged serious looking man was standing.

Bob smiled. 'Welcome to you all. You are here this evening so that you can brush up on your skills in readiness for your shooting test. First I will go over with you how to look after your guns and then we will have some practice at the range.'

'I haven't got my own gun,' said Freya, 'but I was told that I would be provided with one.'

'Come with me, I will sort out one for you now,' said Bob.

They disappeared into the back room and then came back ten minutes later with Freya holding a rifle.

Bob stood with his feet slightly apart. 'Right, everyone, can I have your attention? We are going to start by looking at health and safety.'

Jennie held her .22-calibre single-shot rifle and watched him demonstrate how to clean, maintain and handle it safely.

'The most important thing to remember about shooting is that you must be in a stable position when you fire. That applies whether you are lying flat on the ground, standing or kneeling,' said Bob.

'I find leaning on something like a tree, gate or fence helps,' said Edward.

Bob lifted his rifle. 'When you are in the right position, hold your gun with a light grip and look through the scope straight at the target. Then put your finger on the trigger, and build up a consistent pressure before releasing it. Any questions?'

No one answered. 'OK, let's all go into the indoor range.'

Inside the large shed there were six firing lanes each twenty-five yards long. At the end of each lane was a large black circular target. Located behind each target were bullet traps, which were designed to stop and collect any projectiles.

'First check that you have attached a good quality scope to your rifle. That will enable you to see the quarry in low-light,' said Bob. 'Next tighten any loose screws with a screwdriver and clean the rifle barrel. When you are ready, fire one shot, clean the barrel again and then repeat. Also make sure you are using the right bullet. When we have done about an hour in here we will move outside.'

'Isn't this all a bit long winded?' queried Tony.

'We aim to get every single one of you up to a high standard so that you can use your rifle efficiently and accurately, especially when shooting an animal at close range,' said Bob firmly.

Jennie prepped her rifle, donned her goggles, ear plugs and earmuffs, and started to fire. Bob watched everyone carefully. He shouted, 'Squeeze the trigger, and don't tug at the bloody thing!' every so often. She concentrated on her own aim, not wanting to embarrass herself in front of the others. Towards the end she relaxed slightly as she felt satisfied with her own performance. She regarded the others standing there, holding their rifles correctly and shooting bullet after bullet at the target. She noticed that everyone except Ian, were firing confidently and accurately.

'Right, last shot now,' shouted Bob.

Jennie lowered her rifle and smiled at Edward in the adjacent lane.

'How come you know how to shoot?' said Edward as they walked together out of the indoor range back into the training room.

'It is my father's hobby – he enjoys shooting as a countryside sport. He taught me as soon as I was big enough to hold a gun,' she said taking a glass off a table at the side. 'As a Londoner, I am surprised that you even know one end of a gun from another.'

'There is a range near where we live in west London and my godfather bought me a set of shooting lessons, so I learnt how to shoot when I was a teenager.'

Freya came up to them. 'Wow that was intense.'

'Where did you learn to shoot, Freya?' asked Edward.

She picked up a bottle of sparking water. 'Believe it or not, I was once an army cadet.'

Jennie tried not to look surprised but there was no time to ask anything further because Bob called for them all to move to the outdoor range.

The brightness of the sun made Jennie blink. It was a late summer's evening and the air was warm and still – perfect weather for shooting practice. The bear shaped targets were over one thousand metres away at the bottom of each lane and in front of a high wall. Jennie looked at them with trepidation. The targets started moving back and forth on a pulley. Oh no, even worse - moving targets.

Bob allocated Jennie to a lane next to Tony who was wearing an expensive brand of polo shirt. The setting sun caught the golden highlights in his well-cut hair. He lifted his rifle and aimed at the target. Jennie could see the muscles in his arms. He fired and hit the centre. A smile of satisfaction spread over his face.

Edward was shooting two lanes along from her, concentrating well in spite of frequent interruptions from Freya. The next hour passed quickly.

At the end, Giles said, 'I was happy with the way that went.'

'I feel very rusty,' said Jennie, 'it is a long time since I last picked up a rifle. I need to practise more.'

'You seem like a natural shot to me,' said Edward.

His praise gave her a warm feeling. 'Thank you.'

Joe wrapped up the session by going through a few tips with them and then said, 'OK, everyone that's it for today. This was just the first of many sessions. You will be taking the practical tests when I deem you to be ready.'

Jennie grimaced at this pronouncement. She followed Giles and Ian back out to the car and put her rifle in the boot alongside theirs.

*

14th August

Jennie's days took on a familiar pattern. Her mornings were spent exercising Bramble and Sukey. She spent her afternoons at the university. Four evenings a week she collected data in the field, and three evenings she trained at the shooting school.

After breakfast one day, with the summer sun high in the sky, she set off across the farmyard with Bramble at her heels towards the fields. All was quiet – without the cows and the daily milking routine, Green Mcadow Farm was like a ship blown off course. Giles moped around bereft without his herd and his friend Douglas who was still missing. She heard a noise from inside the cow shed. She went in and found Giles cleaning the stall where Zoe Mudmaker had been kept in isolation.

'You've made a start on cleaning the farm then?' she said lingering just inside the door.

He looked up. 'Might as well – I have nothing else to do.'

'You haven't heard about the compensation yet?'

'Apparently they usually drag their feet.'

'No word from Douglas either?'

He shook his head. It was like living in limbo. She left and went through the gate into the field. She threw a ball for Bramble who chased it. Her phone pinged.

David

Am in Rio de Janeiro for the next month or so - fly out and join me for a couple of weeks xxx

She stared at the screen. Why hadn't she suggested that herself? She could spare the time surely? There was no doubt she needed a holiday. She stopped and stood still for

89

a moment collecting her thoughts. She sensed that her relationship was at stake. The solution was to pack her bags and to be on a flight out to Brazil. But she just couldn't bring herself to do it.

Jennie

I can't – sorry

Chapter 6

29th August

Jennie lifted her rifle and fired at the target. She hit the centre. A smile spread across her face. It was the end of the final practice session at the shooting school. She put her rifle back into its sheath. Joe came up to her.

'Jennie, I want you to sit both the theory and the practical tests,' he said.

A look of amazement passed over her face. 'I never thought that I would be taking them,' she protested.

'I need you to,' he said, 'as a member of the team.'

'But I don't want to kill badgers,' she said. 'That was never my intention.'

'You won't have to – I just think that you should have a licence,' he said. 'Think about it.'

As she made her way out to the car park, she wrestled with herself as to the right course of action. Edward followed her, sensing that her subdued farewells had indicated that something was wrong.

'Jennie, has Joe asked you to take the tests?' he asked as he caught up with her.

'How did you guess?' she said with a troubled look.

'I sort of sensed it – but I agree with him – you should take them when we all do,' he said. 'It won't necessarily mean that you will actually have to do any shooting.'

She hesitated, still unsure. It was flattering that both he and Joe were urging her to undertake the assessments but it went against her principles to start killing the animals she had dedicated herself to.

'It is difficult,' she said, 'I want to help save the dairy herds but also the badgers.'

'Why not sleep on it?' he suggested.

Jennie took his advice. By the morning she had made up her mind.

*

10th September

In the end, Jennie was pleased that she had decided to take the tests. It was satisfying when an email arrived in her inbox:

British Shooting Association
(results@britishshootingassociation.org.uk)
Dear Miss Jennie Cliffe, We are pleased to inform you that you have passed Level 3 Shooting Proficiency with Distinction.

That evening, Giles drove her and Ian in his Range Rover to Oakfield Shooting School to start work with the badger culling team. Freya, Edward and Ibrahim were already there, chatting in the car park, when they arrived. Shortly after, Tony at the wheel of a brand new car with personalised number plates pulled up.

'Wow,' said a clearly impressed Freya.

Tony switched off the ignition and climbed out.

'How does it handle?' asked Ibrahim.

Tony beamed with pride. 'Super. Really smooth, with great acceleration.'

Jennie tried to look interested but kept quiet whilst the others discussed it's performance. Seeing that all the team members had assembled, Joe joined them in the car park.

'First of all,' he said, 'I would like to congratulate you all on passing both the theory and practical tests. You are now licensed operators.' A spontaneous round of applause broke out.

Edward whispered to Jennie. 'You took the assessments?'

She turned towards him and nodded. 'But I don't intend to kill any badgers – I would never do that.'

'You just want to make sure it is done properly?'

She smiled her agreement.

'What we are going to do today is to drive out to a particular sett,' said Joe, 'and we are going to establish a baiting point. As the sett is quite isolated, I suggest we all go together in my four-by-four.'

Edward peered into the BMW SUV. 'Will the cages fit in as well?'

Joe opened the back. 'They should, if we pack everything in tightly.'

Whilst Joe loaded the wire cages, Giles got in the front, Jennie squeezed in the middle next to Ibrahim and Ian, and Freya manoeuvred herself into the back row, alongside Tony and Edward.

As Joe drove them out of Oakfield, the landscape changed to fields and woodland. The trees were still in full leaf and from time to time flashes of late summer sunshine flashed through them. He headed south on the secondary road towards Beesnest Farm before turning down a country lane which became a bumpy track until they were far from the sounds of modern life.

Jennie leant forward so that Joe could hear her instructions above the good natured banter that the others were engaged in. 'Right – the sett is fairly near here, so pull in anywhere you can.'

Joe stopped the car in a grassy area near a small wood. He got out, opened the boot and started unloading.

'These are quite heavy, so carry them in pairs,' he said.

Jennie found herself partnering Tony. They lugged the rectangular cage, which was about a metre long and half a metre wide, along a narrow path taking care to avoid the stinging nettles and the brambles heavy with ripe blackberries as they went.

'What do you usually do on a Monday evening?' he asked.

'I don't have a fixed routine – if I'm not doing my research, then I ride my horse, walk my dog or read. What about you?'

'I ride sometimes as well.'

'You have a horse?' she asked adjusting her grip on the cage's handle.

'Gladiator – he's a fine stallion.'

'I'll have to meet him sometime.'

After another thirty metres, Jennie said, 'Right we are here.'

The cages were dumped on to the ground. Everyone looked around for the sett. It was well hidden by undergrowth and wouldn't have been spotted if Jennie hadn't been there to point out the group of large holes nestling in a sandy bank.

'How on earth did you find that sett?' asked Tony.

'I've fitted GPS collars to the badgers I find.'

Joe scuffed his boot in the ground in front of the sett to make a location marker. 'How many badgers live here?'

'Probably a dozen,' Jennie replied.

'Right, let's place the cages around the entrance.'

The cages, each of which had a spring loaded door that could be raised and hooked to a latch under a brass roller, were hauled into place. Peanut butter sandwiches were placed on the trip plate to tempt hungry badgers. The door would close behind any animal stepping on to the plate trapping them inside.

Joe surveyed their work. 'Great. Thanks everyone. Early tomorrow morning, we will return to see if we have caught anything.'

Reality hit Jennie. Trapping badgers. So far she had devoted her life to protecting them, and now she found herself in a previously unthinkable situation.

*

11th September

At dawn with a light mist hanging over the fields, Jennie arrived at the shooting school accompanied by Giles and Ian. She kept yawning but Giles and Ian were wide awake as they were used to rising early. Joe greeted them in the car park and indicated that they should get into his BMW. When everyone had fastened their seatbelts he drove them back to the sett. Daylight broke as they arrived. With trepidation Jennie approached the cages.

'There is something inside two of them,' said Edward.

Jennie examined each cage. In each was a healthy male wearing a GPS collar that she had fitted. Their eyes pleaded with her to let them free.

'What do we do now?' asked Freya standing back.

Joe looked around at the team. 'Any volunteers?'

There was a short silence. Jennie wondered who would be the first to kill and wasn't surprised when Tony, showing no compunction, stepped forward. He lifted his rifle, aimed and fired at the trapped animal in the nearest cage. The badger slumped forward, killed instantly by a clean shot to the heart. The second badger was dispatched in a similar

95

manner. Jennie suppressed a sob, finding it hard to witness the finality of death. It was brutal and unfair.

'Good riddance,' Giles muttered under his breath. Dismay filled Jennie's eyes.

Edward went forward and examined the corpses. 'That was cleanly done.'

Jennie slipped on a pair of gloves and a protective suit over her clothes. She opened the first cage and with Joe's help pulled the badger out. She removed its collar and ear tag, and took a blood sample. She repeated the procedure on the other badger. Joe and Edward hauled the dead animals into body bags and carried them back to the car while she rebaited and reset the cages.

On the way back to the shooting school, she sat absorbed in her own thoughts. There had to be a way of determining which badgers had bovine TB, so that only the diseased ones were killed. This indiscriminate slaughter of innocent creatures was heart-breaking.

*

12th September

The Department of Ecology's laboratory contained banks of microscopes; drying cupboards full of specimens; a walk-in freezer packed with a miscellaneous collection of fauna and fauna; and shelves of bottles containing items ranging from tree sap to a dead bat. Jennie put on her white lab coat and tipped out the contents of her bag onto the wide bench in front of her. The blood samples, GPS collars and ear tags from the two badgers they had shot the evening before tumbled out. She logged onto one of the laptops positioned along the bench and transferred the data from them into a spreadsheet.

Jennie compared the previous weight of each badger with last night's readings. There was no doubt. The badgers had lost weight since the spring. They should have been fattening up ready for the leaner months ahead. Something was causing their weight loss. Intrigued she clicked on the maps showing the results of the GPS trackers and examined the movements of the badgers in the weeks before their deaths. She noticed that they had been moving freely across and around Liltford.

'Hi Jennie, how are things going?' asked Sana who had just wandered into the lab carrying a rack of test tubes.

'Is there a test to differentiate between a badger with bovine TB and one without?'

'Not sure,' replied Sana. 'Ask Amina, she will know.'

At that moment Amina swept into the lab. 'What will I know?'

'Whether there is an antibody test for bovine TB,' said Jennie.

'Not yet,' said Amina.

'So if I need a test, I am going to have to develop one myself?'

'If it were that simple it would already have been done.'

'But I can try?'

Amina considered this request carefully. 'Go ahead, but I will need regular updates on your progress.'

'Of course,' said Jennie heading towards the freezer where the blood samples she had collected from the badgers in the field was stored. She took out a labelled test tube and returned to the bench. There she smeared a speck of blood onto a slide, added a drop of water and put it under the microscope. She could see many different antibodies swimming around. But which ones were produced in response to the bovine TB infection? She sighed. She would need to go to the library and read the latest research. It was going to be a long job, but one she needed to do.

*

13th September

The next morning dawned fine and clear. Jennie woke early. It had been a month since she had ignored David's entreaties to join him in South America. The memory of their time together was fading. Working with the badger culling team she had met some new people. She couldn't deny that the three men – Edward, Tony and Ibrahim – were all attractive and good company or that every time she saw Edward and Freya together she felt a stab of jealously. Which was nonsensical, as theoretically, she was still in a relationship with David. At least her research was going well. Maybe, just maybe, this new work on the antibody test would give her thesis the extra element it needed to win the prize and her dream job.

Jennie put Bramble's lead on, and together they set off in an easterly direction down the Green Meadow driveway to the public footpath across Hightree Farm. Amongst the grasses were humming bees and butterflies fluttering from flower to flower. She noticed that the oak tree at the corner of the field was laden with acorns. For the previous two years it had been barren. It was nature's way of ensuring the survival of the food web – the same number of acorns each year would be too easy for the fauna dependent on it. Resilience was built by learning to cope in times of famine.

There were more dog walkers than usual. Many were dressed in new hiking gear, in the style of retired, Guardian reading, English teachers. Their pedigree dogs were clearly unused to the smells of the countryside. Ahead the path was blocked by two ladies consulting an Ordnance Survey map.

As Jennie drew nearer, the one with short grey hair barked. 'Do you know where Hope Bottom is?'

'Keep following this footpath for about twenty minutes,' Jennie replied pointing to the east.

'We don't know this area at all –it's our first time,' said a very tall woman with auburn hair.

'Are you ramblers?'

'We're from Bristol and we are helping…'

A nudge from the grey haired woman prevented the tall woman from finishing her sentence. She blushed with embarrassment. Jennie looked at them sharply. Could they be working on behalf of the anti-cullers?

A pigeon-sized long-winged bird flew overhead. 'Look, there's a kestrel,' said Jennie.

Both the ladies craned their necks, excited to see a bird of prey. The grey haired woman whipped out her phone and took some photos.

'If we don't protect our natural world, it could all be lost within a generation,' said the tall woman.'

'It's dreadful that they've extended the badger cull to this area,' said the grey haired woman.

'And badgers are a protected species. Do you know where any of their setts are?'

Jennie's suspicions were confirmed. The ladies were activists. She shook her head.

'I don't,' she lied.

She took her leave of them. In the distance she saw Ian walking along with someone. As she drew nearer she could see that it was the girl from Fauna Protection. She wondered what they could be discussing. Bramble recognising Ian, tugged at her lead, wanting to catch up with him. Jennie increased her pace

'What are you doing here?' she asked.

Ian reddened. 'Dad asked me to check on Hightree.'

Jennie shot him a direct look, doubting the truth of his reply. The girl beside him was looking prettier than last time she had seen her.

'Sophie?' said Jennie. 'You were at the meeting.'

She nodded. 'You seemed like the ideal recruit.'

'Until I made my escape.'

Sophie's eyes danced with amusement. 'Oh yes, I remember how miffed the guys were about that.'

They started to walk along together. A breeze blew in and some clouds rolled in front of the sun bringing down the temperature by a couple of degrees.

Sophie gazed around at the fields which usually would have been grazed by the dairy cows belonging to the Sitwells. 'This land has been ruined by farmers,' she said vehemently.

'Wow – that's harsh,' said Jennie wondering where this view had come from.

'Jeremy says that compared to the past the countryside is a barren wilderness,' said Sophie.

Jennie felt defensive. 'It's a farm.'

'Soon our food will soon be made in laboratories and farming will stop,' said Sophie.

'I don't believe that,' said Jennie.

'Horse riding, hunting, fishing and shooting will go as well. They are cruel and cause animal suffering,' said Sophie.

'Farmers do look after their animals,' protested Ian.

'Maybe there are some that do. But definitely not all of them – farming is a business and the animals are just a means to making a profit. Anyway eating or using animal products is wrong and also harms the planet.'

Jennie kicked a large stone off the path. 'We can't eat grass, if we could we wouldn't need to eat meat,' she said.

'But badger cullers kill for money,' said Sophie. Her remark struck Jennie to the bone.

'That's not fair,' said Ian, 'the government has authorized the cull not the farmers.'

Tired of the way the conversation was going, Jennie changed the subject. 'Oh look – there is a corn marigold,' she said pointing to a fleshy leaved daisy-like bright yellow weed growing at the side of the footpath.

Sophie bent and picked it. Her breathing became less rapid. 'I ought to learn the names of wild flowers.'

They came to a camping and caravan site, which was located in a large field adjacent to the footpath, Sophie went through a gate leading to the site. Jennie and Ian watched her go inside a large modern caravan.

Jennie turned to her brother. 'You are not convinced by her arguments are you?'

'Of course not,' he said, 'but she really cares about animals – she doesn't want the badgers to be killed. She is a true vegan as well – she only eats a plant-based diet with no meat, dairy, eggs or honey.'

'Bully for her,' said Jennie. Had Ian fallen for the girl? He seemed so enamoured with her opinions.

'She also says that people can catch diseases from animals.'

'That's true, but that is more common in developing countries that don't have the strict controls that we do.' A thought occurred to her. 'Are you sure she wasn't searching for the baited setts?'

'Of course not,' said Ian crossly. Abruptly he turned away and starting walking back to Green Meadow.

Jennie was satisfied with his answer – she trusted Ian, but she wondered where his unlikely new friendship would lead. She continued along the public footpath acknowledging that there was a lot of truth in what Sophie said – the countryside had been damaged – there was no denying it. The question was could the damage be repaired?

That evening Jennie went down into the kitchen to lay the table for supper. Nancy opened the hot oven to take out the steak and kidney pie just as Giles came.

'Any post?' he asked.

'On the side,' said Nancy.

Giles opened it and read it slowly.

'What a cheek!' he exclaimed.

Jennie and Nancy paused and listened as he read the letter aloud.

Oakfield
10th September 2018

Dear Mr and Mrs Cliffe,

I am writing to you on behalf of my client to offer to purchase Green Meadow Farm. My client is willing to pay above the market rate for your property provided that the sale is completed within the next thirty days. Please contact me as soon as possible if you wish to proceed.

Yours sincerely,
Khan Solicitors

'Do you think the purchasers are locals?' asked Nancy.

'Highly unlikely. They are probably Londoners who fancy a life in the country but have no idea of the realities of running a farm,' said Giles. He screwed up the letter and threw it accurately into the waste paper basket. He went to the fridge and pulled out a beer. For all the irritations and annoyances that the farm threw at him, he would never sell it.

'They asked you to name your price,' said Jennie taking a seat at the table. 'By the way, has the Animal Health Agency given you a date when they will pay the compensation money?'

He scoffed. 'I received yet another email from them saying that due to the volume of claims they haven't processed ours yet.'

'Perhaps you should ring them up,' said Jennie but the look on his face displayed his opposition to that suggestion. He hated dealing with bureaucracy and avoided doing so if he could. Yet the longer it took for the money to come through, the further the farm was falling into arrears.

When the kitchen had been cleared, her parents and brother set off in the car to Oakfield. Jennie was left on her own. Needing time to process the day's events, she pulled on her boots and grabbed her new solar-powered torch. She tramped across the fields until she reached Bullitt's sett. Whenever she needed to time to reflect, this was where she found refuge.

Arriving at the steep sandy bank she looked for signs of badger activity. She spotted piles of soil and stones recently dug out from the underground tunnels. Badger hairs were caught on twigs and paw prints were evident on the paths radiating out from the sett.

She climbed up onto the tree platform and sat down to wait. She was soon rewarded by the emergence of Bullitt who started scrummaging around for worms and browsing for early blackberries. He was joined by another female that she didn't recognize. He must have roamed into adjacent territories to seek out another fertile sow to add to his family.

He raised his tail upright and strutted around on stiff legs in front of the female badger. They started grooming each other removing the fleas, lice and ticks lodged in their fur. Suddenly he mounted her and impregnated her. The act was all over in two minutes. Pocahontas would have to fight to maintain her position as the dominant female this winter.

The sow returned to the sett and Bullitt ambled off on a solitary stroll.

Jennie walked home checking her phone for a message from David as she went. There was none. Ever since she had decided not to join him for a summer holiday, the time between their communications had become longer and longer. When she arrived home she found the farmhouse in darkness. She let herself in and Bramble came bounding up to greet her. As she climbed the stairs, her feet seemed heavier than usual. Her phone pinged.

Edward

Survivor has had a third negative test for bovine TB and will be released back into the wild

Jennie

Fantastic news! Thank you!

Edward's message cheered her up. He shared her concern for Survivor. Her phone pinged again.

David

Off to Buenos Aires tomorrow on the overnight bus

Jennie

Have a good journey xx

Chapter 7

15th September

Elms and hawthorns in the hedgerows either side of the road swayed in the evening breeze as Jennie drove to the shooting school. As she approached the entrance, she swerved to avoid a dead rabbit lying in the middle of the road. Ahead were several vehicles roughly parked on the grass verge. A large group of activists dressed in black with balaclavas covering their faces were gathered outside the gates banging drums, chanting and waving placards proclaiming 'Stop the Cull', 'Save the Badgers' and 'Murderers'.

As she drove into the car park, projectiles hit the car's windows and roof. Shouts came from the mob and someone banged on her bonnet. When she got out of the car, flash cameras went off and she instinctively raised her arm to cover her face.

She pushed open the entrance door to the small reception area where Joe and the others were gathered. Tony smiled at her and Edward and Freya, who were standing together, broke off from their conversation to say hello.

'I could have run someone over,' she exclaimed, her face flushed from the shock of the encounter.

Ibrahim arrived just after looking flustered. 'That was like running the gauntlet.'

Joe frowned.

'Are they allowed to be here?' asked Jennie.

'Unfortunately, yes,' he replied. 'They aren't breaking any laws. They're not trespassing and this isn't a residential area so they can't be charged with anti-social behaviour.' He bent down to check the contents of a couple of kit bags.

'But throwing stones could have caused criminal damage,' protested Jennie.

'The police only press charges if they have sufficient evidence.'

Tony peered through the glass door at the group of protesters that was growing in number.

'They're determined to stop us.'

A chill went through Jennie. 'I've seen them patrolling the fields.'

'Probably to find the baited cages,' said Edward.

'But so far they haven't found any and let's hope it stays that way,' said Joe picking up the holdalls. 'Are Giles and Ian coming tonight?'

'No,' said Jennie, 'only me.'

'Ok, let's go,' he said.

Jennie climbed into Joe's BMW and fastened her seatbelt. When everyone was on board, he powered through the gate and out into the lane. The shouting and drumming increased. She covered her ears as the commotion became deafening. She looked through the rear window and watched several of the younger protesters chase the car until they gave up, puffed and exhausted.

'That was seriously scary,' said Freya.

On the alert for people hidden in the hedgerow Joe switched on his lights. 'Just noise though.'

He drove along the main road until he turned off and headed down a bumpy track, past Hightree Farm, towards the first baiting point. Arriving at their destination, he stopped the car and they got out and walked over to a sloping bank devoid of vegetation but surrounded by tall grasses and bramble tendrils. Three wire cages were arranged around the entrances to a well-used sett. They were empty – the bait had been removed – and the doors were shut.

'Oh no,' exclaimed Jennie, 'they have been sabotaged.'

'Bastards,' swore Tony.

Ibrahim rattled one of the cages. 'What shall we do now?'

'We could rebait them and then come back tomorrow,' suggested Jennie.

Suddenly a loud noise disturbed them. Out of the gloom appeared half a dozen people dressed from head to toe in black, blowing horns, banging drums and shouting for the cull to be stopped.

Jennie froze as an object hit her chest. She looked down and saw a broken egg running down her jacket. Edward stepped out in front of her to protect her.

'Hey, stop it!' he shouted.

More eggs were thrown, and the drums continued to be beaten until abruptly the ambush was over and the activists slipped back into the darkness. Jennie pulled out a tissue from her pocket and tried to wipe the yolk off.

'Are you alright?' Edward asked solicitously.

'It's only egg,' she said as the paper tissue disintegrated.

Tony listened for more sounds. 'Have they gone?'

Edward picked up a stick from the ground and thrashed the surrounding bushes. Nobody came out of hiding and quiet descended.

Joe turned back to the car. 'Right, let's call it a day,' he said.

Jennie followed him and climbed into the back seat. Her thoughts were sombre and confused. Freya got in and fastened her seatbelt. 'That was horrible.'

Joe switched on the ignition and headlights. 'Unpleasant people.'

'That's an understatement,' said Edward.

'How did they find the baiting point?' asked Tony.

Joe started to drive back down the track. 'They have their own intelligence network. People working on the ground, making observations, tracking our movements.'

'What are we going to do now?' asked Jennie.

'We will have to be better organized,' said Joe. 'We need to outwit them, but first we must inform the police.'

'The police?' asked Tony sceptically. 'Aren't they only interested in rape and murder?'

'None the less, we need to report the incident,' said Joe adamantly, putting his foot down on the accelerator as he hit the road.

Darkness had fallen and everyone fell silent. Mobile phones came out of pockets and bags. Social media was scrolled through.

'Wow!' exclaimed Ibrahim, 'they have already posted pictures of the ambush online.'

Jennie clicked on Twitter and saw the blurry images of the activists. It was too dark to pick out any individual faces. The posts were attracting many retweets, likes and messages of support and encouragement.

'They are asking for more donations in order to carry on the fight against what they say is "the wanton slaughter of innocent animals by the agents of the right-wing government protecting the obscene profits of farmers and landowners",' she cried indignantly.

'They're winning the propaganda war,' observed Tony.

Freya shifted in her seat. 'Shouldn't we post an explanation of why the cull is taking place?'

'We could – but I doubt whether it would make much of a difference,' said Edward.

Joe's eyes were on the road ahead. 'It's best to keep a low profile – in spite of any provocation you receive or any outrageous posts you see online,' he insisted. 'Let's meet tomorrow.'

*

16th September

The following evening Giles drove Jennie and Ian in his Range Rover to a meeting at the shooting school. They took their seats in the training room. Fresh air was blowing in through the open windows. Joe was at the front setting up the laptop and projector. Edward and Freya came in and sat down next to each other. Last to arrive were Ibrahim and Tony – they came in apologetically – saying that they had been caught up in traffic.

'Right everyone, thank you for coming. The police are due any minute,' said Joe just as the door opened and two policemen entered. Jennie recognised them as the same two officers who had been investigating the disappearance of Douglas Sitwell.

'Good evening, I am Police Sergeant Miller and this is Police Constable Allen. As you know, we have been instructed to advise you in how to carry out this whole operation as smoothly as possible,' said PS Miller standing at the front facing them.

'There are well organised people out there who know how to operate within the law and also how to evade detection,' interjected PC Allen,

'However, they have already disrupted one lawful activity,' said Miller. He looked at Joe. 'I understand from

Mr Friend that the incident occurred yesterday evening at a baiting point?'

'It happened at seven o'clock at a badger sett in south-east Liltford,' said Edward.

'This means we have two questions to answer – firstly who are the activists and secondly how did they know where to target?' said Allen.

Miller stood with his feet apart. 'Let's start to examine the evidence of who the activists might be. I understand that you have some footage?'

'Yes,' said Joe, 'we have a video taken by Jennie at Oakfield Market and also some rather blurry pictures of them from a Fauna Protection recruitment leaflet. Let's have a look.'

He switched on the projector and played the video. It was a very short sequence of a group of people on a protest march. Next he showed the scanned pages of the leaflet that Jennie had been given. Everyone sat and watched with a sense of fascination.

Jennie stood up and typed a URL into the laptop's search engine. 'They have a website.'

When the home page of the Fauna Protection website loaded, everyone studied it noting the strident claims and misinformation about a range of environmental issues.

'Their logo is a purple dragonfly,' said Edward.

'Jeremy Boyle is their leader,' said Jennie.

'Thank you,' said Miller moving back to the front, 'so, all the evidence is pointing to the Fauna Protection group being responsible for disrupting your activities. We know that they have been seen in and around Oakfield during the last few months but they are doing nothing illegal.'

'Really?' said Tony. 'How can that be?'

'They have a right to protest peacefully.'

Freya rolled her eyes. 'But they banged our cars and threw eggs at us!'

'But so far they haven't caused any actual bodily harm or committed any criminal damage,' said Allen.

'Is there nothing you can do?' asked Edward.

'When we have evidence that they have perpetrated a crime, then we can call the suspects in for questioning.'

Miller cleared his throat. 'This operation should be as safe and secure as possible so let's turn our attention to their sources of intelligence.'

'I have met people walking around the fields looking for setts,' said Jennie.

'So they have used observation. Any other ideas?' said Miller.

'An informant?' suggested Freya.

Jennie noticed Ian shifting uneasily in his chair and wondered if he was going to admit to anything.

Miller looked keenly at everyone. 'Possibly – but I am sure you have all been warned to keep your actions confidential.'

Jennie racked her brains trying to remember if she had inadvertently let anything slip. She was sure she hadn't.

'Another possibility is that they have fitted GPS tracking devices to your cars,' said Allen.

'Isn't that illegal?' exclaimed Edward.

'At the moment, no – having intent to steal is an offence but these devices are so new, that as yet there is no law against them – it is a grey area,' said Miller. 'So I suggest we check your vehicles now.'

Along with the others Jennie trooped outside to the car park. In the twilight everyone waited besides their cars for instructions.

'Switch on your torches. Look over and under your vehicles,' said Allen.

Jennie, Giles and Ian shone their smartphones inside the wheel wells, behind the bumpers and on to the roof of the Range Rover.

'There's a large box underneath my car,' shouted Edward, 'it seems to be attached with a magnet.'

Jennie aimed a beam under the chassis. 'There's one here too.'

Giles and Ian craned their necks to have look.

'Well, I never,' said Joe, 'who would have thought that someone would go to all this trouble?'

Allen brought over his tool kit. 'You'd be surprised at the lengths determined people go to.' He knelt down, detached the tracker and handed it over to Miller who put it into a plastic bag. He moved onto another car and continued until all the devices had been removed.

'We will take these away for analysis but we will keep you updated. In the meantime, try to outwit them,' said Miller.

As the police drove off, Giles zipped up his fleece. 'How are we going to do that?'

'Confuse them with decoys,' replied Joe.

*

17th September

The rain was falling softly and steadily, when late the next morning Jennie was picked up at Green Meadow Farm by Joe in his SUV packed with wire cages. The windscreen wipers rhythmically moved back and forth clearing the raindrops away.

'So we aim to bait four different setts?' he said.

She dipped her head and unfolded her map of Liltford District on which she had marked the location of all the setts known to her. She directed him towards the south along a narrow country lane beyond Beesnest Farm. The rain became so heavy that he turned on his headlights to see through the gloom.

'Pull up over there,' she said pointing to a passing place at the side of the road. When the engine had been switched off she got out of the car and pulled her hood over her head. Together they lifted a cage out of the boot and carried it through a farm gate and down a path to a sett dug into the side of a ditch. She was glad of her waterproof as the rain continued to pour down. They placed the cage near the sett on some level ground. From a plastic container in her backpack she took out some peanut butter sandwiches, put them in the cage and set the trap. Overhead was a humming sound. She and Joe looked up.

'It's a drone.'

'It could be the activists carrying out some surveillance,' he said.

Jennie shivered. They checked that they had left nothing behind and returned to the car. She directed Joe to the next two setts. At each, they left another baited cage. Once or twice they thought they heard the drone overhead again.

The fourth and most remote sett lay in a wooded dell located in the south-east of Beesnest Farm. Instead of leaving a cage, they scattered peanuts mixed with treacle over the ground. Using a trowel, Jennie buried tempting bite-sized morsels of badger food just below the surface for the badgers to dig out with their snouts and long claws. Leaving with a satisfied feeling, she returned to the car and was dropped back at the farm in time for lunch.

Early that evening Giles drove her, Ian and Bramble to the shooting school where the rest of the team were already assembled. After a quick conference in the car park, everyone transferred into Joe's car. With Bramble sitting between her knees, Jennie sat in the rear row next to Edward, with Ian on the end. She held her backpack on her lap. Holding their rifles, Giles took his customary seat in the front passenger seat. Tony was in the middle row with Freya and Ibrahim on either side of him.

Joe drove them directly to the first location. Leaving Bramble in the car, they got out and walked to the sett. The cage was empty and shut. It was both annoying and disappointing. Undaunted, Joe drove them onto the second and third setts only to find that the same thing had happened there as well.

Giles scowled. 'This is a bloody waste of time.'

'They keep beating us to it,' said Tony a look of frustration crowding his handsome face.

Freya rubbed her arms as she gazed at the empty cage sitting forlornly in the undergrowth.

'It's getting cold,' she complained.

'What now?' asked Edward.

'On to the next sett,' answered Joe. He sounded upbeat.

Ian hesitated, showing his reluctance. 'I think we should call it a day.'

'But the night is yet young,' said Ibrahim.

'Only one more to go,' said Joe firmly.

He drove for another twenty minutes to the most remote sett, where he parked the car.

'Bring your rifles,' he said.

Jennie clambered out into the darkness and put her rucksack on her back. Bramble leapt out, sniffed the night air and strained at her leash. All was silent except for a hooting owl and a jet plane flying through the thick clouds. The earlier rain had stopped leaving the ground wet and muddy.

Holding their torches, everyone followed Jennie and Bramble along the path to the sett where she and Joe had scattered food earlier in the day. Arriving at the small clearing overhung by trees, Edward busied himself setting up the infrared field camera to record the whole session, whilst Jennie scattered fresh peanut butter sandwiches around the sett's entrances.

Freya glanced around. 'I can't see the cage.'

'There isn't one,' said Joe. 'We are going to free shoot. Pick out any animals hiding in the shadows with your thermal imaging goggles, but first find somewhere to lean against and prep your rifles.'

Nervous looks were exchanged. Jennie watched as silencers were fitted to rifles and suitable vantage points found. She chose a safe position for herself and Bramble to wait. After thirty inactive minutes, Freya complained of boredom.

'Keep still,' hissed Joe, 'something should happen soon.'

Quiet fell again. Bramble's ears pricked up. A mature badger with short legs and a long spine appeared from its underground home, sniffed the air and ate one of the sandwiches. Jennie recognised him. In quick succession six other badgers, the rest of his family, emerged, snuffled and gobbled the peanuts down. She remembered tranquilising them all earlier in the year in order to fit their GPS collars and ear tags, and to take blood samples from them. They still looked fit and well.

When Joe was sure that the badgers were completely unaware of their presence, he indicated to each team member which badger they should target. The shooters adjusted their firing positions, aimed at the badgers' heart and lung areas and raised their guns. Jennie watched from a distance. He waited until everyone was ready before he gave the signal to fire.

Simultaneously their bullets flew through the evening air taking the badgers by surprise. Giles hit the largest boar, which fell straight to the ground. Joe, Tony, Edward, Ibrahim and Freya cleanly shot a badger each. The smallest one was wounded by Ian, and it instinctively ran back to the sett. At Jennie's command Bramble intercepted it and trapped it against a fallen tree, where Giles killed it with a decisive shot. She put Bramble's lead back on and gave it to Ian to hold.

As the dead badgers lay immobile on the ground, a wave of sadness swept over her. She suppressed a sob. She had been observing the badger family for many months with the aim of protecting them and now she had witnessed their execution. It was so unfair. Pulling herself together, she put on her protective gloves, went over to the corpses and examined the seven badgers for any signs of life. There were none. She took off their GPS collars and ear tags. After taking a blood sample from each she packed her backpack. Everyone helped to lift the dead badgers, which each weighed the same as a large dog, into body bags and to carry them back to the car to be squashed into the boot.

'Where do the corpses go?' asked Freya.

'They will be collected by the hazardous waste service in the next few days and taken to the incinerator,' answered Joe.

Jennie was subdued on the way back to the shooting school. Bramble lay down on the floor at her feet. Her knee touched Edward's, sending a frisson through her. Having them both close to her was comforting.

'I hate seeing the badgers killed,' she whispered.

'So do I,' said Edward.

She fell back into silence. Her quest to find an antibody test had become even more urgent. However, there were only so many hours in the day and her involvement with the cull was squeezing her time for research. It was a juggling act.

'I am annoyed with myself for not firing a cleaner shot,' said Ian.

Joe reassured him. 'Don't be, these things happen.'

After a period of reflection Ibrahim started talking and couldn't stop. He was buzzing with nervous energy. At the wheel, Joe radiated a quiet satisfaction.

'The first battle of the war has been won,' he said.

*

18th September

Up at the crack of dawn the next day, Jennie cycled as she fast as she could to the university. She went straight to the lab, logged onto her laptop and reviewed her research results so far. Her search for the antibodies, produced by the immune system to fight off bovine TB, was like hunting for a rare plant in a tropical rainforest. Methodically she transferred the data from the GPS collars and ear tags belonging to the badgers killed the previous evening into a spreadsheet. She was preparing a slide to examine their blood when Sana entered carrying some clean flasks and beakers.

'Have you found what you are looking for?' Sana asked.

Jennie shot her an appealing look. 'I need some caffeine to get my brain working.'

Sana laughed, 'I'm not your gopher, you know.' But she plonked the equipment down and disappeared into the prep room, returning with two steaming mugs of coffee.

'Thank you so much,' said Jennie.

Sana pulled out a lab stool from under the bench and sat down beside her.

'Have you heard from David lately?' she asked.

The mention of David's name took Jennie by surprise and she realised that she had hardly thought about him at all in the last few days, so involved had she been with the cull and her research.

'The last I heard he was going to Argentina.'

117

'Still on the move then,' said Sana. 'When is he coming home?'

Jennie had no idea. She lifted her mug, drank some coffee and changed the subject.

'What about Dylan?' she asked.

'He has a new job,' Sana replied.

Jennie's interest was aroused. 'With more money and responsibility?'

Sana nodded. 'I've given him an ultimatum.'

'And?'

Sana sighed. 'He says we need to save another £5, 000.'

'How are you going to do that for heaven's sake?' asked Jennie indignantly.

'I am going to have to extend my hours. Amina has agreed – she says the department's new sponsor will pay.'

Jennie tried not to look sceptical. 'So let me get this right – if you save enough money by say the New Year, he will agree to a wedding?'

Sana shrugged. 'Well, he didn't say that in so many words but that is what he implied.'

'Sana, can you help please?' shouted a researcher at the other end of the lab. She shot Jennie an apologetic look and went over to investigate what assistance was required.

Jennie sat drinking her coffee. Her attention was drawn to a purple dragonfly on a poster pinned to the noticeboard on the wall. She got up and went over to it. It was advertising a Student Union event at three o'clock that afternoon – representatives from Fauna Protection would be outlining the objectives of their organisation. She immediately reserved a ticket online.

At two forty-five, she headed to the university's theatre. Once there, she squeezed along a row in the middle of the modern auditorium to her seat. The atmosphere was already febrile and several undergraduates were enthusiastically waving placards and banners with the usual familiar slogans and emotive statements. She looked around and to her surprise, she saw Edward seated a couple of rows in front of her.

After a short delay, the fresh-faced President of the Students' Union came onto the stage to introduce the speaker.

'Welcome everyone. Thank you for coming. It is my great pleasure to welcome our guest today. Originally from a council estate in south London, he grew up a member of a first generation immigrant community, and during his formative years experienced the cruelness of deprivation and austerity. After taking a Business degree at the University of Warwick, he changed tack and became involved in the fight for social justice and animal rights. Today he leads a national campaigning organisation that takes proactive action. It is my great pleasure to introduce today - Jeremy Boyle,' said the youthful host, his voice rising to a crescendo at the end.

To loud cheers, Boyle came onto the stage. He stood still and opened his arms out wide, like an evangelical speaker.

'Good afternoon. Thank you for inviting me to speak to you today. I am the leader of Fauna Protection, which was formed in 2001, in response to the wicked slaughter of millions of defenceless animals after the outbreak of foot and mouth disease, which was caused by the careless feeding of contaminated foodstuffs to farm animals and poor hygiene standards in our abattoirs. We are now fighting the atrocious culling of innocent wild creatures in this locality. We are taking direct action to stop these injustices against defenceless animals,' he said with a great deal of passion. He paused, to allow time for the spontaneous and enthusiastic clapping and cheering from the audience.

'The government has gone against the advice of experts and has ignored the science so we are forced into action to prevent the further culling of our native species – the badger – which is a noble creature! We have no choice!' he exclaimed ardently. 'But it's no good just stopping the slaughter – we have to tackle the root causes which have led to another outbreak of a deadly disease. We need to act now to change our food production systems before it is too late! The enclosures of the common land led to ordinary people being forced off the fields their ancestors had cultivated for centuries. In their place came wealthy landowners who care only for profit!'

'Here, here!' shouted an audience member, lifting his arms above his head like an act of worship. Others followed, caught up in the heat of the moment, and soon there was a mass of raised hands.

'Many of our modern day ills and problems such as climate change can be traced back to the day when the common people were thrown off the land to be replaced by the landowning class - privileged people who only take, and give nothing back,' continued Jeremy convincingly. 'We must act now to stop the badger culling in the districts around Oakfield and we must band together to stop the testing of new products on animals. To achieve our aims we are asking for donations - please make sure you give generously today.'

He sipped some water from the glass in front of him and waited for the clapping to die down.

'Now, I have some pictures to show you of animals being left in distress - dying in pain and misery,' he said, starting the slide show of pictures of animal cruelty. Jennie noted that they were obviously taken in a foreign country and in many cases appeared to have been staged. She sensed that each slide had been carefully chosen to ratchet up the emotional response of the audience.

After the last slide, the President of the Union came back on stage and stood on the podium.

'Thank you Jeremy, for your interesting and inspiring speech. Now we will take questions from the floor. State your name and organisation and wait for the roving microphone to be brought over to you,' he said.

A few bold people put their hands up straightaway. Jennie hesitated before raising hers. Several questions were asked and answered, and she was beginning to give up hope of being selected when the President indicated that the young lady in the red jumper would be next. She took the microphone and stood up.

'Jennie Cliffe from the Department of Ecology. Badger culling is a lawful activity commissioned by the government in order to try and halt the advance of bovine tuberculosis, which in any species- human or animal - is an insidious cruel disease that steals their humanity. How can you justify trying to bring a halt to the cull?' she said and sat down noticing that several people were taking photos of her on their mobile phones.

Jeremy beamed benevolently at her and said, 'Well Jennie, so far, there is no evidence that the cull is working at all - in fact there is some research which shows that in areas where the cull is taking place, the incidents of bovine TB are actually going up. This is because the spread of TB is mostly through cattle to cattle and not through badger to cattle.'

A ripple of applause broke out.

'Can you elaborate on the means your organisation is using to bring about an end to the cull?' asked Jennie.

'Fauna Protection prides itself on the peaceful methods it uses - we believe that change is brought about through persuasion and argument,' said Jeremy commanding his audience.

Jennie sat down, feeling the disapproving gaze of hundreds of pairs of eyes on her. After several more questions, the event came to an end with a plea from Boyle:

'Fauna Protection is welcoming new members and donations – please pick up our literature which our members will hand out at the door or visit our website.'

The Union President then ended the session: 'Thank you everyone for coming today – I am sure you will all agree that we have found today's talk both informative and enlightening.'

Boyle then left the stage to a big round of applause. The buckets started to be rattled as people filed out. Jennie sat there motionless. She contemplated the ecstatic faces of the converted. She felt that she still hadn't found out the truth - Boyle was presenting Fauna Protection as a genuine organisation that only used peaceful means but she knew otherwise from her own experience. In the queue for the exit she bumped into Edward.

'You certainly put yourself into the spotlight,' he said with a frank look.

'I felt so annoyed,' she said. 'By the way, what are you doing here?'

'I am an Associate Fellow at the School of Veterinary Medicine,' he replied edging forward.

She advanced an inch. 'Oh – I hadn't realised.'

'It is only part-time,' he said, 'but I find it informs my professional practice.'

'What did you think of Boyle's speech?' she whispered.

'Very persuasive,' he replied.

They reached the door and went out into the fresh air. It was starting to rain. She looked around to make sure that she was out of anyone's ear shot. 'Do you think they are fighting a class war?'

He unfurled his umbrella. 'It's difficult to tell what their real aims are,' he said. 'I don't trust Jeremy Boyle an inch.' He headed off across the quadrangle. She gazed after him wishing that she could spend longer talking to him.

Chapter 8

25th September

It was early evening. Jennie was sitting with Giles and Ian in the front row of the shooting school's training room waiting for Joe to start another team briefing. Outside a commotion was going on. Noisy animal activists were blocking the gate. She turned and saw Edward sitting behind, his abundant hair brushed back off his forehead. For a second his eyes caught hers until Freya pulled at his sleeve and he looked away. Tony and Ibrahim were lolling in their seats at the back, their legs stretched out in front of them.

Joe cleared his throat. 'To sum up our progress so far, several baited cages have been successfully sabotaged but we have had more success with free shooting. However, to cut the risk of attack and to sow confusion, we should now go out in smaller teams and in different vehicles.'

'How small a team?' asked Giles.

'In pairs.'

'To four different setts?' asked Edward doing his arithmetic.

Joe nodded. 'Jennie has left bait at each of them.'

'And a small transmitter, so you can use your mobile phone to locate them,' she added.

'At any sign of the saboteurs, just abort and return here at once,' said Joe. 'Now I am going to pair you up. Ian, I want you to come with me. Ibrahim you go with Giles. Tony and

Freya – you two go together. That leaves Jennie with Edward.'

Freya pouted. 'I want to go with Edward.'

'It is up to me to decide our teams,' said Joe with a firm look.

Jennie agreed with him. She didn't want to be paired either with her father or her brother. Freya appeared as if she was going to protest but seeing Edward's look of disapproval, she decided against it.

Tony pulled a face. 'My car is brand new. If I had known, I would've bought along an old banger.'

Jennie handed out the maps of Liltford on which the locations of the setts were marked by the first letters of the alphabet. 'Sett A isn't far from the main road,' she said to Tony. 'Go to that one.'

'Keep in touch via WhatsApp. We'll leave from here at ten minute intervals,' instructed Joe.

He and Ian were the first to depart. From the shooting school Jennie watched as the SUV inched its way through the gate, out in to the lane before speeding off. Some of the protestors piled in to a small minibus and set off in pursuit.

Last to leave were Jennie and Edward. His car smelt of mud and medication. He headed down a country lane towards Beesnest Farm. Once she realised that they weren't being followed, she relaxed and used a navigation app on her mobile phone to direct the way. After thirty minutes she pointed to a narrow turning.

'Follow that track,' she said, 'for about half a mile.'

The car bumped along the uneven surface which petered out as the grass grew longer.

'We're here,' she said.

He stopped and turned off the ignition and lights. They sat in silence, their eyes adjusting to the gloom. At the far end of the field she could just about pick out the outlines of three silver-grey badgers, foraging for their evening meal. They were digging small holes in the ground, searching for the tasty smelling morsels that Jennie had buried earlier.

'A mature male and two females,' she whispered. 'We mustn't scare them off.' She got out of the car and put on her night vision goggles. She surveyed the field and hedgerows looking for hidden protestors, grazing cattle or other wildlife. Satisfied that there were none in the vicinity, she crept forward.

Edward donned his goggles and followed her. Inadvertently he stepped on a twig, which split in two with a loud crack. He froze. The badgers looked up, sniffed the air and listened carefully. Deciding that there was no imminent danger, they lowered their heads and resumed their scratching of the soil. He fitted a silencer to his loaded rifle and sized up possible lines of fire.

With a hand signal, Jennie indicated to him that everything was clear. He took aim at the largest badger and fired. Then in rapid succession he shot the other two. They waited a few minutes before approaching the cylinder shaped bodies. Jennie choked back her tears. Seeing them up close, still and lifeless, was heart-breaking. Kneeling on the ground, from each in turn, she took a blood sample before removing their tracking collars and ear tags. Together they lifted the badgers into body bags, zipped them up, hauled them back to the car and hurled them into the boot.

Jennie sighed with relief. 'I'm glad that's over.'

'You did a good job,' he said.

In the car on the way back, her phone pinged several times. She opened the group's WhatsApp and read the messages aloud:

Ian

Trouble here - mission aborted

Ibrahim

Freya

Two badgers shot

She typed an update from her and Edward to the rest of the team. Carrying out the cull wasn't going to be straightforward.

Street lights illuminated the road through Oakfield but petered out as they approached the shooting school. When Edward turned into the entrance, Jennie saw Freya waiting in the car park.

Edward stopped the car and got out. Freya rushed over to greet him and was rewarded with a kiss. Jennie helped him carry the body bags over to a large wheelie big where they would stay until collected.

'See you early Saturday for a recce?' he asked Jennie. She nodded as Freya leapt into Edward's car and turned her face to receive a kiss. Jennie watched his car until it had disappeared back down the lane towards the town.

*

27th September

Jennie peered down the microscope at a drop of blood taken from one of the badgers that Edward had killed a couple of evenings before. For weeks, she had been searching for the antibodies which indicated the presence of bovine TB in an infected animal. Under the lens something caught her eye. Her heart started to beat faster. She raised her head. At her side was a textbook which she had borrowed from the university library. She leafed through it and found a photograph of bovine TB antibodies. She examined the blood smeared on the slide and consulted the magnified image again. A look of satisfaction spread over her face.

At that moment Amina passed by. She saw the gleam in Jennie's eyes. 'Any results to share?'

Jennie nodded. 'I've just found the bovine TB antibodies I've been searching for.'

'Excellent. You'll need post mortem evidence.'

'I know.'

'And don't forget to submit an outline of your thesis to the judges of the Luminosity Prize by the end of the week.'

'I won't,' said Jennie turning back to her microscope.

Amina carried on walking.

Sana came up to Jennie. 'I heard you tell Amina that you've found them,' she said.

Jennie gestured that she had. 'Do you want to have a look?'

Sana stared down the microscope.

'Are they y-shaped?' she asked.

'Yes,' she replied, 'quite beautiful aren't they? But it means that some of the badgers do have bovine TB after all.'

Sana gave her a sympathetic look. 'That's dreadful. Are you sure? You've always been adamant that they were healthy.'

Jennie sighed. 'I was wrong. Edward warned me that it is very difficult to diagnose bovine TB in badgers. I should have listened to him.'

'So the government was justified in extending the cull area after all?' said Sana starting to wipe the workbench down.

Jennie nodded. At her side, her phone vibrated. She picked it up and opened the message. Silently she absorbed its contents. She gazed out of the lab window.

'What is it?' asked Sana sensing something was wrong.

'It's David. He's breaking it off with me.'

'By text?' said Sana, 'that's so mean.'

Jennie stared at her phone. 'He says he met someone on the coach trip to Buenos Aires. I don't know what to think. I thought we would be together for ever.'

'Well, I didn't,' said her friend, shooting her a meaningful look.

*

29th September

Saturday dawned at Green Meadow. Jennie sprung out of bed. Edward was coming to do a recce. She had thought that she would be devastated if her relationship with David ended. While he was away travelling she had kept her promise to remain faithful to him. Being in a long distance relationship had enabled her to concentrate on her research. The end when it came had not been entirely unexpected. Since then she had shed some tears but in truth her love for David had simply faded away. Now, she was single again. It was a strange feeling.

Outside the ground was damp after the overnight rain and the sky overcast with a gentle wind. When Edward arrived she led him across a pasture, dotted with cowpats and bounded by ancient hedgerows towards the same sett near the River Fogle she had visited with Sana in the spring.

As she tramped along she kept a look out for signs of badger activity. 'It's a busy time of year for them,' she said, 'they know winter is coming.'

'They fatten up to survive the cold,' he said.

She pointed out some bare patches at the side of the field. 'It's mild today, but the undergrowth has already started dying back.'

'That makes it easier for them to grub for juicy earthworms,' he said.

Jennie smiled and gazed around. 'I'm looking out for badger latrines. The cows like to sniff at them. But there is the risk that they could be infected with TB.'

'There are so many possible sources of infection. The science isn't properly understood,' he said.

They walked along chatting and enjoying each other's company. On the left they passed Oakfield camp site where a stream of loaded cars towing caravans were arriving.

'It's too early for half term holidays,' said Jennie.

Edward grinned. 'I daresay that they are the type of well-heeled people who combine protest duties with a short break in the country – you know the sort of thing – a morning march against the cull, followed by a long pub lunch, a visit to an antique shop and then a gentle hike.'

Jennie laughed. 'You are mean – most of those people are very sincere and well meaning.'

'They are lucky to have the time and money to be able to pursue their interests – I sometimes wonder why they haven't anything better to do.'

She gave him a sideways glance. 'Perhaps they feel passionately that killing badgers is wrong.'

The breeze intensified and he walked more briskly. 'Maybe. Or are they just jumping onto a bandwagon that they don't fully understand?'

'Can pressure groups force politicians to make knee jerk reactions?' shouted Jennie as the wind strengthened.

'Undoubtedly,' he replied. They entered a deciduous wood. It was sheltered from the wind but was wet underfoot.

She looked up at the green canopy. 'I just love the colours of autumn – the yellows, oranges and reds – they are so much more subtle than the bright greens of summer,' she said. 'Shorter days, lower temperatures and less chlorophyll and hey presto the leaves turn these beautiful shades.'

'It's the natural rhythm of life,' he said as the path became muddier and slippier.

'Until I did A-level Biology, I never knew that the trees lose their leaves because a layer of cork forms across their base, cutting off their supply of nutrients.' Suddenly she slipped. Edward grabbed her hand to steady her. She regained her balance but was unaccountably reluctant to let go. After a few seconds delay, she released his grasp and flashed him a smile of gratitude.

They continued for a short distance, kicking away the brown leaves which were covering the ground in an insulating blanket, until the path became too narrow for them to walk side by side. Within a mound of bare earth overhung by brambles, she spied a ribbon of freshly dug soil. She pulled the vegetation away.

'Oh no, the entrance has been blocked with builders' rubble.'

He peered at the pile of broken bricks filling the hole the size of a football. 'It's illegal to interfere with a badger's sett.'

'Some people just don't care,' she said. She took her camera out of her backpack.

After she had taken some shots, they moved on until a bit further into the wood they alighted on the sett she was looking for. It was sheltered by an overgrown bush and was undisturbed.

'This is it,' she said. She slung her backpack down and pulled out her notebook and pen. 'I have sampled the badgers that live here. I'm pretty sure that they have the bovine TB antibodies.'

'You found them in their blood?'

She nodded and waved a sheet at him. 'We have to do the risk assessment.'

It didn't take long to tick the boxes and afterwards from her bag she produced a large tub of peanuts mixed with treacle. These were sprinkled several metres away from the sett entrance and any dense undergrowth that a wounded badger could take refuge in. She finished, stood up and stretched.

'Do you mind if we take a detour to Hightree Farm?' she asked. 'I want to check on Mrs Sitwell – she didn't seem that well the last time I saw her.'

He looked at his watch. 'OK. I'll check their biosecurity whilst I'm there.'

'Douglas hasn't returned so there haven't been any improvements because,' she said.

They walked across the fields to the farmhouse. She knocked several times on the dilapidated front door. There was no response. Edward followed her around the back to the garden. She turned the handle of the kitchen door. It opened and they went in. The house was cold.

'Mrs Sitwell? Are you in?' she called.

A muffled sound came from the first floor. They bounded up the stairs two at a time and inspected all the bedrooms before finding the old woman lying very still in bed covered with a crocheted bedspread. Her breathing was shallow and her face was deathly pale.

Jennie moved to the side of her bed with Edward just behind. 'Mrs Sitwell – are you all right?' she asked. 'It's Jennie Cliffe here.'

There was a faint murmur and Mrs Sitwell's eyes opened slowly.

'Jennie, I'm not well,' she said in a faltering voice. 'Can you feed my cat?'

'Yes of course,' said Jennie. She turned to Edward, who signalled his compliance before disappearing back downstairs. She opened the curtains and the light flooded in. 'Have you heard anything from Douglas since he left?'

'Nothing,' whispered Mrs Sitwell.

'Do you have any idea where he might be?'

'I haven't a clue,' she said. She struggled to sit up. 'The police don't know either.'

Jennie pumped up the pillows. 'But the police looked for him?'

'They searched the whole farm,' said Mrs Sitwell.

'Did they find anything?'

'They took away some documents. They've told me that as they haven't found his body he has been classified as a missing person. They said that it's quite common for people to disappear – leaving their families with no trace,' said Mrs Sitwell. 'I know that my uncle came home from the war only to leave immediately. Nothing was ever heard from him again.'

'What are you going to do?'

Mrs Sitwell's face fell. 'I've no idea. But I know that I can't run the farm on my own.' She coughed again.

'Have you anyone to help?' asked Jennie.

'A boy from the village comes from time to time to do odd jobs – there isn't much to do now that the cows have gone. I will have to leave the farm if Douglas doesn't return.'

'Where will you go?'

'I shall join my sister in Minehead. She has a cottage there. We'll finish our days looking out to sea.' She coughed and held her stomach, 'I'm not well, you know,' she repeated with a pained expression on her face.

'Shall I call an ambulance?' asked Jennie.

Mrs Sitwell slumped. 'I don't want to go into hospital,' she said sounding frail. She coughed into her handkerchief.

Jennie was dismayed to see blood. 'I'll get an ambulance,' she said. She took out her mobile phone and dialled 999. Her call was answered quickly. She turned to look at Mrs Sitwell.

'How's my cat?' asked the old lady anxiously.

'I'll find out,' said Jennie. Downstairs she found Edward searching the living room for the missing cat. In exasperation he pulled out an old chair from a dusty corner.

Behind it was a black cat curled up asleep on a woollen blanket. Smiles of relief spread over Jennie and Edward's faces.

'It's alive,' he said. 'I'll find something for it to eat.'

Jennie followed him into the kitchen. He opened some cupboards looking for tins of cat food. She filled the sink with hot water and washing up liquid, and washed up the empty pet bowls. After she had dried them, he spooned the food into one bowl and filled the other with fresh water.

'Kitty, kitty,' he cried, putting the bowls down on the floor. A few seconds later the cat came slinking and meowing into the kitchen. It went straight to the food and started gobbling it all up.

'It's ravenous,' said Jennie.

Edward nodded and when the cat had finished feasting he gave it a quick examination.

'Apart from being all skin and bone there's nothing wrong with it,' he said with satisfaction.

Jennie looked around at the kitchen surfaces piled high with dirty plates and saucepans. With time on her hands, she started washing up. Edward helped to dry up. When everything had been cleared away Jennie wiped down the kitchen surfaces. On the side she noticed an letter lying open. She picked it up and as she read it her eyes widened.

Oakfield
12th September 2018

Dear Mr D Sitwell and Mrs A Sitwell,

I am writing to you on behalf of my client to offer to purchase Hightree Farm. My client is willing to pay above the market rate for your property provided that the sale is completed within the next thirty days. Please contact me as soon as possible if you wish to proceed.

Yours sincerely,
Khan Solicitors

'The Sitwells have received an offer on the farm,' she exclaimed. Edward took the letter from her and read it. His brow furrowed.

'I wonder why they want to buy a farm with no cows?'

Jennie racked her brains. 'Maybe they want the land?'

Outside a noise indicated the arrival of the ambulance preventing any further conversation. Two paramedics came in and went up to attend to Mrs Sitwell.

'Will you look after my cat?' she whispered as she was carried out.

'Of course,' said Jennie. She and Edward accompanied the stretcher to the ambulance. She waited until Mrs Sitwell was safely loaded on board and being driven off before she looked at her watch.

'Do you think we should do the cull another day?'

'We have set the bait up now,' he said, 'so no – we should go out tonight as planned – unless the weather deteriorates.'

'OK,' she agreed as she pulled the front door behind her.

At Green Meadow on her return Jennie found everyone in the kitchen.

'Edward and I found Mrs Sitwell looking really ill,' she said. 'We called an ambulance and they took her to Oakfield Hospital.'

'What's wrong with her?' asked Nancy who was busy at the stove.

'If I'm not mistaken she has TB.'

'That wouldn't surprise me unduly,' said Nancy. 'I know for a fact that she has always drunk unpasteurized milk straight from the cows. She knew the risk she was taking but she preferred it that way – she said it was more natural.'

'That would explain it. It's a good job that we have had our BCGs. What about Douglas Sitwell – shouldn't he be told that his mother is unwell?' asked Jennie, looking at Giles who was watching the afternoon racing on a small television.

Giles looked exasperated. 'Well of course,' he said, 'but I don't know where he is or what he is doing.'

'They haven't found a body – so he is probably still alive,' said Ian who was leaning up against the side.

'What about social media accounts? Haven't you tried to find him through those?' asked Jennie.

'I know he had an online gambling account,' said Giles.

'Why don't you try messaging him?' she asked. 'Someone needs to tell him about his mother.'

'I will – later,' he said turning back to the television.

At dusk Edward returned. The dark clouds overhead darkened the landscape. He drove the car to the entrance of the wood and parked it. They continued on foot through the trees carrying their kit bags along the woodland path using powerful torches to guide their way. Jennie was glad of her heavy duty boots with their high grip soles as she walked over the wet leaves. When they arrived at the sett, all was quiet and still except for an owl hooting. She pulled out her handheld thermal imaging device and surveyed the scene. They were alone. They settled down to wait.

After a time, three emaciated badgers emerged, sniffed the damp air and scratched their bellies. They started to forage half-heartedly around. Edward prepared his rifle and leant against a tree trunk. He aimed at the heart and lung area behind the shoulders of the slightly larger one and fired. It fell motionless to the ground. He then cleanly shot the other two.

They waited a moment or two before pulling on their rubber gloves and approaching the dead bodies. Edward checked to see whether their chests were rising and falling, their eyes blinking or their muscles having spasms.

'They look very thin to me and their fur is dull and patchy,' said Jennie as she removed their GPS collars and ear tags, which she and Sana had fitted only a few months ago. With a tape measure she calculated their lengths and took blood samples from all three badgers. Together they put the carcasses into the body bags. One by one they carried them back along the path to where the car was parked and lifted them into the boot.

On the drive back Jennie felt too emotional to speak. She stared out of the windscreen into the evening gloom. Edward respected her internal struggle and left her to her own thoughts. She appreciated his consideration.

She sighed. 'Their blood samples showed that those badgers had the bovine TB antibodies but I need to be sure,' she said, 'I just wondered if you wouldn't mind performing autopsies on them?'

'Me?' he said, 'isn't there anyone at the university that could do it?'

'No – the cuts mean that there is no one in post at the moment. You are the only person I know that is qualified to do it,' she said in a persuasive tone.

'It's an unusual request,' he said as he changed down a gear.

'But you are an Associate Fellow of the university and your clinic does have a laboratory.'

He glanced across at her and then returned his eyes to the road. 'As a matter of fact I am building up the research facilities at the clinic,' he said slowing right down as he reached a bend.

'So that's a yes?'

He nodded. She grinned with delight.

'I do appreciate it,' she said as they arrived back at Green Meadow.

*

30th September

Late the next afternoon Jennie's phone pinged.

Edward

Post mortem shows that all 3 badgers killed last night had lesions on their lungs – the main indicator of bovine TB

Jennie

Thank you so much

She jumped with joy. It was brilliant news. Her goal was a step closer. She had identified the right antibodies. Now she had to find the specific protein which indicated the presence of the bovine TB bacteria inside of which the deadly virus lived. With the correct protein, she could develop a quick and easy field test to determine whether a badger had the bovine TB antibodies. But finding it would be as difficult as identifying the oldest ant in a colony. Many hours in the lab lay ahead. But it would all be worthwhile if only the diseased badgers were culled.

Chapter 9

6th October

There was an autumnal chill and a slight drizzle in the air as Jennie cycled into Oakfield on Saturday morning. Every evening the previous week she had been working so late in the laboratory that she had only left when the caretaker had come round jangling his set of keys. Overturning her initial ideas and misconceptions had been hard. She had been convinced that the badgers were disease-free but now her work on the antibody test was progressing well. She had been taught a valuable lesson - a scientist needed to keep an open mind.

Then there was Edward. She couldn't forget how she had felt when he had held her hand to prevent her from slipping on the muddy path in the wood. Plus he had been so helpful in agreeing to do the post mortems on the badgers. He was still dating Freya though and they seemed to really like each other.

There was a convenient bike rack outside the Café del Rey which was her favourite coffee shop on the High Street. However when she arrived she realised that a group of protesters was blocking the narrow pavement. They were waving Fauna Protection placards and shaking tambourines. As she pushed her way through a tall young man shoved a collecting can in front of her.

'Give generously to save the badgers,' he said.

Ignoring him she secured her bicycle lock and pushed open the café door. Inside it was warm and cosy. Young couples accompanied by their babies in buggies, and senior citizens with their shopping trolleys, were jostling for space between the wooden furniture. Seated at a round table in the bay window was Sana gazing out, with a look of fascination, at the noisy melee gathered outside.

Jennie queued at the counter to order her drink. Having been served with a cappuccino, she sat down opposite Sana. 'The agitators are back,' she said with a groan.

'Some people say that they are a cult and if you join them, they make you give up everything – all your possessions and money – and then you can't leave,' said Sana. She continued to look with curiosity at the odd assortment of people gathered outside. Some were hippies, others were respectable rambler types and there were a few teenage girls resembling Greta Thunberg.

'When I went to one of their recruitment meetings, I thought it was akin to becoming a nun,' Jennie observed stirring her coffee.

Sana laughed. 'Do you mean like devoting your life to a messiah?'

'Something like that,' said Jennie with a laugh.

Sana returned her gaze to her friend. 'How's Green Meadow?' she asked.

Jennie sighed. 'Still pretty awful – losing the herd has hit Dad very hard,' she said, 'plus it means that the farm's income has fallen drastically.' A tear welled up in her eye.

Sana opened her mouth but before she could speak a middle aged man carrying a tray stopped next to their table.

'Excuse me, but may I join you?' he said, 'there are no other seats free.'

Jennie shifted her chair round to make more room for him. 'Of course,' she said.

The man took his coffee, toasted sandwich and a complimentary copy of the Oakfield Times off his tray and placed them on the table in front of him and sat down.

'Thank you. I have just driven down from London this morning,' he said.

'To visit?' asked Sana.

He nodded his head. 'Do you know Oakfield well?'

'It is a wonderful town – so much to see – there are layers of history here – Roman, Anglo-Saxon, Norman, Georgian – not to mention modern day monstrosities,' said Jennie with a note of pride in her voice.

He gazed out of the window. 'I wasn't expecting to run into a demonstration,' he said. 'I had heard that the cathedral was the main attraction.'

'It is normally,' said Jennie.

He sipped his drink. 'I'm researching a travelogue for The Daily Update – you know the sort of thing – where to stay, what to do and see during a weekend in a picturesque market town.'

Sana looked impressed. 'Oh – you're a journalist,' she said. 'Do you have to tow your paper's editorial line?'

'Usually, but it depends. Sometimes the truth needs to be told,' he said. He peered at the photograph on the front page of the Oakfield Times, 'This photo is of activists pelting eggs at badger cullers arriving at their base. Are they connected with the protestors outside?'

Jennie inclined her head. 'They are from an organisation called Fauna Protection.'

The man took a bite out of his toasted cheese sandwich. 'Have they been causing trouble?' he asked.

Jennie hesitated, remembering Joe's words about being discreet.

'They march about the town from time to time making a lot of noise,' she said.

The man frowned. 'That's not what weekenders want to read about. They look for a range of independent shops, a farmer's market, and Michelin starred restaurants.'

'Oakfield has plenty of those,' said Sana with a smile.

He drained his coffee cup, stood up and pulled out his business cards from his jacket pocket. He handed them one each. 'I'm in town for the next few days. Contact me if you can think of any recommendations you would like to make.'

Sana read his card aloud:

'Stuart Brown. News Reporter. The Daily Update. Tel: 07355571544. Email: sbrown@dailyupdate.org.uk.'

'Thank you,' said Jennie. She put the card into her bag wondering if she would ever need to contact a journalist.

'Right, I must press on,' he said. He collected up all his belongings including the newspaper and headed for the door. He pulled it open and stood aside as two young men wearing jeans and casual jackets entered. Jennie's face brightened when she recognized them.

She waved at them. 'Hi, come and join us.'

Ibrahim smiled back. 'We'll be with you in a minute,' he said as he and Tony joined the end of the queue.

Sana glanced their way. 'They are both good looking guys,' she said, 'how do you know them?'

'I haven't known them long,' replied Jennie. She shifted her chair further around to make space for them as they approached holding their steaming coffees

'Hi, Tony and Ibrahim – meet Sana,' she said as they sat down.

'Gosh, it is busy in here this morning,' said Ibrahim.

Tony removed his jacket. 'So Sana, what do you do?'

'I'm Jennie's dogsbody,' she replied with a warm smile.

Jennie protested indignantly. 'Of course she's not. She is a Senior Lab Assistant at the uni.'

Tony smiled. 'Don't tell me – you spend your days looking at badger poo?'

'Amongst other things,' she admitted.

Ibrahim grinned. 'How do you two know each other?'

'We were at school together – the local comp,' said Jennie.

'Oh – so were we – but our alma mater was Wealthman College,' said Tony.

'Where all the posh boys go,' remarked Sana.

A flicker of embarrassment crossed Ibrahim's face. 'Well actually, I was one of the lucky ones - I had a bursary,' he said.

'Oh,' said Sana, 'well good for you.'

They chatted together for the next twenty minutes or so until Ibrahim stood up.

'Guys, I have to get back to work now. Bye.'

Sana stood up as well. 'I am just going to pop to the loo.' She headed towards the back of the café and disappeared into the Ladies. Tony and Jennie regarded each other suddenly finding themselves alone. His phone pinged. He picked it up and read the message. His eyes filled with annoyance.

'My date has cancelled on me,' he said. Jennie tried to look sympathetic. He paused and looked persuasively at her. 'Would you like to join me for dinner tonight? I've reserved a table at a little place I know in Church Street.'

Jennie hesitated. She thought of David's brutal text breaking off their relationship. She was now a single woman free to date whom she pleased. Besides which it was Saturday night and another Saturday evening alone at the farmhouse was not appealing. On an impulse, she said, 'Yes why not?'

Tony smiled. 'Good, I will pick you up at 7pm,' he said. 'You live at Green Meadow Farm don't you?' He got up and put on his jacket. She nodded. He left and walked off down the road.

'Has Tony gone?' said Sana on her return.

'You will never guess what - I am going on a date with him tonight,' said Jennie with a broad grin on her face.

Sana's eyes widened with surprise. 'Gosh. Well good for you! I thought he was very good looking. They both were. But are you sure? David has only just broken it off with you.'

Jennie paused in contemplation. Maybe it had been a rash move to agree to go out with Tony and she couldn't fully explain why she had said yes. Maybe it was big mistake but the truth was that she needed to feel some love again.

'I've got nothing to wear,' she said running her fingers through her hair.

'Try Posh Stuff,' said Sana.

A few minutes later Jennie marched along the High Street to the most fashionable boutique in Oakfield. She stopped in front of the enticing shop window before entering and seeing the racks of dresses, tops, trousers and skirts and the neatly arranged shelves of accessories. An unexpected greeting rang out.

'Jennie! Good morning!'

She looked to see who had recognised her. It was Freya wearing a similar outfit to one of the mannequins in the window display. Jennie walked into the well of the shop.

'Freya. Hi, I didn't know that you worked here.'

'I have for the last year or so. The staff discount is very good.'

'Oh,' said Jennie. So that was the reason why Freya always well dressed.

'How can I help you?' said Freya. 'I have a date with Tony. I need something suitable for dinner at a restaurant - nothing too expensive though.'

Freya's eyebrows shot up. 'You've come to the right place,' she said. She came out from behind the till and browsed through the rails. After a few minutes she selected three different dresses. She led Jennie to the changing room and pulled the curtain behind her.

Jennie tried on a tea dress but decided that it was too demure. The longer shift dress was rejected for being shapeless but the third dress was just right. Fortunately it also happened to be the cheapest. She changed back into her own clothes and took the three dresses back to the counter.

'I will take the light green one,' she said.

'A good choice,' said Freya, 'the colour complements your eyes.' She wrapped it up in tissue paper. 'It's in the sale, which means an additional twenty per cent off.'

'Brilliant. Thank you. I would never have considered this one for myself,' said Jennie with a beam on her face.

'Are you going anywhere nice?' said Freya ringing the sale up on the cash terminal.

'Somewhere in Church Street,' said Jennie.

Freya's eyebrows shot up and she stiffened. She fell silent for a moment and passed her the car reader. 'It will be The Virtuoso.'

'Maybe.'

'Edward doesn't like fancy restaurants,' said Freya with a sigh. 'I thought Tony had a girlfriend?'

Jennie tapped in her pin number. 'She cancelled their date so he asked me instead.'

Freya fixed a smile on her face to hide her annoyance. 'Oh,' she said as she put the dress into a carrier bag and handed it over.

'Thanks,' said Jennie. She turned on her heel and headed back down the High Street.

That evening, she blow dried and styled her hair, put on the new dress and applied some green eyeshadow which highlighted the colour of her eyes and matched the dress. She checked herself in the mirror. Satisfied with her appearance she went downstairs to the kitchen.

Nancy looked up from the stove where she was frying some liver and bacon. 'Very nice, she said, 'that dress suits you.'

Ian, who was lounging in the comfy chair in front of the fire, raised his head and paused his game on his tablet computer.

'You look good, Sis,' he said.

'Going somewhere nice?' asked Nancy.

'I hope so,' said Jennie as a car roared to a stop outside the farmhouse. She grabbed her coat, headed out of the door and slid into Tony's sports car tucking her long legs. He kissed her cheek and then put his foot down on the accelerator. As they sped along the country road into Oakfield she was glad of her seatbelt. He turned down Church Street and came to a stop outside the expensive façade of The Virtuoso. When they had both got out, Tony handed the keys to the driver who drove the car round the back.

The doorman took their coats. 'Welcome,' he said. He regarded Jennie with an appreciative gleam in his eyes.

The maître d' wearing white gloves approached them and beamed. 'Mr McKensie how nice to see you again and Miss?' he said. He directed his gaze at Jennie.

'Miss Cliffe,' she replied. He led them across the chic restaurant to a table in the window. It was laid for dinner, with a white tablecloth, sparkling glasses and cutlery, and a red rose in a crystal vase in the centre. Jennie was conscious of admiring looks from the other diners, who were wearing what looked to her eyes to be designer clothes and jewellery. Beethoven's Moonlight Sonata was playing in the background and the subdued lighting added to the ambience. The maître d' held the chair out for Jennie, and she sat down. He handed her an open menu and placed a large white serviette on her lap. She smiled at him. He then went to Tony and repeated the procedure.

'You are looking beautiful tonight,' said Tony.

She blushed and her eyes met his for a moment which was broken by the arrival of the sommelier with the wine menu.

'Shall we start with champagne?' he asked.

Jennie relaxed. 'Why not?'

'How's your week been? Mine's been horrendous – quite horrendous – a series of ups and downs - but business is like that, you know?' he said. He broke his bread roll in half and buttered it. He was looking good with a suntan, clear brown eyes and a friendly expression.

'What does property development involve?' asked Jennie.

'We buy, build and rent homes and offices all over the west of England. My grandfather started the company over sixty years ago and it has been going strong ever since. We employ over a hundred people and we recently won several design awards,' he said with a look of pride on his face. Jennie sipped her drink. 'That's so impressive.'

'I plan to double its turnover within the next five years.'

The waiter came and stood by the side of the table ready to take their order.

'I will have the calamari followed by the duck,' said Jennie.

'The pate and steak for me.'

The waiter scribbled on his order pad. 'Thank you, Sir,' he said, 'anything else?'

'That's all for now,' said Tony. The waiter took their menus and turned towards the kitchen.

Jennie picked up her glass and took a sip of champagne. 'What about the cull- how do you find the time to do that as well?'

'It takes place in the evening so I can fit it in. What about you?'

'I seem to be spending all my time these days involved with badgers one way or another,' she admitted.

He laughed as if it had suddenly occurred to him that Jennie was not typical of the girls he normally dated. She smiled and raised her glass to her lips.

The meal passed quickly and at the end Tony asked for the bill. When it came, Jennie picked it up. She winced.

'I can pay half,' she offered.

'Of course not. It's my pleasure. You are my guest,' he said as the waiter came over with the card reader.

'Well, thank you. While I am still a student, I have to watch the pennies.'

He stood up. 'Let's get our coats.'

It was pelting down with rain when they arrived back at the farm. Tony drew up outside and switched off the ignition. He pulled her into his arms.

'You are gorgeous,' he murmured. His lips met hers. Their kiss was long and passionate. Finally she pulled herself away.

'I have to go,' she said breathlessly. She opened the car door and pulled her coat over her head.

'See you soon,' he shouted after her as she rushed inside to avoid getting too wet.

That night in bed her thoughts whirled. Her unexpected date with Tony had been fun – after all those years with David she was unused to being wined and dined. She had to admit that he had been good company. He was totally different to David. She needed to broaden her horizons – to date different men – well date men full stop. Having just a one track mind – developing an antibody test – was maybe not a wise thing to do.

*

8th October

Breaking glass and a yapping dog woke Jennie up. She looked at her alarm clock. It was only two o'clock in the morning. She threw on her dressing gown and rushed out of her bedroom to be met on the landing by her parents. Nancy flicked the light switch on. A brick flew through the glass panel in the front door and landed in the hallway.

'Careful!' shouted Giles heading straight for the gun cupboard. Jennie and Nancy followed him as he ran out into the farmyard brandishing a rifle. He fired two warning shots into the air. Bramble woofed ferociously.

Anonymous figures clad in dark clothing melted away into the inky darkness. A car engine revved and tyres screeched followed by an eerie silence. Jennie could hear her heart beating. Torch in hand she helped check the yard for any remaining interlopers but they had all departed. Giles nailed some wooden planks across the shattered front windows of the farmhouse. At last Jennie could climb back into bed but she lay awake unable to sleep as she thought of the untoward events of the last twenty-four hours – an unexpected date with Tony and now an attack on the farm.

When daylight broke, she was jolted awake by Giles yelling from the farmyard. She opened her bedroom window and leant out. He was standing next to the chicken coop waving his arms in agitation. Besides him was carnage. Scattered around the yard were the bodies of decapitated chickens. A few survivors were running around in circles squawking with fear as Bramble chased them.

149

'Nancy!' Giles shouted again. He swerved to avoid stepping on a flapping bird. Nancy, Jennie and Ian came running out, tugging on their coats.

'Oh no, my chickens,' said Nancy with a look of dismay, 'what happened?' She sprang into action trying to catch the remaining chickens.

Giles frowned. 'Someone opened the door of the henhouse and a fox got in.'

Jennie called to Bramble to heel. There was a trail of destruction everywhere. As well as the dead birds lying on the ground there were doors wrenched off their hinges and walls daubed with graffiti. Several windows had been reduced to shards and farm machinery upturned. Ian disappeared into a storeroom and reappeared with a power screwdriver in his hand. He started fixing the door back on to the henhouse.

'Who would do such a thing?' asked Nancy, retrieving her prize bird from a high perch.

'Maniacs,' said Jennie trapping a chicken in a corner.

One by one, the remaining fowl were caught and shoved back into the safety of their straw strewn quarters. The door was closed securely behind them and a collective sigh of relief rang out.

Jennie walked around taking a closer look at the vulgar words and graphic images that had been sprayed willy-nilly over the farm's buildings, vehicles and machinery. The crude drawings of hands smeared with blood made her shake her head and the sight of the word MURDERER drew an expletive from her. At the back of the milking parlour she noticed a purple dragonfly sprayed onto the wall. She went up closer and for several seconds she was transfixed. Ian came round the corner and saw her staring.

'Maybe it's a warning of some sort,' she said.

'Let's hope not,' he said.

Jennie and Ian walked back to the farmhouse. Nancy was watching Giles pacing back and forth with his phone pressed to his ear.

'No one is hurt – it is just damage to our property. Ok – come when you can,' said Giles. He finished his call and said, 'The police will be here sometime today but in the meantime we should leave things as they.'

Ian scowled and glared at Giles. 'I can't do this anymore,' he shouted, 'this has happened because we are taking part in the cull - killing badgers for fuck's sake.' Bramble barked in alarm at his raised voice.

The mention of badgers set Giles off in a rant. He waved his fist in the air. 'Those wretched creatures infected our cows. We have lost not only our herd but our whole livelihood.'

'We don't know for sure that the anti-cullers are responsible for this vandalism,' said Jennie calming Bramble down by stroking her.

'Who else could it be?' asked Ian.

'I don't know, but what I do know is that bovine TB is bad news for all animals. The cull is a necessary evil,' she said.

'Even so I hate being part of it,' he said. He started to cough violently.

'Dropping out of the cull, won't change anything, you know – it will still go ahead because that is what the government has decided. Come on, it's cold out here, let's go inside and have some breakfast,' said Nancy. She pulled her coat more tightly around her and headed towards the open front door. Everyone followed her in. Ian rushed upstairs to his room. Jennie went into the kitchen and filled the kettle. Shortly after, Ian clomped back down the stairs trailing a small suitcase behind him. He grabbed his coat from a hook in the hall.

'I am leaving,' he shouted from the hall. Jennie and Nancy rushed to talk to him but the front door slammed shut behind him.

Jennie stared after him, stunned. She turned back in to the kitchen.

'What will he do?' she asked Giles.

'Probably get a better job – I can only afford to pay him a pittance at the moment,' he answered.

Just after breakfast, a police patrol car drove up the drive and drew to a stop in front of the farmhouse. Jennie and Nancy followed Giles outside. It had started to rain and there was a brisk wind.

PS Miller, PC Allen and a female officer got out of the police car. 'This is our crime scene investigator,' said Miller indicating his colleague. 'You have reported an incident?'

'We were attacked in the early hours,' said Giles his face full of indignation.

Miller opened the boot of the patrol car and lifted out a large locker bag. The investigator donned a white protective suit, swept her hair up into a hairnet and put on some latex gloves. Giles led the way around the house to the farmyard where most of the graffiti and vandalism had occurred.

'If it is any consolation,' said Allen as he surveyed the damage, 'you are not alone. Recently we have had several reports of attacks on dairy farms around here.'

'There isn't a pattern so far but you need to be vigilant,' said Miller

First the crime scene officer photographed everything and then she dusted many surfaces for foot and finger prints.

'Does this belong to any of you?' she asked holding up an aerosol can.

'Definitely not,' said Giles.

'In that case this must be one of the spray paints that the graffiti artists used – they have been very careful to remove all the other cans. We will take it away and see if it can give us any further information,' she said. She slipped it into a plastic bag and sealed the top.

Miller walked around having a look at the damage. 'Hopefully this was a one off incident, but if you take my advice there are a couple of things you can do to improve security here on the farm,' he said to Giles. 'I suggest you install a camera – these days digital camera technology is much more affordable and reliable. Also put up some more lighting - you know the sort that is activated by movement and make sure you update your insurance policy.' He pointed out suitable places where cameras and lights could be installed.

'Yet more expense,' grumbled Giles, He connected the pressure washer to the outside tap and opened a tub of graffiti remover. 'Can we start the clean up?'

'It's all yours,' said Miller. He ambled over to the police car where he was joined by his colleagues. They drove off down the driveway passing the mail van on the way. The postman handed Giles a letter. He ripped it open.

'Blow me down, Khan Solicitors write that their clients have repeated their offer for the farm,' he exclaimed.

Jennie peered over his shoulder. 'They must really want to buy it.'

'They obviously don't know how difficult it is to be a dairy farmer,' said Giles with an air of exasperation as they walked back inside the farmhouse kitchen.

Later that morning Jennie cycled into the university. On her arrival in the department, Amina opened her door and gesticulated to her to come inside her office.

'Shut the door, will you,' she said. 'I hear that you were at the Fauna Protection meeting last month?'

'Yes,' admitted Jennie wondering why that should be of concern to Amina.

'Well, a polite request – could you refrain from attending any more such meetings?' she asked her lips in a straight firm line.

Jennie knew that it would be pointless to argue or to try to explain. Instead she nodded and said, 'Of course Dr Ahmed.'

'Right, good, I am glad that we have sorted that out,' she said. 'You may go, but don't forget to keep submitting the reports on your research.'

Jennie made her escape and went to the postgraduate common room where she made herself a strong cup of tea. She leant against the kitchen worktop and steadied the thoughts which were racing around her head.

*

9th October

The shooting school's training room was becoming very familiar to Jennie. It was Tuesday evening and she was sitting on one of the wooden chairs waiting for Joe to start his weekly briefing session. She had come with Giles in his Range Rover. Afterwards she had another date with Tony. The ceiling light flickered on and off. While she waited she studied the pictures of different types of gun on the wall. Eventually all the team were present.

Joe came to the front and stood with his feet slightly apart. 'Welcome everyone,' he said, 'first of all - Ian won't be joining us tonight. He is going to take an indefinite break from the cull.'

Ibrahim's eyebrows shot up and he looked along the row of chairs at Giles who was sitting next to Jennie. Giles shrugged and remained silent. Jennie kept her eyes on Joe.

'Has he chickened out?' asked Tony in a scathing tone. The right words needed to defend her brother failed to spring to Jennie' lips.

Joe ignored Tony's question. 'I understand that there has been an incident at Green Meadow Farm?'

'It happened last night. The bastards vandalized the farm and plastered graffiti everywhere,' said Giles his voice resonating with anger and indignation.

'Do the police know who's responsible?' asked Edward.

Giles grimaced. 'Purple dragonflies were sprayed onto a couple of the walls, but that is all that they have to go on at the moment.'

'How is the clean-up operation going?' asked Tony.

'Spray paint on the side of the cars is proving hard to get off,' said Jennie.

Ibrahim sat back. 'Have you used nail polish remover? That usually does the job.'

'Did they key the cars? Key marks on my cars have been hard to remove which is very annoying and inconvenient,' said Tony eliciting a look of sympathy from Freya.

'Fortunately no,' said Jennie, 'but the police aren't sure why we were targeted. It could be because we are a dairy farm or because they have found out that we are involved in the cull.'

Freya was baffled. 'Why would they target cows?'

'Because the activists believe all animals should be set free,' explained Edward.

'That's just plain weird,' she said with surprise, 'where would the cows go?'

Jennie glanced at her to see if she were serious and concluded that she was.

Edward glanced at Jennie. 'Why do they suspect that you are involved in the cull?'

She hoped he wouldn't remember what she had said at the student union event but she could see from his face that he had.

'Who knows? We haven't told anyone. The perpetrators could be cull saboteurs or just local vandals,' said Giles.

'True,' said Joe. He stood more upright and pulled back his shoulders. 'But the police have contacted me to remind you again not to post any comments or images on social media platforms. I would also suggest that it would be unwise to speak to the press. There may well be unintended consequences if you do so. There is a good reason why I have asked you all to keep our activities confidential – it is for your own safety.'

'Well, I for one, would never post anything on the internet,' said Giles, 'I don't even know how to.'

'They seem to have the public's support,' sighed Jennie.

'People hate badgers and foxes being killed,' said Ibrahim fiddling with his phone.

'Fauna Protection has launched an appeal to raise more money,' said Joe, 'the cash must be pouring in.'

'Don't forget, we are involved in a legal activity undertaken on behalf of a government agency,' protested Giles.

'Only a few people know that – everyone just hears that it is cruel and unnecessary,' said Tony.

'Shouldn't we counter their arguments? We could explain that we want to eradicate a deadly disease so that the future is better for all animals,' said Jennie.

'No,' said Joe firmly, 'we have to remain silent.'

Jennie felt rebuked but she continued nonetheless, 'There was an article in last week's The Daily Update defending country sports. Science has shown that both hunting and shooting play a major role in the conservation of the countryside and the management of wildlife, because they pay for both.'

'That article,' said Edward, 'made some good points but the fact remains that opposition to the cull is growing - they claim that it isn't working, and actually they are right - we haven't any evidence to show that the fall in badger numbers is bringing about fewer cases of bovine TB.'

'Ok guys; let's leave it there for now,' said Joe. 'Collect your rifles and go through to the range. You will need your coats – it is freezing in there.' He headed out of the door followed by everyone except Giles who made his excuses and left.

Freya chose the lane next to Tony's. Even in a bulky jacket her figure seemed trimmer than before. She aimed her rifle at the target, pulled the trigger and hit the bull's eye. There was a round of applause from the men. She turned round, ignored Edward and beamed straight at Tony, who responded with a thumb's up. In a fit of pique, Edward picked up his rifle and shot at the target hitting the centre cleanly.

'Gosh, it is a very high standard tonight,' said Jennie. She unlatched the safety catch on her rifle. Standing in the correct position, to her satisfaction, she fired away hitting the centre of the target time after time. At the end of the evening she felt pleased with her performance.

'That was good tonight,' said Freya as they packed up, 'I think I am getting more accurate - maybe because I am fitter.'

'From walking Lola?' asked Jennie expecting an affirmative reply.

'Oh no, I have taken up running,' said Freya, 'walking was too slow.'

Edward overhead this last remark as he came up to them. 'Lola's jabs are due next week,' he said in a low voice. 'Ring the surgery for an appointment.'

Freya pursed her lips. Her laugh sounded fake and Jennie noticed that her response failed to impress him. They left the range and passed through the small lobby where Tony and Ibrahim were standing.

'Before you all rush off,' said Ibrahim. 'Do any of you have any plans for Sunday? I'm thinking of organising a mixed doubles tournament. My partner Maisie and I need the practice.'

Tony nodded. 'Good idea. We could hold it at Beddis Grange – there are a couple of courts there that could do with some action.'

'Brilliant,' said Freya brightening up, 'as it happens, I have Sunday off.'

Jennie wasn't sure. It had been a long time since she had played tennis. 'Who would take part?' she asked.

'Well – there's you and Tony, Edward and Freya, myself and Maisie plus another couple,' said Ibrahim. 'That's four pairs.'

There was a short pause.

Edward said, 'Sounds fun – count me in.'

Jennie hesitated. The cull was already taking up a lot of her time and she didn't want to fall behind with her research. But the silent appeals of the others were hard to resist.

'It is just a knock about.' Ibrahim reassured her.

'OK, I will give it a go,' she said. Smiles broke out on the assembled faces.

'Brilliant,' said Ibrahim.

Jennie looked down and noticed some mud on the bottom of her black trousers. 'I won't be a minute,' she said to Tony. She disappeared into the Ladies for a quick wash and brush up. She slipped off her boots and put on a more elegant pair of shoes. Her trousers were brushed up and a cream silk blouse buttoned up. Instead of her anorak she slipped on a smart jacket. She stuffed her shooting clothes into her tote bag, tidied her hair and reapplied her makeup.

When she reappeared Tony gave her an admiring look and they walked out together to his car. Jennie could feel Freya's eyes boring into the back of her head. They sped off down the winding lane towards Oakfield. Daylight had faded and a stronger breeze had taken hold. It was late, but not too late.

'Where are we going?' she asked as she fastened her seatbelt. The smell of his aftershave triggered a frisson of excitement in her as he put his foot down on the accelerator.

'The pub first, and then dinner at my place.'

Tony drew up outside the Fat Goose, an eighteenth century coaching inn in the High Street. Inside it was noisy and jostling with people. Jennie followed him to a table at the far side. She sat down and took her coat off while he went to the bar to order some drinks. She surveyed the bar to see who was there. In the opposite corner she spotted Jeremy Boyle and four other people, including Sophie, sitting at a table, engaged in an animated conversation. She moved her chair so that her back was turned away from them – she didn't want them to see her.

The pub door opened and a gust of wind blew in, followed to her surprise, by Ian, who went straight to the bar. He shot a greeting at Tony who was being served by a pretty barmaid. He looked around and saw his sister. She waved at him and he gestured back. Tony returned with their drinks.

Sophie joined Ian at the bar. They pretended to ignore each other but Jennie could see that they were whispering something. The tall man with long untidy hair, who had been sitting next to Boyle, went and stood next to them. He glared at Sophie. She abruptly turned and slunk back to the table, like an obedient dog. Ian's face clouded over with disappointment. The barmaid plonked a pint of beer in front of him. He took two or three long gulps and left, pausing only to nod a farewell to Jennie.

'That's Jeremy Boyle over there,' she said softly to Tony. He raised his eyes and spent a few minutes studying him carefully. His face turned a paler shade.

'What's wrong?' she said.

'I know him. We were at uni together.' He picked up his glass. 'It was ten years ago and he has changed a lot but it's definitely him. We didn't part friends,' he said. He looked away. 'Ignore them. Tell me about your research instead.'

She hesitated as she knew it would be hard to talk about it in lay terms.

'I am enjoying it – lots of data collection and looking for patterns but it is fun,' she said, a wide smile spreading over her face.

'Whatever floats your boat,' he said with a chuckle.

'What's happening in your world?'

He launched into a description of the pitfalls that confronted him on a daily basis. She feigned interest but her mind kept wandering. Her attention strayed across the room to Boyle and Sophie. To her dismay, they were casting suspicious looks their way. Suddenly Boyle got up and approached them.

'I remember you,' he hissed and thrust his jaw into Tony's face. 'Don't think I haven't forgotten what you did to me. And I know exactly what you are involved in now. If you don't stop, there is going to be trouble.'

'Don't threaten me,' said Tony in his public school accent and with a look of disdain on his face. He stood up and pulled himself up to his full height. He towered authoritatively over Boyle, who took a step back. Tony laughed in his face. Boyle was furious. There was a short standoff. Sophie came over and pulled Boyle away. She shot Jennie a sympathetic look.

'Come on let's go,' said Tony. He drained his glass and rose.

Jennie needed no encouragement to leave and she followed him to the exit.

'That was scary,' she said.

Tony drove very fast out of Oakfield before turning off the highway and heading down a narrow road. Large iron gates marked the entrance to Beddis Grange's long driveway. It was pitch black when they arrived and Jennie could see very little but she had the impression of a grand house nestling in an open vale. They went into his bachelor suite of rooms in one of the wings. He led her through to the dining room where a large table in the middle of the room was set for dinner. It was adorned with two silver candlesticks and a crystal vase full of golden chrysanthemums. She studied the décor – classic and timeless with curtained sash windows, picture rails and a glass chandelier.

'Champagne?' he said.

She nodded and he disappeared through a side door to a small kitchen beyond. He returned with a bottle, which he popped open. He poured her a glass and opened a bottle of beer for himself.

'I need this,' she said. 'Boyle looked as if he was going to murder you.'

'He is a nasty piece of work. I've come up against him before. But don't let him spoil our evening.'

The alcohol started going to her head. She relaxed and buried the image of Boyle's angry countenance in her psyche.

'Hungry?' he said. She nodded and he disappeared back into the kitchen and returning with two plates of bruschetta.

She hungrily scoffed the food down, entertained by his amusing banter. The main course of carbonara was followed by strawberry meringue. Afterwards, she went into the sitting room, kicked off her shoes and sat on the long sofa. He sat beside her and pulled her towards him. His lips were soft and eager. When his hand moved up her thigh, her flesh tingled and her inhibitions deserted her. It had been months since she had made love and his experienced caresses overcame her scruples and relieved her pent up sexual desires.

Afterwards he lit a post coital cigarette. 'You are lovely,' he said.

She giggled at the strangeness of the situation.

Naked, he got up and walked over to the drinks trolley. He poured himself a whisky and another glass of champagne for her. They made love again and sat and listened to music talking and laughing until the early hours of the morning.

'Can you call me a taxi?' she said.

'What's the rush? Stay the night,' he said squeezing her hand.

'I have a busy day tomorrow,' she said, suddenly keen to leave.

A cross expression appeared on his face.

'Badger research?'

She bowed her head.

'I don't know why you are so interested in them,' he said, 'they are just wild animals that are causing a lot of trouble.'

'You don't care for them?'

'I wouldn't be killing them if I did.'

His callous remark hit her like a sharp arrow and shocked her into a temporary silence. She had been naïve – she had thought that the others were killing the badgers because they believed it was the best way to protect their future. But now for the first time it occurred to her that some of them were possibly doing it for other reasons – maybe the money (after all she had initially being interested in earning some extra cash herself) or for the sport (maybe some actually got a weird sort of buzz from killing). Maybe it was only Edward who felt like her – that the badgers were a mammal that deserved to be protected but unfortunately were as much victims as perpetrators in a human world that needed food. It was so complicated that it made her head ache.

Chapter 10

14th October

Jennie searched through her wardrobe for her only tennis dress, last worn at least five years previously. She found it wedged at the back. It was crumpled and rather grubby. Hopefully it would fit. She took it downstairs and threw it in to the washing machine. After much rummaging in the under-the-stairs cupboard, she located her tennis shoes and racket. Neither was in pristine condition. When the washing cycle had finished she hung the dress out to drip dry. Fortunately it didn't need ironing.

After Sunday lunch, she threw a coat over her tennis clothes and cycled to Beddis Grange, which was about five miles north-west of Green Meadow. She turned off the road and went through the gates down a long drive towards the elegant Georgian-style slate roofed house which was surrounded by a mixture of rolling farmland and deciduous woodland. It was a dull afternoon with a slight breeze blowing the leaves off the trees.

On her arrival, Tony came out to greet her. He kissed her lightly on the lips. It was good to see him again. She leant her bike up against a wall and followed him to the well maintained grass courts at the side of the house. Edward and Ibrahim were already there having a practice. Tony introduced her to three people who were standing chatting. There was Maisie, a medium-sized woman with a jolly grin; Darren who was tall and broad, and Allison, a lean and muscular lady.

Jennie took off her coat and laid it onto a bench. Tony examined her tennis dress with a critical eye. It was too tight in several places. She laughed nervously and coloured with embarrassment.

'It was such short notice, this is all I have to wear,' she explained as nonchalantly as she could.

'This time it doesn't matter,' he said. Which means that next time, I need to get something new she thought.

Freya came bounding up wearing a flattering tennis top and skirt which showed off her long legs to advantage. Jennie blinked and bit her lip.

Freya gazed around at the house and gardens. 'So this is where you live, Tony,' she said, 'what a super place.'

'It is my parents' home,' he said, 'it has been in our family for generations.'

'You are so lucky – to have such a property,' she said with an appreciative look.

'Yes we are,' he agreed. He sounded pleased.

Ibrahim looked their way and seeing that everyone had arrived, came over. He took his smartphone from his pocket.

'Right everyone. Listen up,' he said, 'my plan is for each couple to play each other couple – so that will be six matches, all one set each. I have an app which will keep track of the scores. Ok? Right, let's go.'

Jennie waited for Tony and together they walked on to the nearest court.

She smiled at him. 'Apologies in advance for my rusty tennis,' she said, 'I haven't played for a long time.'

'Don't worry,' he said, 'try to stay at the net.'

When Ibrahim and Maisie joined them on the court they had a few practice rallies until the match began. Tony served the opening ball from the back of the court. Jennie was relieved when she returned Ibrahim's volley. The first game was close with Tony just about holding his serve. Ibrahim, who was full of energy, won his service games easily. Jennie noticed that he used his height and strength to hit the ball hard and straight using the full width and depth of the court whilst Maisie had a useful backhand responsible for several winning points. Both couples critiqued each other in a positive way, in an effort to improve their style and technique.

Jennie was reasonably fit and she ran and returned the ball competently but she lost one of her service games. The standard of play was higher that she had anticipated. Her hatred of losing returned and she upped her game fighting back to win the next few points but the superior skills of Ibrahim and Maisie meant that in the end they triumphed 6-4.

After a short break for lemonade and wedges of orange, Jennie and Tony next faced Edward and Freya on court. They tossed a coin to see who served first. Tony won and everyone took up position. He took a ball from his pocket, bounced it and then threw it up into the air bringing his shoulders back to give it a massive whack. It was an ace and 15-0. He took his service game comfortably. Edward's service game went to love as well. Next it was Jennie's turn to serve and she hit the ball accurately for an ace. Tony shot her an approving glance.

'Keep it up,' he muttered between points.

Jennie noticed that Freya and Edward seemed to be at odds with each other – they were not playing at all harmoniously. The two couples were evenly matched and it went to a tie break with Tony winning the deciding point. Jennie was pleased – it was only tennis but her competitive instinct had come to the fore again.

Their last match was against Darren and Allison who played like semi-professionals winning the both the set and the tournament comfortably. Ibrahim declared himself and Maisie as runners up. 'Thank you guys, I hope you have enjoyed the afternoon,' he said.

Jennie nodded. It had been fun even if she and Tony had only come third, a placing which Tony didn't seem to mind. Edward was also unperturbed at coming last, but Freya threw her racket down on the ground in annoyance.

'Edward and I just didn't gel,' she complained.

Jennie walked with Tony into the conservatory at the back of the Grange, where assorted sandwiches, cakes, cups of tea and jugs of soft drinks filled with ice cubes were laid out on a large trestle table. A buzz of happy conversation broke out as everyone chattered about the points missed and the games won and lost. Tony wandered off. She poured herself a glass of lemonade and dithered over her choice of sandwich. She caught Edward gazing at her as if he were trying to make up his mind about her. He came over to her.

'You played some good shots,' he said. 'I thought you said that you hadn't played since leaving school?'

'I hadn't.'

Freya approached them with a cup of tea in her hand.

'You need a new tennis dress Jennie,' she said, 'pop into Posh Stuff sometime, we have a good selection.'

Jennie smiled and promised she would. She scanned the conservatory to see where Tony had got to. He was out in the garden. She joined him.

'I am going now,' she said, 'I have some work to finish off.'

Tony accompanied her to her bike and kissed her goodbye.

'I'll be in contact,' he said.

*

15th October
The sun's rays were shining as weakly as a low voltage torch through the laboratory's windows when Jennie arrived

167

early the following morning. She flicked the light switch. The ceiling lights spluttered into life but it was still too dark, so she switched on the spot lamp plugged into a socket at the back of her work station. That's better she thought. She lined up a series of blood stained slides and examined them under the microscope. The bovine TB antibodies could clearly be seen swimming around in the solution.

She opened a large fridge and pulled out a rack of test tubes filled with blood taken from the same badger. A pipette in hand, she drew up some blood and dropped it on to a small plastic lateral flow testing stick. She added two drops of buffer liquid and waited five minutes. Just like a pregnancy test, the horizontal blue line changed to red, indicating a positive result. Antibodies were present.

She punched the air and cried, 'Hurrah.' She felt exhilarated and excited. It actually worked. After weeks of painstaking effort she had made a breakthrough. She had developed an antibody test that could be used quickly and effectively in the field. She now needed to test its efficacy.

Sana heard her cry and came over. She took off her washing up gloves. 'Success? Have you done it?'

Jennie nodded with a broad smile on her face.

Sana gave her a tight hug. 'That's brilliant,' she said, 'well done.'

'Can you send the design and specification to the manufacturers?' asked Jennie.

'Amina will have to authorize the order as it will be quite expensive. How many shall I order?' said Sana.

Jennie thought for minute. 'Five hundred to begin with,' she said as her phone pinged.

Tony

Are you free to meet for lunch?

Jennie

Yes

Tony

Meet you outside in twenty minutes.

Jennie had not planned to meet him that day but the sound of his voice made her change her mind. She exchanged her lab coat for a warm jacket. Taking two steps at a time she raced downstairs and across the courtyard. Tony's car pulled up just as she ran through the university's gates. Without hesitation she opened the passenger seat door and leapt inside.

He put his foot down on the accelerator. 'I have only got an hour.'

'Where are we going?' she said fastening her seat belt. His car smelt of his aftershave – a mixture of oak moss and vanilla. He revved up the engine, opened the windows and put on his shades.

'To Ibrahim's – he has a flat in the centre of town – I have ordered in pepperoni pizza,' he said as he navigated through Oakfield's midday traffic to the High Street.

Tony parked outside an office with the name Khan Solicitors displayed on the fascia. He opened the main entrance to the flats above the parade. She followed him upstairs. The front door of the flat opened straight into a open plan living room with a kitchenette along one side, white walls hung with framed prints and bookshelves full of paperbacks. There was a modern fireplace in front of which were a black leather sofa and a coffee table, piled high with magazines and papers. A rolled up prayer mat, a black dining table and chairs completed the scene. She sat on the sofa and picked up a magazine.

'Ibrahim doesn't mind you using his place?' she asked.

'We go back a long way,' he said as he wandered over to the kitchen area to find a bottle opener for the beers he had brought up from the car. He popped the tops off and handed her a bottle.

'A good friend then?' she said.

He sat down next to her and pulled her into his arms. The magazine slipped onto the floor. His lips met hers and he kissed her long and hard, his tongue exploring her mouth. Her defences melted away as his hand started to expertly explore her body. She threw caution and inhibitions to the wind. Their love making was fast and furious. The doorbell interrupted them. He went to the door and came back carrying two takeaway pizza boxes. Their aroma made Jennie ravenous. She sat on the sofa and tucked into a large slice washed down by the rest of the beer.

'I wasn't expecting this to be so delicious,' she said.

Tony picked up the remote control and switched on the flat screen television which was installed over the mantelpiece. He flicked through the channels until he found some wrestling. He turned the volume up so loud that she found conversation to be impossible. Not that he seemed that bothered about talking – he was more interested in the match and was championing one particular wrestler with bulging muscles called Brent Hardman. She suppressed a feeling of boredom. She stretched out her elbows and knocked a wodge of papers off a side table. A letterhead caught her eye – Khan Solicitors. She remembered that Ibrahim was a solicitor working in Oakfield. She wondered if he worked for the Khan Solicitors – the ones that were acting on behalf the company offering to purchase Green Meadow and Hightree.

'Does Ibrahim work for Khan Solicitors?' she asked.

Tony's attention was on the wrestling but he grunted an affirmative. Jennie pondered this interesting fact. Maybe Ibrahim knew more than he was letting on. An urge to be back in the laboratory came over her and she stood up. She was unaccountably glad when soon afterwards Tony dropped her back at the university.

'See you later,' he shouted after her as she slammed the car door shut. As she walked back into the lab she saw Sana giving her a puzzled look.

'What?' said Jennie. She glanced away and put on her white lab coat.

Sana gave her a knowing glance. 'Don't tell me that Tony has just been servicing your equipment?'

Jennie laughed and replied, 'I needed something to break up my day.' At that they both giggled and the other people in the laboratory looked up to see what was so amusing.

She returned to her bench and concentrated on refining the antibody test. As the afternoon wore on, it became darker outside and dimmer inside. She decided to call it a day. She saved her documents, stood up and stretched. She read the time – if she put a move on, she just had time to grab a sandwich and a cup of tea in the canteen before setting off for the shooting school.

It was after six and pitch-black when she cycled down the lane. She was due to meet the rest of the team for a quick briefing. She knew that Tony was going to be there and she thought about their lunchtime tryst. Certainly it was good to have some male attention again.

She turned into the car park. Her bike lights picked out a small group of people dressed in black milling about in front of the building. They were brandishing baseball bats and rattling drums. Edward was talking to the two men who were standing at the front. Joe came and joined him but Tony hung back reluctant to get involved. Edward shouted at her to stay clear. A scuffle broke out. Blows were exchanged.

Jennie's heat beat faster. She leant her bike against the hedge, grabbed her mobile phone from her bag and dialled 999.

'Police please,' she said to the emergency operator.

'Where are you?'

'Oakfield Shooting School....we're under attack,' she said clearly.

'Our response team will be with you as soon as possible,' said the operator in a calm voice.

Jennie waited in the shadows, resisting the temptation to join in the melee. Within minutes a police siren blasted upon her consciousness. The patrol car screeched to a halt outside the school. Miller and Allen tumbled out, holding raised truncheons. There was a clap of thunder and rain started to pour down. Seeing the police, some of the protestors made a beeline for a white van, which sped off into the dark. Others turned on their heels and ran down the lane with the two policemen in hot pursuit. Jennie rushed towards Edward who was wincing with pain.

'Are you alright?' she asked.

'The bastards punched me in the stomach,' he said.

They headed into the building. Miller and Allen returned, breathless and wet.

'They got away,' said Miller.

'We got their number plate,' said Allen.

Jennie led the way into the warm dry reception where everyone else was congregated.

'Right, what's the damage?' asked Miller. He took a notepad and pen from one of his pockets.

'Thankfully I have just got some cuts and bruises – nothing broken,' said Joe shaking his head with relief.

'It was a close run thing,' said Tony. He leant against the wall. 'For a minute or two that got quite hairy.'

Giles scoffed, 'You ought to be grateful to Joe and Edward – they took the brunt of the attack.'

Tony looked as if he were about to deny this but then he said, 'You're right – they reacted so quickly that by the time I waded in it was all over.'

Jennie's nerves were unsettled by the whole episode which for a split second had seemed in danger of escalating out of control. If the police hadn't arrived when they did, Edward could have been seriously injured. She went into the small kitchen, put on the kettle and made some tea.

'Right, everyone, we see that these people will stop at nothing to frighten you. From now on be extra vigilant,' said Miller accepting the hot mug that Jennie offered him. She saw that the faces of the team had hardened – the reality of the situation that confronted them had sunk home.

*

16th October

The next morning, after a restless night, Jennie pulled on her riding boots and a warm jacket. At the stables, she saddled up Sukey for a hard canter across the fields towards Beesnest Farm, which was south-east of Green Meadow Farm. As she rode along, she kept her eyes open for any signs of badger activity such as soil scuffed up by pointed snouts searching for acorns recently planted by jays and squirrels, or cowpats turned over for the worms underneath.

Her thoughts turned to Tony. He was handsome and came from a good family, yet she was beginning to realise that maybe they should have waited longer before their relationship had become intimate.

In the distance she saw the Nelsons' red-brick farmhouse nestling in the landscape. A wisp of smoke was rising from the chimney. Within a few minutes she was there. Outside the farmhouse were upturned flower pots spilling soil and plants onto the ground. Ugly graffiti was scrawled over the walls and a smashed window was waiting to be boarded up. Dismounting, she tethered Sukey to the wooden fence and had a look around. Sure enough the signature purple dragonfly of Fauna Protection had been sprayed onto the sides of an outbuilding.

She rang the doorbell. It was opened by Mrs Nelson, a large woman with a kind face.

'Jennie. Nice to see you. Come on in,' she said.

Jennie entered the hall, which was full of coats and wellington boots on the floor and followed her into the kitchen at the back of the house.

'We are in a right pickle here,' she said. 'Coffee?'

'I won't say no,' said Jennie with a smile.

'You look quite grown up,' said Mrs Nelson switching on the kettle, 'but I don't know why I'm surprised – I hardly recognise my own two these days – they have changed so much since they left home.'

'I see that the vandals have been,' said Jennie.

'They attacked last night,' said Mrs Nelson. 'We've a lot of clearing up to do.' She opened the fridge, took out the milk and spooned instant coffee into two mugs.

'Did the police come?' asked Jennie.

'First thing this morning,' said Mrs Nelson. 'Fortunately most of the damage is minor – our alarms frightened them away before they could do more than splatter slurry everywhere and break a few windows. How are your parents? ' She poured the boiling water onto the coffee. 'Do you know when will they be allowed to restock the farm? Milk?'

'Yes, please. They are still in limbo really – they haven't heard anything yet. How long was it before you got the go ahead?'

'It took three months – but we had spent a fortune on our bio security. It was a great feeling when the cows came back but now we are both agreed that if we get another outbreak, we will sell up – we couldn't go through all that stress again,' she said. She handed Jennie a mug of steaming coffee and indicated that she should take a seat at the table.

'That's rather drastic, isn't it?' said Jennie, 'I mean – after all the time you have been here.'

Mrs Nelson sat down as well. 'Someone has already made a very handsome offer on the farm. They sent a letter only last week,' she said. 'What with the ridiculously low price of milk, this awful bovine TB and now this, it may be time to call it a day.'

Jennie's eyes widened with alarm. 'Who made you the offer?' she asked, not expecting a reply. After all it was an impertinent question.

'I'll find the letter.' She turned round and pulled open the middle drawer of the oak sideboard and rifled through until she found it. Turning back to face Jennie, she put on her reading glasses and read it carefully. 'It doesn't actually say who the prospective purchasers are, just that Khan Solicitors are acting on their behalf. But they seem very keen to buy the farm.'

'I know that this is a bit of a cheek, but as I am the middle of my research would you mind letting me know if you do decide to sell?'

'Of course my dear,' said Mrs Nelson with a warm look, 'we would never just up and go without telling your parents.'

Jennie breathed a sigh of relief – one of her worst nightmares was waking up one day and finding Keep Out notices and barbwire everywhere preventing her from accessing the badger setts.

When she had finished her coffee, she was on her way again, hoping to arrive back in time to catch Edward. He was due to visit that day to assess the farm's readiness to be restocked. She felt pleased when she saw that his car was still parked outside the farmhouse. She went to look for him and found him with Giles in the empty milking parlour.

'So have I done enough to regain TB free status?' Giles was saying.

'No - I'm sorry, there is a lot more to do – you still haven't implemented half my recommendations.'

Jennie kept her lips tight – this assessment came as no surprise to her – she knew that Giles was unconvinced that the necessary changes were needed. He had reluctantly and half-heartedly fixed some of the holes in the fences but that was all.

'Hrrumph,' said Giles. He stomped off before he was told anything else that he didn't want to hear leaving her to exchange wry looks with Edward.

'Well that didn't go well,' he said, 'your father will have to do a lot more before he can welcome the cows back. Can't you persuade him?'

'I've tried but it is like moving a juggernaut with one finger. It doesn't help that the Animal Health Agency is dragging its feet over paying out the compensation money.'

'Hasn't the money come through yet?' asked Edward putting his clipboard back into his document bag. 'That's odd. Usually it's a straight forward process.'

'Apparently they have a backlog of claims,' she said. They ambled out of the milking parlour into the weak sunshine.

'Are you all right after last night? It was scary – I was worried that you were going to get hurt.'

'So was I.'

Jennie stepped sideways to avoid a muddy puddle. 'They are horrible people – they have even posted my name and address online.'

'That must be against Data Protection – you should report it.' Edward headed towards his car.

'Someone is trying to buy up the dairy farms around here – Green Meadow, Hightree and Beesnest have all received very handsome offers.'

'Any idea from whom?'

'No, but Khan Solicitors of Oakfield are acting on their behalf.'

'That's worth investigating,' he said.

Chapter 11

15th November
The mid November weather was predictably dull and damp. No bright blue skies, no warm sunshine – just day after day of low cloud, half-light and strong winds. Without the usual routine of a dairy farm it felt strange at Green Meadow – normally as the days shortened and the weather turned colder, the cows would be brought into the sheds to overwinter, and the stocks of fodder would be replenished.

'Bramble,' Jennie called, expecting to see an eager dog appear. But nothing. She checked her usual haunts - behind the sofa, on the bed and in her basket – but there was no sign of her. She went out to the farmyard where a desultory Giles was brushing wet leaves into small piles. His face was more lined, and his hair thinner than only six months previously.

'Hi Dad, have you seen Bramble?' she asked. He shook his head.

Feeling increasingly more anxious, she searched the yard and the farm buildings and finally she spotted the dog sitting under a viburnum bush at the end of the kitchen garden. She was shaking in anguish and scratching her right ear. Jennie went over to her and saw that her eyes were as dull as ditch water. She murmured reassurances and stroked her but the dog continued to look forlorn. She picked her up, carried her to the Range Rover which was conveniently parked outside the farmhouse and gently bundled her in.

'Dad – is it alright if I borrow the car?' she cried.

'Why?' he asked looking up to see what the problem was.

'Bramble's not well – I need to take her to the vet's.'

'Of course,' he said, 'go right away.'

Jennie drove as quickly as she could. Edward would know what was wrong. She parked in the car park at the rear of the clinic and led Bramble very slowly round to the front. The bell rang when she opened the door. Alpa was sitting in front of her monitor, typing away, with a pile of Manila folders by her side.

'Good morning Jennie – how can I help you?'

'It's Bramble – I'm really worried about her.'

Alpa smiled sympathetically. 'Take a seat – you won't have long to wait.'

Jennie sat down with Bramble quivering at her side. She patted her soft coat and whispered words of comfort. The door of Edward's consulting room opened. Freya, looking slimmer and more sophisticated than even a few weeks ago, came out.

'Anything wrong with Lola?' Jennie asked her.

Freya kept on walking, her eyes straight ahead and her face expressionless. 'She's Edward's now – I've given her to him,' she said sweeping out before Jennie could question her further.

The intercom buzzed.

Alpa lifted her eyes from the computer screen. 'You can go through now,' she said.

Jennie led Bramble out of the reception and along the corridor to Edward's consulting room. He was sitting at his large desk staring out of the window with an expression of disappointment on his face.

'What's happened?' asked Jennie.

'Lola used to be a healthy puppy full of beans and confidence. But now she's the total opposite.'

'Do you know why?'

'We need to run some tests.'

'You're keeping her in?'

'For some TLC. Our veterinary nurses will give her bucket loads.'

'Freya doesn't want her anymore?'

'No – she told me that she only bought her so that she had an excuse to see me,' he said. 'But now there is no need. We've finished.' He looked down at the papers in front of him, his neck turning a deep shade of pink.

Jennie fell silent. How could anyone do that? She had suspected that Freya was faking her love of animals but she hadn't dreamt that she would neglect Lola. And to walk out on Edward? That was madness.

'But enough of Lola – what's the matter with Bramble?' said Edward. He lifted the quaking dog on to his consulting table.

'She keeps shaking her head, pawing at her ear and whining.'

'Sounds like an infection to me,' he said, 'spaniels with their long floppy ears are prone to them. I'll take a look.' He picked up his otoscope and peered down her right ear. Bramble wriggled and tried to get free of Jennie's hold.

In a soothing voice he reassured her. 'There's a good girl. It's alright. There. There.'

He examined the other ear carefully. Satisfied that he had seen enough he placed the instrument to one side.

'As I thought, she has a parasite – an ear mite – that is causing some inflammation,' he said.

'That's horrible,' said Jennie. She held the dog firmly whilst Edward cleaned both her ears with a damp cloth. He picked up a small bottle and squeezed a couple of drops into each ear. When the treatment was complete, he lifted Bramble back on to the floor and wrote out a prescription.

He handed the piece of paper to Jennie. 'There you are – that should sort her out for now, but any reoccurrence of the problem just bring her straight back in.' He turned round to his computer and typed in some notes.

Jennie patted Bramble's head. Already she was calmer and her eyes were brighter. The treatment had started to work already. Jennie relaxed and gazed around the room. A bank of filing cabinets filled one wall and behind the door was a stack of unopened cardboard boxes. Edward saw her looking at them

'Phil has finally agreed to upgrade our computers,' he said. 'We're installing new hardware and software.' He went over to the sink and washed his hands thoroughly. 'We're going to transfer our client records into the new database. Alpa is over the moon. She's been keen to start a proper system for some time – she even went on a course.' He pointed to the filing cabinets. 'Those are heading to the skip.'

'You will be able to run all sorts of queries once you have a decent database in place,' said Jennie.

He nodded. She stood up, went over to the window and looked over the rear of the clinic. In what had once been a garden laid to lawn and flowerbeds, there was an overflowing skip and men constructing an outbuilding.

'You're having building work done?'

'Our laboratory is being extended,' he said.

'You back on to Oakfield Business Park?'

'There are some empty units there,' he said, 'I am hoping to….'

Before he could finish his sentence the door burst open and a veterinary nurse rushed in.

'Edward, can you come? There's an emergency,' she said. He got up immediately.

'Of course,' he said. He shot Jennie an apologetic look. As she left leading a happier Bramble she wondered what he had been about to say.

*

16th November

Early the following morning, Jennie cycled into Oakfield and past the veterinary clinic. She reflected on the reasons why Freya had dumped Edward. It must have been for another man. But who?

Arriving at the university, she chained her bicycle to one of the bike racks just inside the entrance and walked across the leaf-strewn courtyard to the ecology department. The spacious lab was slowly filling up with researchers and technicians.

Near her work station was a large cardboard box which she opened. Inside were the new antibody test kits which Amina had been reluctant to order until something had changed her mind. Jennie checked them over. They were correct and ready to be deployed. A drop of blood squirted on to the indicator pad would give an instant result. If a badger tested positive for bovine TB it could be culled straight away in the field. She switched on both her microscope and her laptop. At that moment Sana came through the lab carrying a tray of dirty containers.

'Hi Jennie, how's it going?' she asked.

Jennie looked up. 'Fine,' she said.

Sana put the tray down next to the sink, turned on the hot water tap and squirted in some detergent.

'How's Tony?' she asked.

Jennie pursed her lips. 'He would like to see me more often but I can't while my research is ongoing,' she replied. 'Have you given Dylan that ultimatum yet?'

Sana sighed and nodded. 'I proposed.'

'You didn't wait until February 29th?'

182

Sana shook her head. 'I couldn't.'

'So,' said Jennie, 'what did he say?'

Sana pulled on a pair of washing-up gloves, piled the containers into the soapy water and started scrubbing them furiously. 'He said no. He didn't want the status quo to change.' Her eyes filled with tears as she rinsed some tubes and placed them into a wooden rack.

'Well?'

'I broke it off.'

Jennie put her arm around her friend and gave her a squeeze. 'After five solid years? Six weeks before Christmas? That's an incredibly brave thing to do.'

A tear trickled down Sana's cheek. 'I'll miss him, but it is for the best really. I wanted to move onto the next stage of our relationship but he didn't.'

'He might come to his senses.'

'He won't - you were right – I needed to force the issue, otherwise I would have become resentful,' she sobbed. 'Oh well, time to move on. Jennie, do you know anybody who would suit me?'

'As it happens, I do,' she replied, her eyes twinkling. 'I know just the man for you. And you have already met him.' She smiled at Sana's querying look and was about to elucidate when Amina moved through the lab like a chief inspector.

'Ah Jennie,' she said, 'I need a quick update on your progress for our sponsors.'

Jennie suppressed a groan and answered as pleasantly as she could. 'Of course Dr Ahmed – I will do it straight away.'

She pulled her laptop towards her and started typing. Her phone rang. Seeing disapproving faces around her, she answered it as quickly as she could.

'Tony. Hello. How are you?'

'Are you free tonight?' he asked.

She hesitated. 'I'm afraid not.'

'Don't tell me, you're working.' Abruptly he rang off. She gave herself a shake and she reminded herself that her priority was gaining an outstanding PhD. Afterwards she would have more time to spend with Tony, but not now.

It was later than normal when she cycled back home with her bike lights blazing away in the dark. Navigating the narrow country road safely required all her concentration. After a quick bite to eat, she dressed in warm waterproof clothes and set off across the moonlit fields, a torch guiding her way. The wind howled around her ears and a tawny owl hooted high in a tree.

The landscape was so familiar to her that it took her less than thirty minutes to reach Bramley Brook the small stream that meandered north-west into the River Fogle. She followed the twisting footpath along the shallow valley to the sett where Bullitt and his family lived. Outside the entrance of their underground home she sprinkled the contents of a jar of large peanuts. She climbed up to the wooden platform nailed securely half way up the overhanging tree. It was still wet after the previous night's rain. She wiped it down before spreading out a plastic sheet and putting down a cushion. Once settled she got out her tranquiliser gun and loaded some darts. From time to time, a drop of water dripped on to her head.

An hour ticked by. Cramp and fatigue began to set in. She stretched her legs. Just as she was about to give up, out of the deep hole, into the damp gloom appeared Bullitt, Pocahontas and the other female. A few minutes later, two well-grown cubs also clambered out but there was no sign of Survivor.

Silently and accurately one by one she fired tranquiliser darts at the five badgers. When they were all fully sedated she scrambled down and administered the antibody tests to each of them. The results were all negative. It was a moment for elation. She had always believed that her favourite badger family were bovine TB free. Now she had been vindicated. All these months she had been justified in shielding them from the cull. Now she had to continue to keep them and all the other healthy badgers in Liltford safe.

Chapter 12

4th December

Jennie sat relaxing and half dozing as Giles drove them both in his Range Rover to the shooting school where Joe had convened an evening team meeting. There were dark shadows under her eyes caused by working late for many evenings trying to test as many badgers as she could. If any badger tested positive for bovine TB, she marked the location of the sett they lived in on to a map. Frequently she had returned home soaked, windswept or frozen as the weather deteriorated with the approach of winter. In the last two weeks, she had only managed to meet Tony on a couple of occasions and she hadn't seen Edward at all.

When Jennie entered the training room she realised that she and Giles were the last of the team to arrive. The wooden chairs, arranged in two rows in front of the instructor's table, were almost all taken. Giles grabbed the remaining seat in the front row next to Ibrahim and Jennie sat down in the row behind next to Edward, who was scrolling through his mobile phone. Tony turned around and smiled at her. She returned his greeting and noticed that Freya, who was sitting next to him, had a new hairstyle which suited her oval face.

'Good evening,' said Joe. 'We have broadly kept to our schedule throughout the autumn although I know there have been some interruptions caused by the saboteurs and the weather. There aren't many weeks left until the end of the season – we pause over Christmas and finish at the end of January.'

'Why then?' asked Ibrahim with a puzzled look.

Jennie leant forward. 'The government bans the shooting of badgers in the field during the breeding season from February to May, in case any cubs are left to starve underground when their mothers are killed.'

Ibrahim sat back in his seat seemly satisfied with this explanation.

Giles thumped his knee in protest. 'But bovine TB in cattle is on the rise around here.'

Jennie glared at her father. 'That is because when their family is killed, the surviving badgers move elsewhere and infect new herds.'

Giles frowned. He was unconvinced. 'Four months is too long a gap,' he insisted.

Joe paused. 'Maybe, but that's the law,' he said. 'Now, for the remainder of the culling season, we are going to target only those badgers that we know have the disease.'

'How are we going to do that?' Giles demanded.

'Jennie has drawn up a list of the setts where the badgers have tested positive,' said Joe.

'Did you develop that antibody test?' Edward whispered. She indicated that she had. 'Wow,' he said with a note of admiration in his voice. 'That's impressive.'

Jennie blushed. 'It's been hard work,' she admitted quietly.

Joe picked up a pile of maps. 'Right guys, this month we are carrying on in our pairs and I have here the locations of the setts I would like you to focus on. Remember to keep me updated on your progress and to do a proper recce of each site.'

Tony and Freya took their map from him and sat with their heads close together discussing their plan for the evening ahead. Jennie turned her attention to Edward and to the map he was studying.

'Well it looks like we are going to a sett in north-east Liltford,' he said.

Jennie glanced at the location. She knew the sett well. She had been there only the previous evening. In front of her, Giles headed for the Gents leaving Ibrahim sitting on his own.

Jennie leant forward and whispered in his ear. 'Ibrahim, you work for Khan Solicitors in Oakfield, don't you?'

He turned to face her. 'As a matter of fact I do,' he said, 'but I'm just a junior partner. It's my uncle's practice. Why?'

'An anonymous buyer has offered to buy Green Meadow and a couple of our neighbouring farms,' she said. 'Khan Solicitors are acting on their behalf. Would you be able to find out who their clients are?'

Ibrahim considered this. 'That would be unethical,' he said after a pause.

Jennie's face fell. 'It was just a thought.'

Giles returned and hovered next to Ibrahim. 'Come on my lad, let's go.'

Ibrahim got up, smiled apologetically at Jennie and followed him out. She zipped up her jacket.

'Ready?' asked Edward as he turned towards the door.

She gestured that she was and looked across at Tony. He was still deep in discussion with Freya. She went over to him.

'Hi Tony, we're off now,' she said trying to catch his eye.

There was a glint of annoyance when he fixed his eyes on her. 'I'll see you tomorrow,' he said before turning back to talk to Freya.

Jennie waited for a couple of seconds to see if he would say anything else but nothing was forthcoming. Abruptly, she followed Edward out of the door without looking back. She slumped into the front seat of his car still thinking about Tony. They had a date the following evening yet he seemed to be more interested in Freya than her. Edward switched on the engine and the car radio. As the upbeat song – Who Loves You Baby by The Four Seasons – played, her mood improved. He drove through Oakfield and down a secondary road.

'You've field tested the antibody test?' he asked, his eyes on the road ahead.

'Amina has peer reviewed the results so I am pretty confident of its efficacy.'

'It's quite a break through if you have,' he said in an appreciative tone of voice as the road became an unlit lane.

Jennie peered out of the windscreen into the darkness looking for the layby nearest to the sett. They rounded a corner and she spotted it.

'Over there,' she said. He pulled over.

When the car was parked, she got out and retrieved her kit bag from the back seat. The temperature had fallen. She pulled on her gloves and her thermal imaging goggles. She pointed to a field the other side of the hedge.

'That's the way,' she said.

Edward opened the rickety gate and Jennie followed him through. After he had closed the gate, they tramped across the field to an area of rough grass and brambles. Hidden in the undergrowth was a sett, in front of which was a mound of fine sandy soil. The badgers would have dug the deep hole with their sharp claws kicking the earth out behind them.

'So all the badgers from this sett have tested positive?' he asked.

Jennie nodded. 'All four of them. I was here yesterday evening and tested them again. I'll top up the bait I laid.'

Out of her bag, came a plastic container full of peanut butter sandwiches. She sprinkled them liberally in a circle a few metres in diameter around the sett.

Edward walked to and fro assessing the best place to fire from. About ten metres from the sett he found a slightly raised area of the field with a good view down to the sett.

'Over here, Jennie,' he said lying down on the ground in a prone position. He lifted his rifle and aimed it at the sett.

Jennie hesitated but then picked up her holdall and joined him. She took out her rifle and lay down on her stomach beside him.

'Wow,' said Edward. 'Are you sure?' He sounded surprised.

She smiled an assurance and made sure that the muzzle of her rifle wasn't in contact with the ground. 'I never thought that killing could be justified but now that I know that these badgers do have bovine TB, I feel that there is no choice. Until there is a vaccine the only way to wipe out this deadly disease is to remove the infected animals from the area.'

She lined up her rifle. They settled down to wait. It was eight o'clock and a slight drizzle had started to fall. She pulled her hat down over her ears. The ground was hard and damp.

A peppery grey badger appeared. It was an adult female. Even in the dark, her dense white underfur and her black nose shaped like a lump of coal were clearly visible. She started shuffling around searching for her evening meal. A large adult male joined her, his head wagging from side to side as he sniffed the ground for worms. Another male scudded out of the sett ignoring the other two. Finally a smaller female badger made its appearance. She trotted over to a tree, stood up on her hind legs and started scratching at the bark in search of beetles.

Without warning, a scuffle started between the two males. The dominant boar flaunted his muscles and sized up the younger animal. A chase began. The older male caught up with the younger badger and noisily attacked its rump with his teeth, drawing blood. The two females raised their heads, distracted from their supper. Jennie and Edward watched with fascination, momentarily forgetting their mission. After a few minutes, calm was restored and the vanquished badger licked his wounds.

Edward signalled to Jennie that the time had come to shoot. She stood still, psyching herself to kill the animals that she had vowed to protect. She raised her rifle, peered through the eyepiece and aimed at the two badgers that were digging the earth to her left. She took a deep breath and fired. They fell immediately to the ground. Her shoulders relaxed and her heart stopped beating so fast. Tears came to her eyes.

Simultaneous Edward shot the other two badgers in quick succession. Jennie waited a few minutes before getting up and going over to the dead bodies. She removed their collars and ear tags, and took a blood sample from each whilst Edward went back to the car for the body bags. She helped him haul the dead badgers into them and to squeeze them into the car boot.

On the way back, a smell of blood, mud and damp enveloped the car. Jennie sat absorbed with her thoughts. She looked across at Edward's handsome profile. His presence was a comfort to her. Arriving at Green Meadow, he pulled up outside the farmhouse.

'Good night Jennie,' he said, 'we've had a successful evening.'

'Of sorts,' she replied as she got out.

He drove off down the drive and she watched until his car turned into the road. After a long soak in a hot bath, she tumbled exhausted into bed.

*

11th December

Jennie opened her bedroom curtains. The blackbirds and greenfinches were already breakfasting at the feeders hanging from the apple trees in the orchard. She picked up her phone and checked to see if there was a message from Tony. There wasn't. He hadn't been in touch since their date the previous week. A police car drew up outside the farmhouse. She descended the stairs to the kitchen where her mother was busy frying eggs and bacon.

'The police are outside,' she said.

Nancy raised her slotted utensil in the air. 'What on earth do they want?'

Jennie went to the front door and opened it. PS Miller and PC Allen were standing on the doorstep.

'Morning, Jennie,' said Miller. 'Is your father here?'

She opened the door wider. 'Come in,' she said. She led them through the hall, which was cluttered with coats and boots, into the front room. 'Wait here. I'll get him.'

Giles was at his desk reading farming magazines with loud music playing in the background.

'Dad, the police are here,' she said, 'they want to speak to you.'

He swore under his breath and reluctantly rose to his feet. He followed her in to the front room. Miller and Allen were waiting in front of the fireplace admiring one of Nancy's paintings which was hung over the mantelpiece.

'Good morning, Mr Cliffe,' said Miller. 'We have come to ask you to accompany us to the police station.'

'There must be some mistake,' said Giles, 'I've done nothing wrong.'

192

'No need for alarm,' said Miller, 'it's just routine questioning.'

Giles held onto the arm of the sofa as his nerves unsteadied him. 'About what?'

'You made a claim for compensation after your herd tested positive for TB?' said Allen.

'I was told to do that by the Animal Health Agency.'

Miller looked up from his notebook. 'They have reasons to believe that there were irregularities with your claim and they have asked us to investigate.'

'That isn't true,' protested Jennie vehemently. 'I checked the claim. Everything was in order.'

'That may well be the case,' said Miller firmly, 'but that needs to be determined.'

'Sir, if you can accompany us to Oakfield Police Station?' said Allen.

'Do I have any choice?'

'I'm afraid not,' he replied.

Giles shrugged. 'OK, the sooner we clear this up, the better,' he said, 'I'll get my coat.'

Jennie left the room and called to Nancy. They watched as Giles left the farmhouse, got into the back of the police car and were driven off down the drive.

'What's that all about?' asked Nancy.

'Something about Dad's compensation claim,' said Jennie trying to sound reassuring. 'I'm pretty sure that it is a mix up of some sort.'

'I just hope you're right.'

Several hours later, a car crunched up the drive and came to a halt outside. Jennie rushed downstairs just as Giles put his key in the front door.

'What happened?' she cried.

A morose looking Giles took off his coat. 'Nothing,' he said, 'at the police station they put me in a cell for an hour or so. Then I was taken to an interview room. They said that I could get some free legal advice but I didn't bother with that.'

He went into the kitchen where Nancy was painting at her easel. She looked up and asked if he was alright. He nodded but Jennie persisted with her questions.

'What did they ask?' she said.

Giles sat in the chair in front of the fire and stroked Bramble who had come up to greet him. 'What symptoms the cows had. When they were tested – that sort of thing. It was months ago but I tried to remember everything.'

Nancy filled the kettle and took a rock cake out of the tin for him. 'Then they let you go?'

'They gave me a charge sheet and sent me home on bail until the court hearing at the magistrates.'

'Did they say when that would be?' asked Nancy.

'After Christmas, they said.'

'It could be to do with Douglas Sitwell,' said Jennie.

Giles scoffed. 'It's got nothing to do with him – what on earth makes you say that?'

'He disappeared, didn't he – just after receiving a large sum in compensation?' said Jennie, in a matter-of-fact tone.

'That was just a coincidence,' said Giles. 'We don't know where he is or why he left.'

'Has he contacted you?'

'Sort of,' he replied.

Nancy regarded him. She poured hot water into the teapot. 'You didn't tell me that.'

A thought occurred to Jennie. 'Could you message him again?'

'I could, but I very much doubt he could be persuaded to come home and testify in my defence,' said Giles.

'You're right,' said Nancy, agreeing with her husband. 'My theory is that he owes money – what gambler doesn't end up in debt? Maybe he committed fraud in order to get the compensation.'

'That might be what the police suspect,' said Jennie. 'But I wonder who reported you?' She took her mug of fresh tea and headed back to her room. There was a lot to think about.

*

12th December

At nine the next morning, a car horn sounded outside the farmhouse. Jennie threw on her waterproof jacket, shouted goodbye and tore outside. She hopped into Edward's car.

He restarted the engine. 'Ready for another recce?' he asked. 'Where are we going today?'

She placed her rucksack on the floor between her knees. 'Bovington,' she said turning to look at him. His dark hair was brushed back off his unlined forehead showcasing his blue eyes and thick eyelashes. He was casually dressed in jeans and a navy anorak. She shivered. It was cold in the car.

Edward turned up the heater. Stopping at the junction of the farm drive with the road, he waited as a lorry thundered past before heading towards Oakfield.

'Have we finished with Liltford?' he asked.

'There aren't any badgers left there anymore.' A remark she knew to be a lie because she had deliberately shielded Bullitt and his family from the cull.

He slowed down when the steeple of Oakfield Cathedral became visible on the horizon and he drove into the town.

'Oh by the way, yesterday the police charged my father – at the police station.'

'Why?' he asked as he stopped at a road junction.

Jennie looked at the signpost. 'They suspect him of making a fraudulent compensation claim,' she said. She took out her mobile phone, loaded a navigation app and typed in the location of the sett.

He fell silent. A pensive look came into his eyes. 'Why do the police suspect that fraud may have occurred?' he asked. He released the handbrake and drove on through the town centre. The streets were festooned with Christmas lights and were thronging with people wearing hats, scarfs and winter coats.

'Keep straight ahead,' said Jennie. 'We don't know, but my mother thinks it's something to do with Douglas Sitwell's disappearance.' She paused. 'Didn't Phil Oldman do the TB testing at Hightree Farm?'

'Yes, but that doesn't mean that anything irregular happened,' said Edward, 'and how does that implicate your father? I carried out the testing at Green Meadow.'

'I don't know,' said Jennie with a shrug, 'and anyway how on earth would he have committed such a fraud?'

'There are a lot of ways - we are trained to be vigilant and if something looks suspicious, I always investigate it carefully,' he explained as he drove out of the built up area into the countryside.

'My father would never do anything dodgy,' she said indignantly.

He glanced across at her. 'I would testify to that.'

She gave him a warm smile, scanned the road ahead and checked the directions on the app. 'Take the next turning on the left.'

He looked in his rear mirror and slowed down. 'I think I know what's going on,' he said.

'What?' she asked curiously.

'I can't say yet – there are a couple of things I need to check out at the clinic.'

He turned down a narrow lane and drove along for a few hundred yards past a large billboard erected at the entrance to a field. Jennie craned her neck to read what it said. It was advertising new homes.

FOR SALE
McKensie Developments
10 Luxury Houses
Coming Soon

The name rang a bell. She could see that the bulldozers were digging the foundations for several buildings.

'McKensie. Isn't that Tony's company?' she asked.

'Yes,' replied Edward.

That was interesting. She pointed to a small layby. 'Pull over there,' she said.

Edward stopped the car. Jennie got out, put on a thick pair of gloves and a woolly hat, and slung on her rucksack. He followed her through a farm gate, along a muddy path, and across a field laid to pasture. At the far end of the field, she stopped and pointed to a rough area of bushes and brambles. He helped her beat the vegetation back to reveal a large hole in the ground. He peered at it, found his camera and took some photographs.

'There are signs of recent activity,' he said.

'Six badgers from here have recently tested positive.'

He walked around the sett having a look at the lie of the land.

'Right, OK, I think we have enough info – let's move on,' he said, 'where are the other two setts?'

'Just over that small ridge - they are close together,' she said picking up her bag. They walked along the hedgerow, up a slight incline and down into a small wooded area. She started humming. He smiled at her. She beamed back. The clouds parted and a ray of sunshine burst through the trees. Her phone rang. She fished it out of her pocket.

197

'Tony? Hello,' she said as a blush spread over her cheeks. Edward looked sharply at her and his expression changed.

'Tonight?' She hesitated. It was such short notice but she hadn't seen him for over a week. She glanced at Edward but he avoided her gaze and walked on. 'OK. See you later.'

Tony rang off and she put the phone away. She caught up with Edward but the camaraderie between them had disappeared. A cloud moved in front of the sun. They worked on, exchanging few words. Finally they finished surveying the setts.

'Can you drop me at the university?' she asked.

He nodded. On the drive into Oakfield Jennie tried to make conversation but his replies were monosyllabic. Arriving at the university she got out of the car.

'Thank you,' she said with a warm smile.

He gave a curt goodbye. She blinked with surprise – normally he was so easy going. It occurred to her that she had become dependent on his approbation. He drove off and she watched his car until it had disappeared from view.

The afternoon passed quickly as she became absorbed in her work. When she finally looked at her watch she gasped, as she knew she would have to rush to get ready in time. Arriving back at the farm she stood under the shower and washed away the smell of the fields, the laboratory and the sweat from her cycle home. Her hair blow dried and styled, she opened her wardrobe and rifled through the rail for something suitable to wear to a smart restaurant. She was starting to despair when her eyes alighted on an old dress she had forgotten about. It was a bit creased but the gold earrings and necklace that David had given her would bring it to life. To complete her outfit, she selected a pair of strappy sandals and carefully applied her makeup. She regarded herself in the mirror. Maybe she wasn't as stylish or as fashionable as Freya but she was passable.

At seven o'clock Tony's sports car roared up the drive. Outside the farmhouse, he tooted his horn.

She put on her winter coat and raced downstairs. 'Bye,' she yelled to her parents as she shut the front door. She opened the passenger door, sat down in the low seat and swung her legs in.

'Hello babes,' said Tony leaning across and kissing her. 'Another green dress?'

He drove straight to The Virtuoso. Jennie got out and followed him into the restaurant. The doorman took their coats and the maitre'd welcomed them and led them to a table in the window. A splendid Christmas tree decorated with hundreds of tiny white lights and shiny baubles had pride of place in the corner by the fireplace. The flower arrangements dotted everywhere were magnificent with red roses mixed with white carnations and scarlet amaryllis. Verdi's La Traviata was playing in the background.

A young waiter came up with their menus and a jug of water filled with ice cubes. He picked up the white crisp serviette in front of Jennie, shook it and laid it on her lap. He filled her glass tumbler with water, inadvertently spilling some onto the table cloth.

'I am sorry, sir,' said the youth with an apologetic look.

An expression of annoyance passed over Tony's face. 'So you should be,' he snapped. Jennie couldn't disguise that she was shocked by the tone of his voice. Tony gesticulated to the head waiter, who came over. 'This oaf has split some water.'

Things were soothed things over but a look of displeasure remained on Tony's face. Jennie crossed her legs and shot a look of apology at the staff. She sensed that Tony was displeased with her as well.

The sommelier approached with the wine list.

'Good evening sir, may I suggest the Neuf de Pape?' he said.

Tony took the list. 'I only want the best you have,' he said. He perused it carefully. Jennie leaned across to have a look. The wines were all expensive. Too expensive.

'You decide,' she said and sat back in her chair.

Tony closed the menu. 'We will have the Chateau Lych-Bages.' He handed it back to the waiter.

Jennie picked up her glass of water. 'Don't you begrudge spending all that money on wine?'

He laughed lightly. 'Not at all – you pay for what you get,' he said. The wine waiter returned with the bottle and a corkscrew. With a flourish the bottle was opened and a small amount of the wine was poured into a glass. Tony tasted it and announced it to be acceptable. The waiter filled up both the glasses with the red wine and Jennie took a sip.

'I am never likely to become a connoisseur of fine wine,' she confessed.

He frowned as the sommelier retreated and the waiter approached with the menus. Having made their orders, they relaxed and looked at each other. She twiddled with her charm bracelet. He noticed her chipped nail varnish. A look of distaste came into his eyes.

'I meant to have a manicure, but I was too busy,' she explained as a light blush spread over her cheeks.

He smiled but his smile didn't spread to his eyes. He changed the subject. 'We're having a Christmas party at Beddis Grange,' he said. 'It's a family tradition – my parents invite their friends and neighbours.'

'Sounds fun.'

'I am going to invite all the team,' he said, 'and your friend Sana.'

She raised her eyebrows.

'I need a couple of gorgeous ladies to help me meet and greet the guests,' he said. 'Tell her to dress up and to be there early with you.'

Momentarily Jennie was taken aback. The invitation to the party was exciting, but the request to help host was alarming, as was the lack of a suitable party outfit in her wardrobe. Tony shot her a quizzical look. She relaxed and smiled. She would go to Posh Stuff and buy a new dress, and as she had a large acquaintance in and around Oakfield, many of the guests would be known to her.

'Sana will be thrilled – she loves big parties.'

Tony seemed pleased. The waiter arrived with a Caesar salad with anchovies and croutons in a white bowl for Jennie and steamed mussels garnished with parsley for Tony. He topped up Tony's glass.

'Have you had a busy week?' asked Jennie when the waiter had gone.

'We have just started clearing a site for a new housing development,' he replied.

'In Bovington? Edward and I saw it on a recce and wondered if it was your company,' she said.

A smile spread over his face. 'It's going to be a prestigious development. It should make us a fortune.'

'Do you include habitat restoration in the design?' she asked.

'Never,' he said emphatically.

'Don't you do any? It can be a good marketing tool – people like to know that some of the money developers make is being used to create landscape features such as small ponds or woodland areas.'

'I disagree,' he said with a look which closed down any further discussion of the topic. She changed the subject but somehow they found easy discourse elusive. The rest of the evening passed uneventfully and she was glad when he dropped her back at the farm earlier than usual.

*

15th December

The next morning, as an icy wind blew around her, Jennie was cycling through Oakfield, when she heard the sound of drums and tambourines. Ahead she could see a sea of placards and banners being held in the air. A crowd of people, huddled together like penguins, were blocking the High Street outside the Town Hall causing the police to redirect the traffic down a side road.

'Damn,' she muttered to herself. She dismounted. As she wheeled her bicycle through the demonstrators she heard a man speaking through a megaphone.

'This government has funded the slaughter of innocent animals. The badger, a British protected species, is being hunted to extinction. Together we must stop this massacre,' he shouted, 'Together we must halt the killing. Sign our petition today, write to your MP, join us on a march through Oakfield.'

She recognised his voice. It was Jeremy Boyle. As she drew nearer she could see him standing on a wooden box. Next to him was Sophie, dressed in a long military-style coat and a bobble hat. Members of Fauna Protection were mixed in with the crowd holding placards in one hand and collecting tins in the other.

'Hear, hear,' someone in the throng cried.

'As well as the badger cull, we at Fauna Protection are working hard to stop the cruel practice of drag hunting,' said Boyle. 'Drag hunting purports to be an event for riders and their hounds but is actually a cover for fox hunting.'

'Boo,' shouted a young woman at the front of the crowd.

The wind ruffled Boyle's hair. 'Oakfield Boxing Day Hunt is billed as a family event,' he continued, 'but it is actually a form of animal cruelty as every year horses are injured jumping the fences and foxes are killed by out-of-control dogs.'

The crowd waved their placards and booed.

'We need to stop this cruelty now. Give generously to our cause,' Boyle yelled. Cheering broke out and people raised their arms in the air. Members of Fauna Protection shook their tins and people squeezed in notes and coins.

Jennie lengthened her stride and pushed her bike forcibly through the rabble. Boyle caught sight of her. His expression changed to one of hatred. He looked as if he was going to leap off his box and attack her. Fortunately, Sophie restrained him. Without looking back Jennie kept on going. Eventually she broke clear of the crowd. She stopped and remounted her bike. She rode on with the sound of their protests echoing in her ears. Her heart was beating rapidly and only slowed down when she was a hundred yards away.

Arriving at the university was like sailing into a harbour after a storm. She rushed to the ecology department. In the prep room she made herself a large mug of coffee and took it with her into the laboratory. She sat on the stool at her work station and stared out of the window. The expression on Boyle's face when he had stared at her had been frightening.

After a few minutes she felt ready to start work. From the fridge she took a rack of barcoded test tubes containing blood samples. She spent the rest of the morning undertaking blood culture tests, entering the results into a spreadsheet as she went. Only a few months remained before she completed her PhD. Eventually she finished, pressed Save and made her way up to Amina's office for her monthly tutorial.

Amina was sitting at her desk. She looked up and welcomed with Jennie with a smile.

'Take a seat. Give me an update on your progress,' she said.

Jennie crossed her legs. 'My field collection is complete. The data from the GPS trackers has been really useful.'

'And the antibody test?'

Jennie nodded. 'That has been invaluable.'

'In your methodology make sure that you reference my input into the creation of the antibody test,' said Amina.

Jennie knew that it was usual for PhD supervisors to be credited. 'Of course.'

'Good.' Amina looked at her directly. 'Your first hypothesis is that the incidence of bovine TB in badgers is linked to age and gender?'

'Yes and I am hoping to be able to accept that,' said Jennie.

'So you are almost ready to start your data analysis? What statistical test are you planning to use?'

Jennie uncrossed her legs. She named a test. Amina drew in her breathe, 'To what degree of significance? It needs to be ninety-nine per cent - less than that is not acceptable. Remember that as your supervisor I will be credited as a being a co-author of your thesis and so I have to approve both your methodology and your conclusions.'

Jennie sighed. She didn't need reminding. But she wondered why Amina was making the point now.

One of the university's caretakers threw her out of the laboratory late that evening. As she rode home via Oakfield High Street she cycled past Posh Stuff. The shop was closed for the day but the display in the shop window was lit up. She knew that she needed a new party dress but if she couldn't find the time to buy one she would have to wear something already hanging in her wardrobe.

Chapter 13

19th December

The Boxing Day Hunt was only a week away. It was an event enjoyed by riders, horses, and hounds from all over the Oakfield area in need of fresh air and exercise after the excesses of Christmas Day.

Jennie, with a determined spring in her step, strode towards the stables thinking of all the camaraderie and fun that the cross country ride normally gave her and the other riders. Usually she prepared Sukey her mare thoroughly for the hunt, but this year she had been less diligent. The double demands of her research and the cull had taken their toll on her time and energies. Hearing her approach, Sukey pricked up her ears, neighed and stuck her head over the stable door waiting for her muzzle to be rubbed.

Jennie greeted her affectionately and was rewarded with another neigh. She filled the feeder attached to the stable wall with pale green hay and the trough with fresh water. While Sukey tucked in, she unhooked the pitchfork from the wall and cleared away the soiled bedding replacing it with fresh straw. That finished, she fitted Sukey with equine cross-country boots to protect her legs from any bashes and scratches acquired when jumping hedges and ditches. Studs were screwed into her horse shoes for extra grip in muddy conditions and her bridle and saddle put on.

Using rein and leg pressure Jennie steered her horse down the drive, across the road and along the bridleway eastwards through the northern part of Hightree Farm. As she passed

Oakfield caravan site, she noticed a steady stream of cars, camper vans and touring caravans arriving.

Turning due south, the horse trotted before breaking into a canter through the sodden fields. A low hedge lay ahead. Jennie leant forward in the saddle and approached it straight on. Sukey jumped it with ease. Another hedge, the same height, was cleared without any hesitation. Gaining in confidence, she steered Sukey towards a higher fence. She sailed over with a foot to spare and landed in textbook style.

Satisfied that Sukey's technique, speed and endurance were improving, Jennie returned to Green Meadow farm, her mind and body energized. Back in the stable, she removed all the tack, rubbed Sukey down and filled the trough with more hay.

Removing her riding hat, her face splattered with mud, she ambled back to the farmhouse. Ahead she saw a parked car. Giles, dressed in corduroy trousers, a Shetland jumper and a baker-boy hat was talking to a tall woman with a commanding air. Jennie recognised Geraldine Waugh, the master of the Oakfield hunt.

She waved at her. 'Good morning Geraldine.'

'Are you hunting on Boxing Day? ' asked Geraldine who was holding an Ordnance Survey map.

Jennie brushed some pieces of twig off her jacket. 'I wouldn't miss it for the world.'

'It nearly didn't happen,' said Geraldine drily.

'I heard that Fauna Protection tried to get the council to ban it.'

'It got the go ahead, but on the condition that the horses and horses stick to the trail.'

I've seen a lot of people are arriving in Oakfield,' said Jennie. 'I hope they don't intend to disrupt it.'

'Bloody protestors,' grumbled Giles, 'why do they want to spoil a fun day out?'

Geraldine shot him a sympathetic look. 'Don't forget that peaceful protest is lawful.'

Giles huffed. 'The trouble is that they don't know when to stop.'

'Have you chosen the route yet?' asked Jennie.

'That's why I'm here. Giles and I need to firm up the section across Green Meadow,' answered Geraldine.

'The ford across Bramley Brook is a good place for a checkpoint,' said Giles. 'Nancy and I could man it.'

'There will be other volunteers and a team from St John's Ambulance to help you,' said Geraldine.

'Let's hope the weather stays this mild,' said Giles.

'The forecast is for high pressure,' said Jennie, 'cold and bright.'

'We are planning for every eventuality. All the local farmers and landowners have contingency plans in place. Well, let's get on. We need to walk the route and make a note of any issues,' said Geraldine.

'OK,' said Giles leading the way across the farmyard towards the fields.

Jennie left them to it and entered the farmhouse.

*

22nd December

Three days later, Jennie stepped in to help Nancy on the Green Meadow stall at the town's Christmas Market, which by tradition was held on the three Saturdays preceding Christmas Day. The young woman, who normally helped serve on the stall, had caught chickenpox from her baby and had rung the night before to give her apologies.

Overlooking the market place was Oakfield Cathedral, decorated with starry illuminations and banners proclaiming the birth of Christ. A large poster advertised the hourly carol services and the nativity tableau in the nave. Aromas from mulled wine, roasting chestnuts and spicy hot food filled the air. Adding to the ambience was the sound of folk music, laughter and revving motorbikes. The sharp wind and the glacial temperatures couldn't deter people from their festive shopping or visits to Santa's Grotto.

'It's going to be a busy day,' said Nancy.

Jennie pinned a garland of fresh holly, dripping with red berries, to the front of the stall and entwined a string of festive fairy lights around the top. 'It'll be fun,' she said. The reality was that she needed a break from writing her thesis. 'Your elderflower sponges and Christmas cakes should sell quickly.'

Nancy hung her paintings of chickens on to hooks around the wooden frame. She stood back to admire the stall with its pyramid of fresh eggs and display stands groaning with sumptuous cakes with their handwritten labels. 'I hope so,' she said.

Trade was brisk and both Jennie and Nancy were kept busy serving a stream of customers. It remained cold and Jennie appreciated the warmth provided by her cashmere forest-green scarf and hat and letterbox-red coat. From time to time, she jiggled her toes and fingers to stop them from becoming numb. Most of the people browsing the stall were locals but a substantial percentage looked like tourists with their expensive clothes and Ugg boots. Their accents were more metropolitan than rural.

A smart looking man wearing a sheepskin jacket stopped in front of the stall. Jennie recognised him. It was Stuart Brown, the journalist from The Daily Update. 'Haven't I met you before?' he asked.

She returned his stare. 'In October –at the Café del Réy.'

'Ah yes – I remember now.'

'You're back in town?'

'I'm researching an article.'

'Oh?'

'On the growing opposition to the cull.'

'How do you know it's growing?' she asked.

'Emails to the paper, social media activity – that sort of thing.'

'And the number of people in town?'

He nodded. 'The activists have won the propaganda war and they have raised a lot of money.'

'Isn't the money going to improve animal welfare standards and to fight all types of animal cruelty?' asked Jennie.

'That's what they would like the public to think,' he said, 'but in reality they are a political organisation that attacks what they perceive to be class privilege. Their next target is the Boxing Day Hunt.'

'But that is a drag hunt – a sports event for riders,' protested Jennie. 'They won't be hunting foxes.'

'That is beside the point – animal activists believe that it is a form of animal cruelty.'

'Why?'

'Jumping fences is dangerous for horses,' said Stuart, 'and they suspect that the drag hunt is just a cover for a real fox hunt.'

'Well, it definitely isn't,' said Jennie vehemently. 'I have been a participant for the last ten years and I know that the dogs only follow an aniseed trail.'

'Nobody believes that,' said Stuart looking at the produce for sale on the stall.

Jennie gesticulated at the myriad of people thronging the market place. 'So these are protest tourists?'

'Call them that if you want,' he said with a smile, 'but don't knock them if they are spending their money at the same time.'

His eyes fixed on Nancy's canvasses.

'Those are quite splendid,' he said. 'Are they the work of a local artist?'

Nancy's attention was alerted. 'Well actually, yes – they are mine,' she said proudly.

He pointed at a painting depicting a yellowish-beige chicken with a heavy body, fluffed-out feathers and a red comb on top of its small head. 'What breed is that?' he asked.

'A Buff Orpington,' she replied.

He pulled out his wallet. 'I will have that one, if I may.'

'Of course,' she said, 'that will be fifty pounds.' She took the picture off its hook and wrapped it up in tissue paper.

He counted out the correct amount in cash. 'I'm looking for a story for tomorrow's Sunday paper. An article about your farm, you and your paintings would do nicely – English folk art is all the rage these days.'

'That would be wonderful – I could do with the publicity – here's my business card,' said Nancy picking one up from a small pile.

Stuart read it. 'Green Meadow - aren't you the farm that was vandalized?'

Nancy nodded. 'My chickens were traumatized by the whole thing – they didn't lay any eggs for three whole days afterwards.' She hung up another painting to replace the one he had just bought.

'How do you know about that?' Jennie asked him. She knew that the vandalism hadn't been reported in the papers or online.

'It's my job to know what's going on,' he said. He put his wallet away and looked around. He beckoned to a young woman who was walking towards the stall holding a long lens camera. 'I will need a couple of photographs. My photographer is here.'

'Now?' said Nancy in a fluster. 'I will have to touch up my makeup.'

'No need - you look great as you are,' he said. He took his purchase from her as the photographer arrived.

'Can you photograph Nancy and Jennie behind the stall but with the paintings and cakes in the frame?' asked Stuart.

'Me?' said Jennie. 'But I don't paint.'

'You look very festive in your outfit,' explained Stuart with a smile that was impossible to resist.

The photographer expertly directed Nancy and Jennie into different poses and clicked away. It only took a few minutes and then the photo shoot was over.

'Can you sign that you give permission for the article and the photos?' said Stuart proffering them a form and pen that he had pulled from his pocket.

Nancy and Jennie both obliged. Stuart took his parcel and went on his way with his photographer at his side. Jennie stared after him. She wondered whether he had enough content for his article. It was interesting what he had said about the Boxing Day Hunt. In the distance she saw Ian and Sophie walking towards the stall laughing and chatting. They arrived a few minutes later and stood side by side in front of the stall.

'Hello Mum,' said Ian.

Nancy beamed at him. 'Ian, lovely to see you.'

'This is Sophie,' he said.

Jennie observed that her demeanour seemed softer than before but that she still had her nose stud and short spiky hairstyle and was dressed in a long military-style coat and a pair of Dr.Martens.

'How are you Ian? Have you had your test results,' Jennie asked. He looked puzzled.

'Your cough?' she prompted.

'Oh that – I had forgotten. It was bronchitis – the doctor checked me out and I had to rest and drink plenty of fluids,' he said. 'But I'm better now.'

'Good – I was worried that it might be TB,' she said. 'What have you been doing since you left home?'

'Working in a garden centre – the money isn't great but it will do for now.'

'Where are you living?'

'In one of Fauna Protection's caravans – but we are hoping to get our own place soon –if we can,' he said with a quick glance at Sophie.

'What do you mean?' asked Jennie.

'I can't leave, said Sophie softly. 'I have been a member of Fauna Protection since I was sixteen and I am under obligation to them.' She wrung her hands. 'I'm not supposed to have a relationship with a non-member.'

Ian put his arm around her. 'The rules are really strict and Boyle is really mean to anyone who breaks them.'

'He wants to stop both the badger cull and the Boxing Day Hunt,' said Sophie looking around to make sure no one was listening.

Jennie wanted to find out more but Ian abruptly pulled Sophie away.

'We've got to go,' he said.

Jennie watched them disappear into the crowd. She wondered how Boyle was planning to stop the hunt. Maybe a protest of some sort? Her thoughts turned to the party that evening at Beddis Grange. Both Tony and Edward would be there. Plus Freya, and Tony's parents. She hoped to enjoy herself but somewhere she wasn't sure that she would.

The day wore on and from three o'clock onwards daylight started to fade, but the customers kept on piling into the market. She looked at her watch and panicked when she saw the time.

It was only with difficulty that she managed to persuade Nancy to pack up the stall and to drive back to Green Meadow. Arriving home, she hastily showered and dressed in a black velvet dress that was too short and too tight for her. Several tiny moth holes, the result of languishing unworn in the dark recesses of her wardrobe for at least three years, were clustered near the hem. Too late, she noticed that the stiletto heels of her black evening shoes were worn through exposing the metal. Hoping that her mother's heirloom necklace would make up for any deficiencies in her outfit, she shouted downstairs a request to borrow Nancy's pearls. An answer wafted up.

'Make sure you don't lose them.'

Finally she took care with her hair and makeup, and squirted her favourite rose and jasmine perfume on to her wrist. The taxi was booked for seven but it was thirty minutes late when it finally drew up outside the farmhouse. A relieved Jennie tore through the front door and leapt inside.

'Sorry, love, but it's been a very busy evening,' said the driver putting his foot on the accelerator and speeding off down the drive.

'We need to collect my friend Sana as well,' she said.

A tractor held them up on the way into Oakfield, resulting in further delay. Finally, an hour late, Jennie and Sana were dropped off at Beddis Grange. The party was being held in a large barn at the side of the grand house. Sounds of merriment and music were emanating from inside.

Jennie and Sana crossed the cobbled courtyard as fast as they could. Inside the entrance, a smartly dressed doorman pointed to the cloakroom. Jennie hung up her coat, and quickly checked her appearance in the mirror before walking into the vaulted barn.

Tony, handsome in a designer shirt and with newly whitened teeth, was welcoming the guests. At his side was a stunning-looking Freya, wearing a fabulous dress.

'You're late,' he hissed at Jennie. 'I told you to get here early. Fortunately, Freya has stepped into the breech and she has sorted out the caterers, who were being very tedious.'

Jennie started to explain but she could see from the look in his eyes that he was not in the mood for explanations. Instead she muttered an apology. A distinguished looking couple approached them. From their resemblance to Tony, Jennie guessed that they were his parents.

'Ah, Tony I see that you have surrounded yourself with a bevy of lovely ladies,' said Mr McKensie with a broad smile. He reminded Jennie of George Clooney.

'Mum, Dad let me introduce you to Jennie, Sana and Freya,' said Tony.

'Welcome,' said Mrs McKensie. Her blonde hair was immaculate and her black lace dress encased a slim figure. She cast an appraising eye over the three girls and Jennie could see that she was impressed with Freya's appearance. Jennie held her evening bag over the moth holes in her dress and wished that she had found the time to buy something new and to get her hair and nails done professionally. Freya smiled sweetly and almost curtseyed. It was clear that she wasn't going to waste the opportunity to ingratiate herself with Tony's parents.

More guests arrived and the McKensies switched their attention to them. With a subtle glance, Tony dismissed Jennie and Sana. They moved into the well of the barn which had a bar at one end and a small stage at the other. A five piece band was playing but no one was on the dance floor. Dozens of finely dressed party goers were milling around with smiles on their faces and laughter on their lips.

A waitress, wearing a black skirt and a white blouse, came over to them with a tray of soft and alcoholic drinks.

Jennie picked up a flute of champagne. 'I'm annoyed that we were late,' she said. 'It meant that Freya took advantage.'

Sana chose an orange juice and looked across the room at Freya who was at Tony's side welcoming guests with a charming smile. 'She does seem in her element.'

Jennie had to agree. It would be churlish not to. Determined to enjoy the evening, she summoned up a more positive frame of mind and admired the decorations adorning the barn. Massive garlands of holly and ivy, studded with dried fruits and fresh flowers, and entwined with thousands of twinkling fairy lights were pinned to the overhead beams and walls.

'It's years since I was single at a party,' said Sana, 'I don't know what to do.'

'Just enjoy yourself,' replied Jennie.

A beaming Ibrahim bounced up to them. 'Hi guys,' he said, 'great party.'

'You remember Sana don't you?' Jennie said to him. 'You met in the Café del Rey.'

'Of course I do,' he said.

Sana smiled brightly. 'You're a solicitor aren't you?'

Ibrahim nodded and sipped his beer. 'I'm on the hunt for a new doubles partner.'

Jennie nudged Sana. 'You play tennis – don't you?'

Sana hesitated. 'Occasionally,' she said.

'You're being too modest - you have played at county level,' insisted Jennie.

Sana shook her head. 'That was a long time ago.'

Ibrahim perked up. 'That doesn't matter,' he said reassuringly. 'Will you give it a try?'

Sana protested. 'But my racket is ancient.'

'That's no excuse,' he said. 'I'll lend you a new one.'

Sana paused but then gave a gentle nod.

'OK,' she said, 'I'll give it a go.'

A huge smile spread over Ibrahim's face just as Edward joined them. Jennie thought he looked very handsome in his smart evening shirt and dark trousers, with his luxuriant hair tamed into shape.

'What are you talking about?' he asked.

'Sana is going to be my new doubles partner,' said Ibrahim.

Edward directed a look at Jennie. 'Why don't the four of us have a game sometime?'

Jennie blushed and the fizz started to go to her head. 'When the weather's better,' she agreed.

The maitre'd announced that dinner was about to be served and could they take their places. After consulting the table plan displayed on a large easel, they made their way to the one of the several large round tables set up in the barn. In the middle of the table was a tall crystal vase filled with silver and red baubles, topped with sprays of fresh roses, carnations and foliage. Crackers, party hats and poppers were scattered over the white tablecloth. Open bottles of red and white wine, still and sparkling water were on the table.

Place cards denoted where everybody was to sit so Jennie found her seat and sat down. Places for Tony and Freya were laid to her right but she could see that they were still welcoming latecomers. On her left was a young couple she didn't know. Edward, Ibrahim and Sana were on the other side of the table and it was hard to talk to them as another couple was in between. Ibrahim set off a rocket balloon and Sana blew one of the party horns. Jennie sipped her wine and kept a fixed smile on her face.

After quite a delay, Tony and Freya joined them at the table.

'Sorry guys for being late,' he said sitting down. 'Host duties I'm afraid.'

He ignored Jennie. He poured Freya a glass of white wine and himself a large glass of red. The waiters and waitresses came out of the kitchen at the back of the barn carrying the starters of melon and Parma ham. Jennie kept smiling even when her attempts of small talk with Tony and Freya failed. She turned to the couple on her left and talked to them instead. The first course plates were cleared away and the main course of chicken in a mushroom sauce or vegetarian lasagne started to be brought out.

At an adjacent table drunken singing broke out. A young man, shaking with laughter, leant back in his chair knocking plates of hot food out of the hands of a youthful waitress. The china plates shattered on the floor and the food splattered everywhere. Tony frowned with displeasure and Jennie hesitated, not knowing what to do. Freya immediately got up and went over to help the waitress clear up the mess. The maitre'd rushed to take over and she returned to the table.

'Thank you, Freya,' said Tony squeezing her hand.

The drink continued to flow. The party noise became louder. Jennie tried again to talk to Tony but his attention was on Freya. She felt excluded. Edward was talking to the others. Sana and Ibrahim were chatting about tennis. Jennie sat and listened to the conversations going on around her. Occasionally she nodded her head in agreement and she kept smiling but inside she was not enjoying the evening at all. The waiters refilled their glasses. Tony began to drink faster while Jennie slowed down her consumption. She could see that he was getting redder and redder. Across the table she regarded Edward who was sitting there with an amused expression on his face.

The conversation turned to the badger culling.

'I like killing vermin,' said Tony in a loud voice. Jennie looked at him with a shocked expression. She knew that he thought that way but none the less it was distressing to hear. He must be drunk. Freya whispered something in his ear. Whatever she had said was effective, as he smiled apologetically and changed the conversation to football.

Their main course arrived and everyone started eating. Dessert and coffee followed. Jennie relaxed and found more to talk about with the couple on her left. She was conscious that Edward's eyes were often on her.

After the meal as the staff cleared the tables the musicians came back on to the stage and started to play. Jennie was hoping that Tony would ask her to dance, but instead he pulled Freya to her feet.

'Come on gorgeous,' he said, 'let's have a dance.'

Freya saw the look of pique on Jennie's face and hesitated, but Tony's encouraging smile overcame her reservations and they headed to the floor.

Jennie sat there expressionless. Suddenly she had had enough. She got up and marched over to Tony where he was dancing.

'I am sorry Tony, but it's over. I'm leaving,' she said. She walked away and headed for the door. He didn't follow her. Instead he pulled Freya closer and kissed her.

Sana chased after Jennie.

'I'll call the taxi,' she said.

Jennie smiled gratefully at her. She looked back at Tony and Freya. They were still on the dance floor. Freya saw her looking and smiled triumphantly at her. Edward was standing at the side watching what was going on. He and Ibrahim came over. Edward started to say something but the doorman announced the arrival of their taxi. Jennie rushed out into the cold air with Sana following close behind. It was only when she was alone in her bedroom that night that she let the tears flow.

*

23rd December

Mid-afternoon the next day Jennie's phone pinged. It was a text from David. Seeing his name again made her heart jolt. What on earth did he want? She opened the message.

David

I'm in Oakfield. Meet me this evening 7pm at the Fat Goose xx

Jennie

OK

She couldn't explain to herself why she had agreed to the meeting. Maybe it was a reaction to what had happened the previous evening. She ordered a taxi. It picked her up at 6.30pm and all the way to the pub she wrestled with her thoughts and emotions. She pushed open the door of the Fat Goose. Inside, people were laughing and talking whilst the silver and gold tinsel decorations pinned to the dark wood panels and overhead beams radiated cheerful light in the dimness.

David was waiting for her just inside the entrance. She stood and stared at him. Memories of their intimate moments together came flooding back. His face was suntanned and his hair thicker and glossier than before. He broke the awkward moment by giving her a quick hug. He was wearing his usual aftershave.

'Jennie, how are you? I saw the photograph of you and your mother in this morning's Sunday paper and I just had to see you again,' he said.

'Today? I missed it. It was only yesterday that the journalist interviewed us,' said Jennie with a surprised look on her face. She watched him. 'How are you? It's been a long time. Tell me all about your trip.'

219

'First let me buy you a drink.'

'A dry white wine, please.'

'Ok – you sit down.' He headed for the bar which was five deep with customers.

She found a vacant table with two chairs and took off her coat and scarf. David looked different but seemed just the same.

'It's very busy here tonight, I guess because it's Christmas,' he said when he returned ten minutes later. He put his pint of beer and her glass of wine down on the table and sat on the chair with his back to the pub entrance. She smiled at him and flicked her hair off her face.

'I see you are wearing the earrings I gave you,' he said looking pleased.

'I really love them,' she said with a smile. 'So how did it go?'

He picked up his beer glass. 'It was a huge adventure – I saw loads, met lots of people, ate a lot of new food – it was fantastic – it was a shame that you didn't come with me.'

'I couldn't,' she said, 'I needed to finish my PhD.'

He smiled into her eyes. 'But you always said that you wanted to see the world.'

'I still do – at some point in the future.'

'South America was fantastic – you would have loved it,' he said waving his hands about. Under the table he reached out and touched her knee. She remembered the pleasure his caresses used to give her. 'And you Jennie? What have you been doing whilst I have been away?'

Hadn't he read her emails? Unconsciously she shifted her chair a few inches away from his.

'Working mainly,' she said.

'How is your thesis coming along?'

She took a sip of wine. 'Fine,' she said. 'The more I got into it, the more I enjoyed it.'

'Don't you have time for anything else?' he asked giving her a questioning look.

Her part in the badger cull was on the tip of her tongue but she remembered Joe's instructions to keep her involvement secret. 'I've been preparing Sukey for the Boxing Day Hunt.'

'Oh yes, I will have to follow it on foot as usual.'

Jennie smiled as she recalled previous years' hunts when David had spent more time in the pub than in the actual field.

'What about you? Are you home for good?' she asked.

He paused for a moment. 'For Christmas.'

'Where are you staying?'

He sipped his beer. 'With a friend.'

'Oh,' she said. 'Anyone I know?'

'I doubt it – but that's not important – when I saw your photo I realised I had forgotten how lovely you are.' He reached for her hand. 'I've missed you Jennie.' He sounded sincere but there was something in his eyes which made her doubt him.

She sighed. 'But David, you went away – you broke it off – remember?'

'You said you loved me.'

'I did,' she said. 'But I'm not the person I was.'

He moved his chair closer hers. 'Come on – let's have some fun together – for old time's sake.' Before she could remonstrate, he leant forward and planted a kiss on her lips.

The pub door opened. Over David's shoulder she saw Edward and Ibrahim come in. She could tell from Edward's expression that he had seen the kiss. She pulled away and shot Edward a look of apology. He turned around in disgust and went straight back out of the door with a surprised Ibrahim hot on his heels. Jennie's face fell and she wrung her hands in anguish.

She stood up. 'I can't stay – I shouldn't have come.' She grabbed her coat and scarf, and rushed outside. A blast of cold air almost knocked her sideways. Without looking back she ran down the High Street to the taxi rank.

*

26th December

The day of the Boxing Day Hunt arrived. Jennie looked out of her bedroom window. Overnight the temperatures had fallen well below freezing resulting in ice covered puddles and a crisp frost. The pale blue cloudless sky indicated a dry cold day lay ahead so for added warmth she dressed in thermal underwear, a long sleeved t-shirt, beige breeches, which showed her long legs off to full advantage, and a black riding jacket with a dark green collar and buttons imprinted with the hunt's emblem of a white oak leaf. To complete her outfit, she pulled on a pair of black leather knee-high riding boots with patent-leather tops. She checked her appearance in her full-length mirror and was satisfied with her reflection - her slender figure and her fair hair arranged in a chignon.

After breakfast Jennie loaded Sukey into the horsebox and drove into the centre of town where the members of the Oakfield Hunt were meeting in the widest section of the High Street. The hunts men and women were dressed in black jackets with green collars embroidered with an oak leaf emblem. Their horses were of different heights and colours – some brown, some bay and others chestnut. Geraldine, in a bright red jacket and mounted on a large horse, was surveying the riders arriving to follow the hunt on horseback. Having parked in the large overflow car park, Jennie slipped a medical band around her arm and donned her black riding hat. She opened the horsebox's rear doors and led Sukey out, before mounting her and riding over to where Geraldine was directing newcomers.

'Good morning,' said Jennie, 'everything all set to go?'

Geraldine nodded. 'I've finished laying the three lines of aniseed. They're two miles long. The checkpoints are all set up with first aid and refreshments. All fox earths and badger setts are unblocked and extra refuges built.' Her horse fidgeted, excited to see the pack of tan and red fox hounds, full of pent-up energy, milling around, sniffing and barking, near the ancient water trough.

Jennie patted Sukey's neck. 'My parents are already at the Green Meadow checkpoint.'

'We're almost ready to go,' said Geraldine, 'just some final checks to be made.' She moved off and went to inspect the younger riders.

Occasionally the red coated huntsman blew his hunting horn to keep the hounds under control. The terrier man dressed in a yellow visibility jacket was sitting on his quad bike all set to follow the hunt, to open and close gates, repair trampled fences and refresh the trail when it became too faint.

The exciting sights and sounds were encouraging people of all ages to join the crowd of several hundred onlookers. Amongst the police presence Jennie recognised PS Miller and PC Allen patrolling and helping to keep order. Out of the corner of her eye she glimpsed someone similar to David holding hands with a red haired woman. They were talking happily. Maybe this was the friend he was staying with. She sighed. On the one hand, she had fond memories of the years they had spent together but on the other hand she now knew beyond any reasonable doubt that she no longer loved him. The man saw her looking at him and he gave her a friendly wave. It was David. She waved back.

'Hi Jennie,' said a familiar voice. 'Good to see you here.'

She turned in the saddle and saw Tony mounted on a fine-looking stallion with a plaited mane. A blush spread over her cheeks as the memories of their last encounter at the party came flooding back.

She held the reins firmly. 'This is Sukey.'

'Meet Gladiator,' he said sitting in his saddle with a straight back. 'He is a grand old horse – much loved by all the family.'

Jennie relaxed her shoulders. 'He's certainly a magnificent creature,' she said. It was their first encounter since breaking up and she was relieved to find that Tony was being civilised about their split. He certainly looked happy.

Ibrahim rode up to them on a brown horse with a red ribbon tied to its tail.

'I see you have hired a kicker,' said Tony with a laugh, 'you know that you will have to stay at the back of the field? Kicking a hound is a cardinal offence.'

A smartly attired Ibrahim nodded. 'The riding stables warned me but it suits me to take it slower than the rest of you considering that I am still a novice rider.'

More horses and their riders arrived, many of them in their late teens and early twenties, riding young horses with green ribbons in their tails to indicate they should be given some leeway. Jennie exchanged cheery 'good mornings' with a number of familiar faces and accepted a tot of whisky offered by a man walking around with a tray laden with small glasses, to warm herself up. In the crowd she saw Freya dressed in fashionable outdoor gear accompanied by an older man coming towards them.

'Hello everyone,' said Freya as Tony beamed down at her. 'This is my father Colin. You all look so smart. When are you starting?'

'Nice to meet you Colin,' said Tony with a smile. 'We are waiting for the starting whistle. Are you following on foot?'

'We plan to, though I don't know if we will make it all the way around the course,' said Freya.

Loud drumming started, causing several of the horses to rear up in alarm. Jennie turned to regard the source of the noise. Several members of Fauna Protection, dressed in their black fleeces, were congregating outside the Fat Goose holding placards proclaiming: 'HUNTING IS A CRUEL SPORT' and 'HUNTING KILLS'. Jennie recognized Boyle, who was wearing a bright purple beanie with a dragonfly embroidered onto it, and Sophie in the middle of the protestors.

A chant broke out: 'What do we want? We want to stop the hunt. What do we want? We want to stop the hunt.'

'Bloody anarchists,' shouted Tony.

Boyle heard his shout and looked over at him. Angrily he broke away from the group and marched towards Tony and Jennie. Sophie followed him, her face grim and fearful. The disturbance attracted the attention of passers-by.

Boyle raised his fist. 'McKensie and Cliffe,' he said. 'I might have known that you two would have been involved with this hunt. You are the idle rich who don't deserve the privileges you have.' He drew himself up and puffed out his chest. Gladiator neighed and stepped back. Tony held the reins tightly and regarded Boyle with disdain. He turned his head away provoking Boyle even further.

With hatred on his face, Boyle advanced. 'You are just a toff who kills for pleasure,' he said alarming the horses even more. Jennie held firmly onto Sukey's reins, patted her neck and muttered calming words.

'That's not fair,' cried Freya. Trying to protect Gladiator she stepped forward but slipped on some ice. Instinctively she maintained her balance by raising her arms.

Tony turned Gladiator away. 'This isn't the time or the place to have an argument,' he said. Edward drove up to them on a quad bike. He was dressed in a navy blue gilet emblazoned with the words EMERGENCY VET. His handsome face flushed with annoyance. 'Back off, Boyle,' he said with a glare.

Boyle hesitated. Sophie grabbed his arm. He frowned and clenched his fists, but after a moment's hesitation, he walked away without a backward glance.

Sophie whispered to Jennie, 'Take care, won't you?' before disappearing into the crowd.

David rushed over. 'Are you alright, Jennie?' he asked.

Edward stared at him and a look of recognition and disappointment passed over his face. He turned his quad bike away and rode off before Jennie had a chance to explain. She gazed after him until he had disappeared from sight.

'Are you OK?' repeated David as the red haired woman joined him.

Jennie looked down at them trying to find the right words to express her emotions.

'Yes, I'm fine thank you,' she replied, 'but Boyle was really scary.'

A whistle sounded and the starter flag was lowered. David seemed relieved. He and the woman stood back and watched the hunt set off. With the other riders, Jennie mounted on Sukey, walked through the town and across the bridge over the River Fogle and down a long road heading south. They hit the rolling countryside, where the weak winter sunshine glistened over the bare brown fields dusted with a thick frost. Here and there red berries in the hedgerows provided flashes of bright colour. The pace quickened and the horses fell into a trot. Looking over her shoulder, Jennie saw that Boyle and Sophie plus a dozen or so activists were following the hunt on quad bikes. They were blowing horns and shouting, in order to unsettle the horses and the hounds. She made sure that Sukey kept her pace up so that she was amongst the front runners and away from all the distractions.

Geraldine, as master of the hunt, was checking that the horses didn't run too fast or hinder the hounds, who were running as a pack alongside the riders. From time to time, she shouted directions and warnings as she ensured no one rode into places where access was denied, or caused unnecessary damage to crops and fences.

As the morning progressed, the temperature struggled into single figures but the fresh air and exercise was exhilarating, bringing colour to Jennie's cheeks. Her legs began to ache as she used them to tell Sukey when to speed up, slow down and when to jump. The riders cried encouragement to each other as they cantered for nearly an hour, across country, jumping easily over the low fences. As they rode towards Green Meadow many of the riders fell behind as the pace of the hunt became too fast for them.

The hunt followers broke up into different groups – some keeping up on their quad bikes, some just jogging behind and some, mainly the family groups, on foot at the back. Most were using the maps of the aniseed trails on their mobile phones. Some were cutting corners and taking short-cuts.

As Jennie traversed a large field, she looked behind and saw Boyle and another man, who was wearing a black hat, suddenly veer away from the others, speed towards a metal gate and exit into a narrow lane.

Jennie and the hunt rode on through the muddy field that been ploughed in the autumn and left fallow. Hundreds of hoofs, paws and feet trampled the soil splattering it everywhere. She felt the wet mud on her jodhpurs. Her riding outfit was no longer in the pristine condition that it had started the day.

Tony was in the lead, riding Gladiator with panache. Jennie and Sukey were just behind. They cantered out of the field and along a well-worn farm track bordered by high hedges. A hundred yards ahead Jennie could see two men each standing either side of the track. Straightaway she recognised Boyle, who was still wearing the same distinctive purple beanie. The other man seemed familiar as well. There was something on the ground laid right across the track. A ray of sun glinted on it. It was a metal wire.

Alarmed, Jennie pulled on Sukey's reins to slow her down. 'Whoa,' she cried, 'watch out.' Her warning came too late for Tony. The wire was raised and pulled taut across the path. It cut into the front legs of Gladiator, laming him and felling him to the ground. Tony went straight over his horse's head, landing on the hard ground with a thud like a bag of potatoes falling from a shelf.

Jennie brought Sukey to such a sudden stop that she was thrown out of the saddle on to the ground. She lay there stunned with her arm caught awkwardly underneath her. Sukey ran off rider-less. Cries of horror and loud warnings cmanated from the other riders as they reduced their speed. The huntsman sounded his horn to halt the hounds but several of them carried on running forward.

Carefully Jennie pulled herself up to a sitting position. She looked across at Boyle. He turned and saw her before disappearing with his companion close behind through a hole in the hedge. A few minutes later Sophie arrived on her quad bike. She sat as rigid as a rock, staring with a look of horror and compassion at Tony lying there injured and Gladiator motionless on the ground emitting a soft moan. She ran over to Jennie to see if she was alright and helped her to her feet.

Jennie brushed herself down. Something was wrong with her arm – it was painful and hanging unnaturally. Her ankle hurt as well. She heard sirens. A rapid response car drove along the track and stopped close to where Tony was lying unconscious in a pool of blood on the ground. A paramedic jumped out and went straight to him. A small silent crowd gathered round.

Edward rode up on his quad bike. Seeing Gladiator lying there, he lifted up his veterinary bag and went immediately over to the stricken horse. He gave him a thorough examination but the expression of sadness on his face told Jennie the situation. He stood up and wiped his brow.

'His leg is broken,' he said to the onlookers. He opened his bag and pulled out a bolt gun. 'Stand back everyone.' He aimed and pulled the trigger. Gladiator gave a spasm and fell still. The people gathered around became silent, their heads bowed with sorrow. Tears ran down Sophie's face. Edward covered the dead horse with a blanket. Jennie sobbed quietly.

A police car arrived and pulled to a stop. PS Miller and PC Allen got out. They told everybody to stand back before taping off an area around Gladiator's body in order to prevent any evidence being contaminated. Sophie got back onto her quad bike and sped off. Edward went over to Jennie. In his eyes was an unmistakable look of tenderness and affection.

'Are you alright?' he asked.

'My right arm,' said Jennie cradling it against her chest, 'it hurts a lot.'

A young woman came up leading Sukey. 'Is this your horse?' she said. 'I saw her run off so I followed and caught her.'

Jennie grabbed Sukey's reins with her left hand. 'Yes, thank you so much for returning her.'

Miller and Allen walked up to her. Miller pulled out his notebook. 'Jennie, can you tell us what happened?' he asked.

'She's hurt her arm,' said Edward. 'Can't this wait?'

'I'm afraid not,' said Allen.

Jennie shot him a look of reassurance. 'It's OK, I don't mind,' she said. 'There was a wire stretched across the track.' She tried to point to where she had seen it but the movement made her wince. 'They tightened it and it brought down Tony and his horse.'

Allen looked to where she had indicated and went over. He put on his gloves and picked up the wire. 'You're right.'

'Who were they?' asked Miller. 'The people pulling the wire I mean.'

Jennie nursed her arm. 'It all happened so fast but I think it was Jeremy Boyle. He was dressed in a black fleece and a purple beanie. I didn't recognise the other man.'

'The horse's injuries have been caused by a sharp wire cutting into its forelegs, causing it to fall and fracture a limb,' said Edward.

Miller took out his police radio and called for a crime scene officer to attend immediately. Allen went over to the paramedic who was attending to Tony, watching by several people standing close together in the cold.

Stuart Brown zoomed up on a quad bike. He stopped and got off.

'I'm a reporter from The Daily Update,' he said, 'do I have your permission to take some photos?'

Miller nodded. 'We may well ask to see whatever you take though.'

Stuart whipped out his long lens camera and started to take numerous shots of the scene. The sound of an air ambulance was heard. It landed in the adjacent field. A couple of paramedics got out, running under the blades towards the gate. They headed straight to Tony who was lying prone on the ground. One of them felt for his pulse, the other checked his breathing and searched for any bleeding. Together they lifted him onto a stretcher. Jennie heard a distraught cry.

Freya, with a look of genuine concern on her face, rushed towards the stretcher. Seeing Tony lying motionless covered with a blanket and with his face deathly pale brought tears to her eyes. Colin held her back.

'Can I go with him?' she asked.

'I'm afraid not, Miss.'

'Where are you taking him?' Freya cried.

'Oakfield Hospital, Miss,' replied the paramedic.

The paramedics picked up the stretcher and carried it across the field and lifted it into the air ambulance. A few minutes later the helicopter took off just as Ibrahim rode up.

'What on earth has happened?' he asked. 'My horse got a thorn in its leg.'

'Sad news, Tony and Gladiator were brought down by a wire across the track,' said Edward with a grim look.

The expression on Ibrahim's face changed to one of alarm. 'Oh no, how are they?'

'Tony is unconscious – he's been taken to hospital. Sadly Gladiator had a broken leg and had to be put down,' said Edward.

Ibrahim's eyes filled with tears. He looked around and saw Jennie with Sukey. 'What about you Jennie?' he asked anxiously.

'I came off but it's nothing serious,' she replied just as the police walked past giving instructions.

'Right everyone, move on now, I have told Mrs Waugh that the hunt can be restarted,' said Miller.

'How can they do that?' asked Ibrahim.

Geraldine rode past on her horse blowing her whistle.

'It's quite normal to restart hunts after accidents and injuries,' said Jennie.

Edward indicated that he knew. 'It doesn't seem right somehow,' he said, 'but there we are. I think you should get some medical attention for your arm Jennie, and get Sukey home.'

Jennie gave a weak smile. ''Don't worry about me. Can you get my phone out of my pocket? I will ring my parents. They aren't far away – Green Meadow is just over there – they can come and get us.'

Freya, her face pale and her eyes red from crying, reached across and fished the phone out of Jennie's pocket. 'I'm going to the hospital,' she said giving it to her, 'I want to be with Tony.' With that, she set off with Colin on foot back to Oakfield. Ibrahim rode off saying that he might as well finish the hunt as he had nothing else to do that day.

Edward revved his quad bike. 'Right, I have to follow the hunt – in case there are more casualties,' he said before driving off without a backwards glance. Jennie gazed wistfully after him.

The sound of hunting horns, yelping dogs, and pounding hooves resumed. Glad to be on the move again, the riders, their horses and all the followers both mounted and on foot streamed forward. They went down the track and past the body of Gladiator which was covered by the blanket. Most had been too far behind the leaders to have been aware of what had gone on. Overhead, crows cawed and a kestrel whined.

Jennie stood on one leg at the side of the track finding it too painful to put pressure on her swollen ankle. A sharp pain shot through her right arm. She slipped Sukey's reins through her left. With some difficulty, she managed to ring home and to speak to Nancy.

'Mum, there's been an accident, I'm injured,' she said. 'Can you come and get me and Sukey?'

'What happened?' asked Nancy.

'I will tell you everything later.'

'Where are you?'

'Three hundred yards down the track from the road,' she replied.

'OK, we will be with you as soon as we can. Hold tight.'

She didn't have long to wait. Giles arrived first on foot, an anxious look on his face.

'Are you alright? What happened?' he asked.

Jennie pointed to the track. 'Someone pulled a wire across and brought down Tony and Gladiator. Tony's been taken to hospital and Edward had to put Gladiator down.'

Giles looked over at Gladiator's body covered by the blanket. 'The bastards,' he said grimly. He took hold of Sukey's reins as Nancy rushed up.

'I've heard what happened. It's dreadful. How are you?' she asked.

'My arm hurts, and my ankle is really painful, but Sukey is OK,' answered Jennie.

Giles put his foot into one of Sukey's stirrups and swung himself into the saddle. 'Right, you drive Jennie to A & E in the car and I'll ride Sukey back to the farm,' he said.

Nancy nodded. 'I've parked the car in the road. It's not far away.'

'The horse box is still in Oakfield,' said Jennie with a worried look.

'I'll ring Ian. He's there. He can drive it home for us,' said Nancy taking her phone out of her shoulder bag. 'Ian? Jennie has hurt her arm. If we meet you in Oakfield and hand you the keys, can you drive the horse box back to Green Meadow?'

Jennie and Giles waited to hear his answer.

Nancy put the phone away. 'Right that's all settled. Let's go.'

Giles trotted off through the gate into the field beyond.

Jennie limped the short distance up the track to the road where the Range Rover was parked.

'Ouch,' she said as Nancy gently helped her into the front seat.

Nancy took off her scarf. 'Let me make a sling for your arm,' she said. 'That should give it some support.'

'Thank you, Mum,' said Jennie, 'I feel as if I am in the wars.'

'Nothing too serious though,' said Nancy. She switched on the engine and drove off down the road towards the hospital.

'I just hope Tony is alright - he had a nasty fall,' said Jennie.

At Oakfield Hospital, a nurse eased off Jennie's riding boot to reveal the swelling around her ankle and bruising up her shin.

A young doctor came to have a look at it. 'It's a nasty sprain,' he said. 'You will have to rest it until the swelling has gone down and you can put your weight on it.'

Her arm was x-rayed and a fracture diagnosed. Painkillers were offered before the doctor manipulated the broken bone back into place. Her arm was encased in plaster and supported with a splint and a sling.

'Here are some more painkillers to take home and a leaflet giving advice on how to look after your cast,' said the friendly nurse.

Finally the doctor discharged her. It was dark when they arrived back at Green Meadow.

'You will have to stay indoors for the next week,' said Nancy, 'you can't go out until you are better.'

Jennie groaned. Upstairs in her bedroom, she undressed with difficulty using one hand. She managed to have a wash taking care not to get the plaster cast wet. How was she going to write? Thankfully she had collected all her data but now she needed to crack on with her thesis. And the badger cull? Obviously she wouldn't be able to continue with that. Her phone rang. She reached across to answer it. It was Edward.

'Jennie? How are you?' he asked with a genuine note of concern in his voice.

She put the phone on to speaker mode. 'A broken arm and a sprained ankle, that's all, but it will mean that you'll have to find another partner for the badger cull.'

'I'll let Joe know, but without your input I expect he will call a temporary halt anyway,' he said as another phone rang. 'Sorry, I've got to go.' He rang off before she could thank him.

She sat on the edge of her bed and gingerly eased her swollen foot into the widest pair of slippers that she could find. From outside, came the sound of a horsebox being driven around to back of the farmhouse. A few minutes later she heard the back door open. Holding tightly on to the bannister rail she hobbled down the stairs and went into the kitchen. Ian and Sophie were standing just inside the door with suitcases in their hands. Nancy was in front of her easel holding her paintbrush. Giles was sitting in an armchair in front of the fire with a newspaper in his lap. Bramble was sniffing Sophie's feet and wagging her tail.

'I have brought Sophie home with me,' said Ian. He gave Sophie, pale from fright, a reassuring look. 'I hope you don't mind but we would like to stay until we find somewhere else.'

Nancy paused to consider this request. She saw Giles nodding his agreement. 'Of course, stay as long as you want,' she said. She took off her artist's apron and washed her hands in the sink. 'I will make up your bed right now.' She disappeared upstairs.

Giles looked across at Sophie. 'You're a member of Fauna Protection aren't you?'

Sophie shuffled her feet and pulled her military style coat tighter around her.

Jennie put on the kettle. 'Have you managed to escape?'

Sophie gave a weak nod. 'How's Tony? I'm so shocked about what happened. Gladiator being killed and Tony injured,' she said as a tear rolled down her cheek. 'I feared that Jeremy would do something awful. He was in a foul mood. But killing a beautiful horse – that's just plain wickedness. So I have left Fauna Protection.'

'Sophie's worried that they will come after her – no one is allowed to leave without permission,' said Ian putting his arm around her.

'You'll be safe here,' said Giles reassuringly.

Jennie nodded in agreement but she had seen that determined look in Boyle's eyes and knew that he was capable of anything.

Chapter 14

3rd January 2019

The beginning of January saw a change in the weather. The high pressure system, responsible for the cold settled days, broke down and towering clouds rolled in from the south-west. The wind howled through the farmhouse's chimney pots and brought down isolated trees. Rain battered on the window panes and soaked into the ground, leaving the fields saturated. The River Fogle flooded and Bramley Brook swelled into a torrent. The days were short and dark. Life for Jennie shrunk to the four walls of her far-from-palatial bedroom. The only messages she received were from Sana. There was plenty of time to reflect. She realised that it was Edward she was missing. She wondered when she would see him again.

Her laptop sat on her desk. She loaded the spreadsheets recording the results of her fieldwork. They were finally complete. She could now run the most important statistical test of her thesis – a correlation test. The calculated value would allow her to accept her hypothesis that the greater the biodiversity of a habitat, the shorter the distance badgers would travel to find food. She would be able to reject the null hypothesis that there was no relationship between the two variables.

Methodically she set up a summary spreadsheet. In the first column was a list of the thirty Liltford badger setts; in the second the number of different species found within ten metres of that sett; and in the fourth the average distance travelled by the badgers in search of food. In the third, fifth and sixth columns were calculations, the outcomes of which went into the final formula which produced a value which indicated whether she could accept her hypothesis or not. She checked the entries and then clicked Run.

Her face flushed with excitement. Staring at her was the result she had been working towards. There was a link between biodiversity and food supply. The result could not have occurred by chance. She sighed with relief, got up and danced around the room. Bramble, sensing a celebration, emerged from under her desk and woofed.

But being able to prove something was only the first step. Making changes to the countryside and to farming practices would be a huge task – one that she wouldn't be able to do herself. It would need a collective effort to show sceptics that creating a wide variety of habitats on farmland would benefit both farmers and wildlife.

Using the index finger of her left hand she typed up her analysis and conclusion. It took longer than expected. She sighed. There were only a dozen or so weeks left before the closing date for the Luminosity Prize and a broken arm was the last thing she needed right now.

Her attention turned to the pile of textbooks, on her dressing table. She sifted through them looking for the one on animal vaccines. It was right at the bottom. Making herself comfortable on her bed, she settled down to read. Occasionally she jotted down some notes in pencil in a small notebook. Finally she finished the last page and put the book down, her head full of ideas. She remembered Amina saying at the beginning of the cull that there wasn't an effective badger vaccine for bovine TB. That was still true, but she realised that if she put her mind to it she could develop one. Now was the perfect opportunity – she had what she required on her laptop and in her head plus plenty of time to fill. Her bedroom would have to substitute for the laboratory.

First she needed to find the essential protein that could neutralise the virus. She opened the picture folder on her laptop. It contained thousands of images of badger blood samples taken with the digital camera. One by one she examined each photograph, looking for the elusive protein. Totally absorbed, the next few hours just flew past.

Her tummy rumbled. She limped downstairs. The kitchen was warm and homely. Nancy was busy at the stove and Ian and Sophie were sitting next to each other at the table reading the Oakfield Times Online on a laptop.

'There is an item here about Tony McKensie,' said Sophie scrolling down.

Jennie hopped over to the table and peered over Sophie's shoulder. 'What does it say?'

'MEMBER OF THE OAKFIELD HUNT INJURED. A man, named as Tony McKensie, was airlifted to hospital after an incident during the Boxing Day Hunt. His horse Gladiator was put down at the scene. An update from Oakfield Hospital on Mr McKensie's condition says that he is at a critical stage of his recovery. The doctors warn that he may have life changing injuries. The next few days are going to be crucial. The death of his stallion Gladiator has been met with a mixture of sorrow and anger throughout Oakfield.'

Tears welled in Jennie's eyes as memories of that day came flooding back.

'I hope that Tony is going to be alright,' she said. She pulled the laptop towards her and re-read the item followed by another article. She frowned.

'It says here that members of Fauna Protection have posted claims on social media that the death of a horse is proof that hunting is a cruel sport which should be banned. How can they say that? It was a trail hunt conducted according to the law,' she exclaimed.

Sophie replied, 'I know that they would blame the death of Gladiator on the organisers of the hunt – in their eyes the accident would never have happened if the hunt had been called off in the first place. That's why they tried to stop it.'

'That's rubbish – it wasn't an accident – that wire was pulled deliberately,' said Jennie.

An expression of unease spread over Sophie's face.

'Haven't the police arrested Boyle yet?' asked Nancy at the cooker.

Sophie looked up with a fearful look in her eyes. 'He's an evil man you know.'

Ian reached over and held her hand. 'He raped Sophie,' he said angrily.

Sophie sobbed. Nancy stopped stirring the gravy. She came over and put her hand on Sophie's shoulder. 'What happened, my dear? Can you tell us?'

Sophie hesitated.

'You don't have to say anything if you don't want to,' said Ian.

Jennie sat still, keen to hear Sophie's story.

Sophie blew her nose. 'The more I talk about it, the better it gets.' She paused. 'I was fourteen when my parents divorced. My mother remarried straightaway and she pushed me out after my new stepfather moved in. One day I heard Jeremy Boyle speak at a rally. He was leading a Fauna Protection attempt to stop the construction of a new road which would destroy the breeding site of a colony of great crested newts,' she said. 'He seemed so passionate and authentic. I hung around afterwards and he spotted me. I was only fifteen. He told me I was beautiful.'

'The classic line,' said Jennie.

'Go on,' said Nancy.

'At first, joining Fauna Protection was the perfect choice for me. My mother gave me some money which I handed over for my living expenses. I felt cared for,' said Sophie. 'I didn't realise it but right from the start Boyle brainwashed me. He made me feel good about myself. He told me that he loved me. I went on the pill. Then a new girl joined. She was younger than me and he did the same to her. When I met Ian I tried to leave but he wouldn't let me. I was trapped. One day Boyle lost his temper and he raped me. After the Boxing Day Hunt I knew that I had to escape. Fortunately Ian helped me. I'm so grateful that you have allowed me to stay here.'

Sophie started to cry. Ian held her hand tightly. Nancy put her arm around her. The back door swung open and Giles stomped in. A gust of wind blew some leaves into the kitchen before he could get the door shut. The fire spluttered in the grate. Nancy returned to the cooker. Sophie dried her eyes but hung on to Ian's hand.

'It's lethal out there,' said Giles. He took off his coat and sat in the armchair to take off his boots.

Ian looked at his father. 'What have you been doing out there in this weather Dad?'

'Feeding the horses and chickens, what do you think?' he retorted.

'Isn't it about time that you started cleaning up the farm and making the necessary changes?' asked Ian with a touch of impatience.

'There is no point, my lad, doing anything whilst the threat of conviction hangs over my head like the sword of Damocles,' said Giles. 'We could very well lose this farm in months if not weeks.'

This statement was met with horrified expressions on those around him.

'But you aren't guilty of fraud – surely the police realise that?' said Ian loudly. He slammed his fist down on the table so hard that Bramble leapt up in alarm from the hearthrug.

Giles scowled. 'They obviously think I'm guilty and I can't prove otherwise.'

'Edward said he would look into it,' said Jennie reassuringly.

'Well he hasn't yet and until he does we are in limbo,' answered Giles.

From outside came the sound of a car arriving. The doorbell rang. Jennie answered it. Standing on the doorstep was a middle aged man, with a suntanned complexion. He was wearing a jacket and boots. He seemed unsure of the reception he would receive. Her face betrayed her surprise. 'Mr Sitwell – you're back,' she said, 'come on in. My father will be pleased to see you.'

She ushered him into the kitchen. Giles stared at him as if he was a ghost. He got up out of the armchair and hugged his old friend and neighbour.

'This is a turn up for the books. I thought you were dead,' he said.

'Douglas!' said Nancy delightedly. 'You are alive! Let me take your coat.'

'I was never dead,' he said slipping it off. 'I just needed to get away.'

Giles stood back and gave him a long look. 'You could have told me – you just disappeared into the blue. I was so worried. We all were.'

'Apologies – I was in such as bad place.'

'But it's been nearly nine months,' said Giles.

'I know – a lot has happened since then,' said Douglas.

'Tell us all,' said Nancy. 'We are just about to have dinner – join us.'

Douglas hesitated. 'Well I don't mind if I do. I must admit I'm ravenous,' he said. He sat down and stroked Bramble whose tail was wagging with excitement. Jennie laid the table with the red gingham check tablecloth reserved for special visitors.

'So,' said Giles as he opened another two bottles of beer, 'what have you been up to?'

'It's a long story and I don't know where to begin,' said Douglas looking around at them all.

Nancy inspected the vegetables boiling in the saucepans on the hob. 'At the beginning,' she said.

'Well it all started nearly two years ago – after some of the cows on Beesnest Farm tested positive 'for bovine TB. Samuel Nelson received a tidy sum in compensation from the Animal Health Agency and it got me thinking – I have to admit, that I'm not proud about this,' he said accepting the bottle of beer that Giles proffered him. 'I had gambling debts and my creditors were breathing down my neck. Phil Oldman came and did the first stage of the tests. After he had gone, I injected a concoction of rancid water and diesel into each cow, to make sure that they developed swellings at the site of the tests.'

Sophie gasped with disapproval.

Jennie looked dismayed. 'That's so cruel.'

'I wasn't thinking straight – I was just thinking about the money. I have no excuses – what I did was wrong. I know that now,' said Douglas with contrition written all over his face.

'Fraud,' said Jennie.

He ignored her remark and continued. 'Anyway, the herd was condemned and sent to slaughter. Phil had his suspicions. He threatened me with the police. When the money came through I settled my debts and paid him.'

'That's blackmail,' said Giles.

'Exactly,' said Douglas. 'Then I left. Somehow I just needed to get away. I needed a change of scenery to straighten myself out – I had been drinking too much – way too much – as well as gambling.'

'Where did you go?' asked Giles.

'As far away as I could – to the Australian outback. I bought a camper van and set off to the interior. It did me good – getting away from people and finding myself again.'

'What made you come back?' said Nancy.

'I checked into a small hotel and connected up to the internet and saw your messages, Giles, about my mother. I felt guilty about abandoning her, so I booked a flight home,' he said.

Nancy put the bowl of roast potatoes on to the table. 'Have you seen her?'

'She is out of hospital and has gone to her sister's in Minehead. I visited her there yesterday.'

Jennie took the plates out from the warming drawer of the range cooker and Nancy served the roast chicken, green vegetables, carrots and gravy.

'Right tuck in,' said Nancy.

'Now tell me what's been happening here,' said Douglas.

Giles cleared his throat. 'I lost my herd as well – last summer.'

'Dreadful. Dreadful,' said Douglas sadly. 'Zoe Mudmaker?'

Giles nodded. 'It has been awful,' he said, 'and what makes it worse is that I have been charged with fraud over the compensation claim.'

'But surely you wouldn't be as daft as me?' asked Douglas.

'Of course not. I wouldn't harm my cows,' said Giles.

A pained look darted over Douglas's face. 'So why do they think you might have committed fraud?' he said with a puzzled look.

'I don't know. Perhaps because they suspect you could have and that by implication, I did as well. Something like that, anyway,' said Giles shrugging.

'Well that's just plain wrong,' said Douglas. 'Have you challenged it? I would if I were you. I assume that you want to carry on with the farm?'

Jennie waited for her father's answer and was relieved to see him nod.

'So is the farm bio secure now?' asked Douglas. 'If you want a new herd, you will have to change your ways round here. I let things go on Hightree – not keeping things as clean as they should have been, not maintaining the fences that sort of thing. I suppose I didn't keep up with the times.'

Giles bowed his head and twisted his rough hands in his lap. 'The old ways worked for my father and grandfather and were good enough for me. I didn't want to change. But now I accept that I have no choice.'

Nancy smiled across the table at her husband. Jennie and Ian exchanged looks of relief.

'I'll help,' said Ian.

'Thank you, my lad,' said Giles. 'Come now, let's celebrate Douglas's return.'

Everyone raised their glasses in a toast. After supper, Jennie carefully climbed the stairs to her bedroom. Her sprained ankle was on the mend but it still gave her the occasional twinge. She checked her mobile phone to see if there were any messages. It was days since she had heard from Edward. She looked out of her window into the darkness at the beating rain, whistling wind and swaying trees. Impulsively, she wrote him a text.

Hi Edward how are you?

His reply came immediately.

I'm in London on business – will explain when I see you

Her heart thumped. She smiled. It was a short communication that raised more questions than it answered but it was a reply. After closing the bedroom curtains she climbed into bed.

*

23rd January

After quite a considerable time cooped up in her bedroom, Jennie had some queries that could only be answered in the laboratory. Her broken arm ruled out cycling. So she had been pleased when the previous evening her father had announced that he would be driving into Oakfield. The early morning mist and murk was slowing lifting when they set out. As Giles drove across the bridge over the River Fogle into Oakfield she noticed that the river was high after weeks of heavy rain. Debris washed along by the flood waters was hanging from the lower branches of the trees growing on the river banks. Giles drove through the town and drew to a stop outside Oakfield University.

'I'll pick you up at four,' he said as Jennie got out of the Range Rover.

'Thanks Dad,' she said.

She passed the bare cherry trees in the central courtyard on her way to the Department of Ecology. The laboratory hummed with the quiet activity of machines and researchers. Her pressing priority was to design a badger vaccine to combat bovine TB. It was a tall order.

'Jennie, long time no see,' said a familiar voice. 'How are you?' It was Sana, her friendly face beaming at her.

'I'm managing,' said Jennie struggling to get her arm, which was still encased in plaster, into her lab coat. 'What about you?'

'Just fine,' replied Sana. 'Here let me help you.' She held the lab coat up and guided Jennie's arm in. 'How's the PhD going?'

Jennie turned on her microscope. 'I think I have identified the right protein which indicates that badgers have bovine TB. Now I need to isolate it and grow it in animal serum.'

Sana gave a low whistle. 'Wow - that's brilliant,' she said. 'If you have, that would be a real breakthrough. Our stocks of serum are low though.'

Jennie grimaced. 'Can't you order some more?'

'Not at the moment. The departmental budget is stretched to its limits.'

Jennie's face fell at the thought of a possible delay to her work. She reminded herself that she hadn't yet separated the protein from the badgers' plasma. With renewed determination she headed to the walk-in fridge and pulled out a rack of test tubes full of blood samples. Returning to the lab bench, she smeared a drop of blood onto a slide and put it under the microscope. She bent her head and resumed her painstaking research.

Later, she sat back and looked at her watch. The time had flown by. Her father would be picking her up soon. She packed away and went out to wait. When the Range Rover drew up she got into the front passenger seat. On the drive back to Green Meadow she kept thinking about the vaccine. The right recipe to make it was almost in place but the design still needed some tweaking.

*

24th January

The next morning Jennie woke early. It was still dark. She lay in bed and thought about the day ahead. At eleven she had to be at Oakfield Police Station. Painful memories of all that had happened at the Boxing Day Hunt filled her mind. She got up, pulled back the curtains and gazed outside. Even though the trees were swaying in the strong breeze, it wasn't raining. That meant she could walk into Oakfield - after so many days indoors, she needed the fresh air and exercise.

After breakfast she set out along the three mile long public footpath which wound its way into Oakfield. Her broken arm, supported by a sling, didn't prevent her from stomping through the puddles and muddy patches. Her thoughts turned to Edward. Her longing for him had grown, although since his last text, there had been no further communication from him. Many times she had been on the verge of contacting him again, only to draw back from fear of being rejected. She walked past the caravan site and noticed that there were hardly any touring vans or tents left. The Fauna Protection supporters must have gone home.

After an hour she reached Oakfield High Street. With time to spare she walked along looking into the shop windows. She saw the sign for the Café del Rey and smelt arabica coffee. Behind her someone shouted her name. She turned around and saw Edward coming towards her. Her heart leapt with joy.

He caught up with her and beamed. 'Jennie. Good to see you. You look well,' he said. 'How is your arm?'

'It's better thank you – the plaster is coming off in a couple of days,' she said hoping that he wouldn't notice her muddy boots and wind-swept hair. 'You've been away a long time?'

'I know,' he said, 'but I'm back now. Do you have time for a coffee?'

'Just about,' she said, 'I have an appointment at the police station. To make a witness statement.'

Inside the café the small tables were full of people chatting and laughing. She stood in the queue behind him. When the barista asked for their orders he requested a black

Americano and she a regular cappuccino. When they had been served, he led the way to a table in the window that had just been vacated.

They sat down.

'Do you think that they have arrested Boyle yet?' she asked.

He picked up his drink. 'I don't know,' he said.

'How is Tony? Have you heard?'

'Ibrahim keeps me posted. He is due to leave hospital in the next few days. He's been extremely lucky and has sustained no permanent injuries. He's got to convalesce but after that he should be fine.'

Jennie sighed with relief. That was good news. She gazed at Edward's handsome face. It was so good to see him again. She had so much to say to him but shyness was holding her back. After a pause she plucked up courage. 'You know that evening in the pub when you saw me with a man? That was my former boyfriend.'

'I guessed,' he said.

'He had just returned from his travels and he wanted to see me.'

'And?'

'I told him that it was over – there was no chance of us getting back together,' she said as clearly as she could.

There was a short silence. Edward started to speak but was interrupted by a small dog sniffing his trousers. Its owner, a short woman with dyed hair, exclaimed, 'Edward, I saw you sitting there and I just had to come over and ask you about Charlie's eyes – they are awfully dry.'

Edward smiled charmingly. 'Mrs Barton, come along to my evening surgery.'

'I've already made an appointment,' said the woman pulling her dog away, 'I just thought you could have a quick look now.' Edward shook his head firmly and turned away.

He apologised to Jennie but the moment for deeper exchanges between them had passed. Seeing the time she stood up. He rose as well. Outside they went their separate ways. She walked along to the police station, which was housed in an unassuming building fronting the High Street. She went in and was greeted by the duty officer. He pointed to where she should wait. She sat on an upholstered chair in front of a coffee table scattered with lifestyle magazines. The door opened and the duty officer summoned her.

She was accompanied along a short corridor and was shown into a compact interview room. Two plain clothed detectives stood up to welcome her.

'Jennie Cliffe?' asked the older one. 'Thank you for coming today. I'm DS Page and this is my colleague DC Friar.'

Friar turned on the microphone. 'Just so you are aware, we are recording this interview.'

Jennie sat down facing them across a narrow table. There was a glass of water in front of her.

'We have some questions to ask you about the incident on the 26th December 2018 in Liltford,' said Page, a stocky man with broad shoulders. 'We understand that you witnessed the event which resulted in an injury to Mr Tony McKensie and the death of his horse Gladiator?'

Jennie composed herself and indicated that she had.

'Can you give us a full description of what you saw? Take your time - there is no rush,' said Friar. He started typing on the laptop in front of him.

She cleared her throat. 'It all happened so quickly, it's hard to remember everything.'

'Just do your best,' said Page reassuringly.

When she had finished her account, her statement was read back to her.

'Do you agree that you have given a truthful and accurate description of the events of that day?' asked Page.

She nodded.

Friar pressed Print and the printer sprung into life and spewed out several pages of text. He gave the sheets to Jennie. In silence, she sat and read them. When she finished she signed her statement on the dotted line at the bottom of each page. She uncrossed her legs and stretched her ankles.

'Is that all?' she asked.

'No. Next is the identity parade,' said Page.

Visions of men lined up in identical clothing flashed through her mind. The worried expression on her face prompted Friar to reassure her that these days all she had to do was to watch a compilation of images.

Page continued the explanation. 'We would like you to watch two identification videos. They both contain images of the two men under suspicion. You will be shown pictures of at least nine other men who are all volunteers and who are similar to the suspects in terms of age, general appearance and status in life. Take your time. At the end of each film I would like you to identify the person you think was responsible for this crime.'

He turned on the TV screen attached to the wall. He pressed Play and Jennie sat and watched as the photographs of several men passed in front of her. All had the same dark complexion, close set eyes and stocky build as Boyle. When Boyle's face appeared, she shuddered and emitted a gasp.

Identifying the other culprit took longer, as Jennie only had a vague recollection of the man who had held the other end of the wire which had tripped up Gladiator. After much consideration she felt confident that she had picked out the right person. He was the tall young man with straggly hair who was always shadowing Boyle.

Finally the detectives indicated that they had finished and that Jennie could go. She jumped up releasing her pent-up nervous energy.

*

31st January

A week later, early one morning, Jennie walked from Green Meadow Farm to Oakfield Hospital. The temperature was barely above freezing but she was warmly dressed and thankful that it wasn't wet and windy. On arrival at the Outpatients department she was directed to a waiting area. It was just after nine o'clock but already there were a dozen or so people occupying the blue chairs. She pulled a queue ticket from the dispenser machine on the wall. It was number forty. She sat down to wait. From her bag, she pulled out her Kindle and started to read. From time to time a member of the medical staff came out of a side room and shouted a number. Someone would immediately stand up and collect their belongings. Number thirty-nine was called. In readiness, Jennie prepared herself for her turn.

'Forty,' shouted a young nurse in a blue tunic.

Jennie followed her into the consulting room and handed over her NHS appointment letter. The nurse read it and typed some information into the computer on the desk in front of her.

'Jennie Cliffe?'

She nodded.

'You have come to have your plaster cast taken off?'

'Yes,' said Jennie. 'It's filthy.'

Expertly the nurse cut the cast off and Jennie's pink arm emerged. The nurse examined it carefully. 'Every day soak it in warm water for five minutes. Rub it with a towel and apply moisturising cream. Repeat until your skin returns to normal. You may find that your forearm aches but try to use your hand as normally as possible,' she said.

Jennie listened carefully and rubbed her arm. Some dry skin flaked off.

'It feels fine,' she said. She thanked the nurse and made her way to the exit. Outside she stood and breathed in the fresh air. The hospital had been hot and stuffy. To her surprise she saw Freya walking towards the hospital entrance. She was wearing a stylish winter coat and high heeled boots. Her hair and makeup were immaculate. Not for the first time Jennie wished that she had more money to spend on her own wardrobe.

'Freya,' she exclaimed, 'what are you doing here?'

'I've come to collect Tony. He's being discharged today.'

'How is he?'

'For a time I was really worried about him but he is well on the mend now.'

Jennie smiled. Embarrassing memories of her dates with Tony momentarily flooded back. She pushed those thoughts away.

'Have you any news of the police investigation?' she asked.

Freya shivered. 'They rang Tony yesterday. Jeremy Boyle and another member of Fauna Protection have been arrested and charged with attempted murder. They've been given a date to appear at the magistrates court,' she replied. 'What about you? What are you doing here?'

Jennie held up her arm. 'I've just had my plaster removed.'

Freya regarded her with sympathy.

'Did it hurt a lot?'

Jennie nodded. 'It was a nasty break but it has healed up well.'

Freya climbed the step. 'Good. I'm afraid I can't stop. See you around.'

'Bye,' said Jennie. She went on her way reflecting that she now understood why Edward had dated Freya for so long. She did have a lot to recommend her after all.

Chapter 15

22nd February

A stiff breeze was blowing clouds across the sky, but the warmth from the morning sun was waking the land up from its winter slumbers. Tiny white snowdrops in the hedgerows were heralding the start of a new season. A robin, with his red breast fluffed out, warbled away just outside Jennie's bedroom window hoping to attract a partner. Her research was going well. That was the one area of her life that was within her control and with which she was satisfied. Frequently she found herself alternating between hope and despair. Hope that Edward would be in contact soon and despair that he hadn't been.

After a particularly intensive session of writing and rewriting her thesis, a flash of sunshine lured her outside for some fresh air. Her arms swinging freely at her side, she walked across the farmyard to a row of tractors and trailers parked in front of a large garage. They were lined up ready to be washed, disinfected and polished. Giles was connecting a long hosepipe to the cold tap; Ian filling a bucket with boiling water from a kettle, whilst Sophie was brushing the cobwebs off an ancient utility vehicle.

'I have come to help,' said Jennie dressed in an old pair of dungarees. 'Shall I start with the manure spreader?'

Giles nodded. 'Remove all the dried on muck first.'

She looked around for a suitable implement and saw a stiff broom leaning against a wall. She grabbed it and brushed off as much of the loose dirt stuck to the machine as she could. Satisfied that she had dislodged most of it, she squirted some detergent into a bucket of hot water and plonked in a yellow sponge. She wrung it out and then used it to wipe off the remaining particles. Finally she hosed the machine down with cold water to wash any soap suds and final dirt away.

At the end of a busy couple of hours, Ian and Sophie emptied their buckets, packed away their waxes and polishes, and stood back to admire the line of clean vehicles shining in the sunlight. Giles indicated his satisfaction just as a delivery truck trundled up the drive and stopped outside the farmhouse.

'That will be the new fencing,' he said. He walked over to welcome the driver.

Ian collected up the cleaning cloths and Jennie started brushing down a red tractor with the broom. In the corner of her eye she saw several rolls of electric fencing being unloaded and stacked against a wall.

'Brilliant,' said Ian as he bounded over to inspect them. 'I'm going to fence off the wildlife pond to stop the cows drinking from it.' He went back to the garage for his quad bike. After attaching a small trailer to the back, he returned and loaded on a roll of fencing before driving off across the field with Sophie following him on another quad bike.

Jennie finished cleaning the tractor, leaving it spick and span. 'Shall I set up a visitor cleansing station, Dad?' she said as Giles pushed a wheelbarrow full of fencing kit past her.

'Yes, you get on with that whilst I put up an electric fence around the farm buildings,' he said over his shoulder. Since Douglas's return, he had been in a better frame of mind. He had accepted that if he wanted to restock the farm, he was going to have to change his old ways.

After scouting around, Jennie decided that the best place for a decontamination zone would be adjacent to an outdoor tap, located in the small visitor car park not far from the farm entrance. She connected a hosepipe to the tap and humped supplies of detergent on to a table rescued from the store shed. Next she erected signs directing visitors to the parking area and instructing them to clean their vehicles and footwear on arrival. It had been a day well spent, she decided, at the end of the afternoon. Finally the necessary improvements were being made to the farm.

The kitchen smelt of freshly baked cake. Nancy was at her easel busy painting when Jennie entered checking her phone hoping for a text or email from Edward. It had been so long since she had seen him. She knew that he had left Oakfield for a while but when was he coming back?

The back door opened. Giles entered came in with grubby trousers and boots. Just as he was changing into his slippers, his phone, which was sitting on the sideboard, rang. He groaned.

'Nancy, answer that for me will you?' he asked. She sighed and put down her paintbrush.

'Hello, can I help you?' she said. 'Yes, Giles Cliffe is here.' She handed the phone over to her husband. 'It's the police.'

His face fell. 'Hello? Yes, speaking.' As he listened to the caller, his eyes began to dance and his shoulders to relax. 'Thank you. That's brilliant news. Goodbye.' The call over: he put down the phone.

'Well?' said Nancy with a look of enquiry.

'They've completed their investigations and dropped all charges against me. My compensation claim is valid after all.'

A tear ran down Nancy's face as she came forward to hug him. Bramble, sensing the happiness in the room, got off the hearthrug and wagged her tail.

Jennie joined in the group hug. 'I'm so pleased,' she said. This must be Edward's doing.

*

1st March

Her shoes splattered with mud and her hair tangled after being blown by the strong wind outside, Jennie returned from her morning walk with Bramble.

'Coffee?' asked Nancy.

'Please.'

'The money has been paid into my account,' said Giles as he entered the kitchen from his office.

'A cool quarter of a million pounds. I thought that the blasted Animal Health Agency would drag their feet and mess around. But they haven't.'

'It's a new beginning for Green Meadow,' said Nancy her face full of delight.

'You can't restock the farm until you regain TB free status,' said Jennie.

Giles sat at the kitchen table. 'You don't need to remind me. As a matter of fact, Edward is coming today.'

Her heart missed a beat. 'What time?' she asked.

He looked at his watch. 'In half an hour.'

Without hesitating she rushed upstairs. She just had time to wash and blow-dry her hair and change into something more flattering. Satisfied with her appearance, she ran down the drive to the farm gate and waited. The wind had dropped to a strong breeze. When Edward drove in, she greeted him as nonchalantly as she could and directed him to the visitor car parking area. Ian came over to his car and hosed down the wheels and sprayed them with disinfectant.

Looking particularly handsome, Edward got out and smiled warmly at her. She handed him a protective coat and a pair of boots which he put on. 'You've have adopted some biosecurity measures,' he said opening his car's rear door and picking up his IPad from the back seat. 'Let's see if the rest of the farm is up to standard.'

'Dad is waiting for you,' said Ian as Jennie and Edward set off towards the farmyard where they found Giles busy fixing the holes in the wire around the chicken run.

Edward gazed around. 'Good morning Giles,' he said, 'everything looks cleaner and tidier than last time.'

Giles paused in mid-task. 'It should do after all the work we have done,' he said. 'Go with Jennie. Ian and I have jobs to do. Let me know at the end what your verdict is.'

Edward followed Jennie as she crossed the yard to the milking parlour.

'Repairs have been made to all the farm buildings,' she said as they entered. 'Hopefully no wildlife can get in and mix with the cattle.'

Inside the improvements were evident. The floor and all the milking cubicles were as clean as new.

'You know that the fraud charges against Dad have been dropped?' she said as they walked down the middle of the parlour. He nodded.

'You wouldn't have had anything to do with that?' she asked, her eyes on him.

'It's a long story,' he said. He scanned the bottom of the walls for any gaps that badgers could squeeze through. He made some notes on his IPad.

She waited until he had finished. 'Well?'

He cleared his throat. 'When I first started at Oakfield I found that the clinic wasn't as profitable as it should have been. The record system was out of the ark and the accounts were full of discrepancies. After the outbreak of bovine TB

259

at Hightree Farm, a payment from Douglas Sitwell went into Phil's account rather than the clinic's.' He paused to write some more notes.

'What did you do?'

'I challenged him and he told me that Douglas was repaying a loan. He said that it was a one off occurrence and reassured me that the accountants had verified the books and there was nothing for me to worry about.'

'You trusted him?'

'I had no reason not to,' he said staring up at the high windows. 'When we transferred the old system to the new database, I was expecting there to be more issues. Sure enough the sums didn't add up. So I confronted him again. Right, I think we are done here. Where next?'

'The dairy,' said Jennie. 'How did he respond?'

'Defensively at first but then it all came out. The practice had made money for twenty years or so until Phil made some clinical errors which resulted in a couple of law suits. The claims were settled out of court but the business was almost bankrupted,' he said as they went into the dairy where all the cheese making equipment stood ready to be reused.

'He was more careful after that?' said Jennie noting with satisfaction that everything appeared very much in order.

Edward checked for any gaps wildlife could squeeze through. 'There were no more law suits but he started accepting payments for turning a blind eye to the dubious practices some farmers were engaged in.'

'Colluding with them you mean?'

He nodded. 'He admitted making a lot of money.'

Satisfied all was in order, Edward indicated that they should move on. She led the way out into the blustery air and over to the cow sheds.

'I had no choice but to inform the police. That was late summer last year. They came and took away boxes of files. Green Meadow got caught up in their enquiries. It has taken all this time to sort it out – that's bureaucracy for you.' He paused and gazed around the shed making sure that there were no holes in the walls and that the doors fitted tightly.

'It's been a very difficult period here.'

'I know,' he said sympathetically. 'Will you show me round the fields?'

Jennie led the way into the pasture next to the farmyard. The wind had dropped slightly but was still buffeting the trees in the hedgerows.

'You've fitted electric fencing,' he said.

'It's supposed to be badger proof, but they may tunnel underneath. We will see,' she said kicking a large stone. 'So both Phil and Douglas are guilty? Will the police bring charges?'

'Probably not: there isn't enough evidence. The carcases have been incinerated so it's too late for post mortems. There are financial records but unless the Animal Health Agency pursues the case, which doesn't look likely, they are off the hook. Anyway Phil has announced his retirement,' he said as they traversed the field in a southerly direction.

The breeze strengthened again, blowing Jennie's hair across her eyes. She brushed the strands back. 'So are you going to stay at the clinic?' she asked.

Before he could reply, they heard the sound of quad bikes behind them. They turned around and saw Ian and Sophie racing towards them.

Ian brought his bike to a temporary stop. 'How's it going? Did you see that I've fenced off the pond?'

Edward smiled. 'There have been a lot of other improvements as well.'

'Enough?' Ian asked.

Edward nodded. Ian whooped and drove around in a circle but Sophie sat on her bike, stiff with disapproval.

'Dairy farming is not sustainable,' she said, 'I don't know why Ian is so pleased.'

Ian rode back to them and seeing Sophie's face he said, 'I shouldn't have reacted like that. Sorry.'

Sophie remained frozen but then relaxed and gave a half smile. 'I know that you are pleased for Giles,' she said. She put her foot down on the accelerator and sped off across the field with Ian racing behind her.

Edward gazed after them. 'Wasn't that Sophie from Fauna Protection?' he asked.

'Ian moved back home a few weeks ago and brought her with him,' replied Jennie.

'Oh,' he said as they continued along the path, 'hasn't she been charged with any offences?'

'She received a police caution - her finger prints were found on a spray can – but that's all,' said Jennie. 'When she first escaped from Fauna Protection she was terrified that Boyle would find her but now that we have heard that he is in custody she feels safer.'

They walked along the hedgerow looking for gaps. A rabbit hopped across the path in front of them and headed straight down a burrow under the hedge the other side of which was the road to Oakfield. Jennie looked over the hedge and saw the entrance to Beesnest Farm. She remembered her last visit to the Nelsons before Christmas.

'Do you mind if we do a quick detour?' she asked.

Edward agreed. Together they walked through a gate in the hedge, across the road and along the lane to Beesnest Farm. The sight of cows grazing in the adjacent fields made Jennie long for the return of a herd to Green Meadow. Arriving at the farmhouse she knocked on the front door. It was answered by Mr Nelson.

'Jennie. Edward. Come on in,' he said. 'What brings you here today?' He led the way down the hall to the kitchen where Mrs Nelson was wiping the dishes.

'We were just passing and wondered how you are,' said Jennie looking around for any signs of their imminent departure from the farm.

'Well as you can see we're still here,' said Mr Nelson, 'although we were sorely tempted to accept their very generous offer.'

'Especially after the attack by vandals,' added Mrs Nelson.

Her husband agreed. 'But when we considered selling all the animals we realised how much we love this place,' he said. 'We think we can do another five years and by that time one of the children might want to come back and take over.'

'That's good news,' said Jennie. 'I am pleased.'

For another twenty minutes she and Edward stayed and chatted with the Nelsons before continuing their walk back to Green Meadow in companionable silence.

After a while Edward asked, 'How is the development of the vaccine going?'

Jennie started to explain. He listened intently as she told him how she had identified the right protein.

'What about the clinical trials?'

'They will start when we have grown enough protein. You must come along to the laboratory and have a look the next time you are at the university,' she said watching a pair of magpies fly to their perch in a beech tree.

'I will,' he said.

His answer prompted her to say, 'You didn't answer my question about staying at the clinic.'

He stopped walking and turned to face her. 'Jennie, I have a proposal for you.'

Intrigued, she searched his face for clarification but he gave nothing away.

Just then his mobile phone rang breaking the moment. 'Edward Hollyer speaking.' He listened before replying, 'Hold tight, I'll be with you as soon as I can.' He put the phone away. 'Jennie, I'm sorry but I have to go. A cow on a farm the other side of Oakfield needs an emergency caesarean.'

He ran back to the farmhouse. Jennie tried to keep up with him. When he reached his car he shouted, 'Tell your father that Green Meadow has passed its inspection. He can restock as soon as he gets the green light from the Animal Health Agency.' With that out he got into his car and sped off down the road.

*

4th March

A proposal. What sort of proposal? All weekend Jennie had mulled over Edward's words, her heart buzzing with possibilities and her head itching to know the answer. Early on Monday morning, as she cycled along the road to Oakfield, she noticed that the slightly warmer weather was encouraging the hedgerows to burst forth with white blossom and new growth. Arriving in the town, she saw the shopkeepers pulling up their shutters and opening their doors in preparation for the new day's trading.

On arrival in the university's postgraduate office, she logged on to a computer and started writing. Her thesis was nearing completion. Finally she pressed Print and waited while a section of her report spilled out. Holding it, she went along the corridor to Amina's office and knocked on the door. Hearing permission to enter she went in.

Amina swivelled her chair to face her. 'Ah Jennie, have you analysed that data yet?'

She nodded. 'I've established that the older male badgers, particularly those living in areas with lots of badgers, are the demographic most likely to develop bovine TB.'

'Any ideas why?'

'Two reasons,' said Jennie crossing her legs. 'They roam further in search of food and are more liable to fight and squabble with other badgers, deer and cattle - over food. As a result they get injured and pick up infections which weakens their immune systems.'

Amina raised her chin and pondered. 'Any recommendations?'

'Habitats can be restored,' said Jennie, 'so that there is wider variety of food available.'

Amina tapped her biro. 'That can be very expensive.'

'Maybe, but making small changes at a time can be like a snowball rolling down a slope getting larger and faster,' replied Jennie.

Amina gave a half smile. 'Put that into a short report for me would you – our donors like to be kept updated. They are pleased with the work the department is doing and have funded new supplies of animal serum.'

This was welcome news. Jennie turned to leave but Amina asked her for an update on the badger cull.

'The season restarts in May,' said Jennie. 'There are still a lot of diseased badgers out there.'

'When do you think your vaccine will be ready?'

'It depends on when the new supplies of animal serum arrive and how successful the clinical trials are.'

Amina pondered this information. 'Oh by the way, Edward Hollyer, an Associate Fellow is coming this afternoon to discuss your work with you.'

Jennie hid her delight.

In the laboratory after lunch she tried to concentrate on her examination of a blood sample but butterflies kept dancing in her stomach. She was gazing out of the window when Sana walked through holding a handful of pipettes.

'Hi Jennie, how are things?'

'Not too bad, thank you,' answered Jennie. 'Have you played that match with Ibrahim yet?'

Sana's eyes danced. 'We lost the first set but won the second and third.'

'So all's going well?'

Sana's eyes lit up and her mouth curled into a smile. 'We like painting and decorating as well as tennis.'

Jennie smiled and bent back over her microscope until she sensed Edward's arrival in the lab. He came straight over to her with eager eyes.

'You said to call in to look at what you have done so far on the vaccine,' he said. 'Hello Sana.'

'Hi Edward,' said Sana, 'let me know if there is anything particular you need to know.' She disappeared back into the prep room giving Jennie a meaningful look as she went.

Jennie's cheeks turned a delicate shade of pink.

'It's over here,' she said standing up. She led him to a whirring machine that was analysing the cell cultures. She pressed a few buttons and the control panel flashed up some figures.

'It's working continuously and the results go automatically into a spreadsheet,' she said as she opened the front of the machine and slid out a tray of Petri dishes.

'Does the vaccine provoke an immune response?' he asked.

She took the lid off one of the shallow glass dishes and slipped it under the microscope.

'You can see the antibodies clearly,' she said.

He peered down the lens for several minutes, then straightened and grinned.

'You are right.' He hesitated. 'Jennie, you know I have something to ask you?'

She wondered what he was going to say. He looked out of the window in the direction of the veterinary surgery. 'I have plans to expand the clinic's lab and to open a factory in the business park behind.'

She fell silent, absorbing this news. 'What are you going to manufacture?'

'Animal vaccines,' he said. 'Jennie, what would you say if we went into business together? We could make bovine TB vaccines.'

'Wow,' she said quite taken aback. 'I wasn't expecting you to say that.'

'Meet me at the clinic later on and we can talk some more,' he said. He left and Sana came over to her.

'What did Edward want?'

Jennie leant back against the bench. 'He is developing an animal vaccine business.'

'Oh,' said Sana immediately understanding the situation, 'and he wants to team up with you?'

Jennie nodded. 'On a purely professional basis of course.'

Sana laughed, 'Oh come off it Jennie, don't you know that Edward is mad about you? I don't know why it is taking you both so long to get it together!'

Jennie grimaced. 'He can't be – he just keeps running away.'

'Just give him time – like you do with those badgers – you are so patient waiting for them to appear – but in the end they always reward and surprise you.'

Jennie sighed. Sometimes when she caught Edward looking at her in a certain way she thought that he had feelings for her. She rued the day she had turned down his invitation to go on a date with him. What had she been thinking? It had been loyalty to David, that was what it had been. And what had David turned out to be? Just a fleeting moment in her life. She had convinced herself that she was in love with him but really it had only been a relationship of convenience. Thank goodness she hadn't gone travelling with him. If she had, it would have been a disaster.

Later Jennie cycled back into Oakfield. School children just released from their lessons were blocking the pavements waiting for buses or walking home their bags on their backs. The veterinary clinic's reception was closed in the lull before evening surgery. Inside she could see Alpa sitting in front of her new computer. She rang the bell and Alpa opened the door.

'Jennie, good to see you. Edward said that you were coming.'

Jennie stepped inside and waited for a few minutes. The door from the consulting rooms opened and Lola came through wagging her tail followed by Edward.

'She looks so much better now,' said Jennie stroking her ears.

'A good diet and plenty of exercise sorted her out,' said Edward. He led her out of the reception area and along the long corridor to the clinic's laboratory.

He opened the door. 'Phil has sold me the clinic - that's why I was away – arranging the finances.'

Jennie went into the laboratory and looked around. It was smaller than the university's and not so extensively equipped but it was perfectly adequate for its intended purpose.

'Later on if the business is successful, we can expand or move to larger premises.'

'It is bigger than I was expecting, actually,' she said. 'And the factory?'

'Let me show you.'

She followed him out of the lab and down the corridor to the back door. A narrow path led to a metal gate. He unlocked it and they walked into the modern business park.

'Conveniently this unit came up for rent and I snapped it up,' he said. He pointed to a large single storey rectangular building. 'It will be kitted out with the manufacturing capability to make animal vaccines in large quantities. The glass vials will be filled, labelled and packed here as well, before distribution in refrigerated lorries.'

Jennie was impressed. 'What if the virus mutates into variants?'

'I am planning to have the platform technology which will enable us to change the components of the vaccine whenever necessary,' he answered. He led the way around the outside of the building.

'My prototype is almost ready to be tested in the field,' she said. 'I plan to start with the vaccination of the healthy badgers with no bovine TB antibodies.'

'Who's going to help you?'

'Sana usually does, but if you are volunteering?'

There was no time for an answer as a voice behind them cried out. They looked round and saw one of the veterinary nurses running towards them waving her hand frantically.

'Edward, can you come? There's an emergency. A badly injured dog has just been brought in.'

Without hesitation he ran back into the clinic. Jennie's eyes followed him. She retraced her steps back out to the street. A gust of wind hit her. She dug her hands into her coat pocket for the key to her cycle lock. Her feet hit the pedals, her mind racing.

*

6th March

Dusk was approaching when Edward's car drew up outside Green Meadow Farm. He got out and smiled warmly at Jennie who was standing in front of the farmhouse. She returned his smile hiding how awkward she actually felt. There was still so much unresolved between them.

His easy banter soon put her at ease. Her rucksack on her back, she led the way along the public footpath across the fields towards Bramley Brook. Overhead the thick clouds darkened and thunder cracked, frightening the birds off the tree tops.

As daylight faded even further, their torches automatically came on. They turned down the ancient track towards the old oak tree. Occasionally Jennie stumbled over a rock but Edward's hand shot out to steady her.

After a while, she said, 'We are here.' She shone a light onto the ground at some large holes surrounded by patches of bare brown earth.

'So this is your secret sett?' he said. 'You told me that there were no badgers left in Liltford.'

In the dark he couldn't see her face redden with embarrassment. She vowed never to lie to him. He would only catch her out. She took off her rucksack. While he held the torches, she sprinkled a jar of peanuts liberally around.

'Let's climb up onto the tree platform,' she said.

Squeezed together, there was just enough room for both of them. He sat down and stretched out his legs. She could smell his aftershave. It was hard to concentrate with him so near. She took out her tranquiliser gun and put on her night vision goggles. They waited in silence. It started to drizzle.

Thirty minutes later, first Bullitt, then Pocahontas and three younger badgers appeared and beetled around in the soil looking for their supper.

Jennie gasped with excitement and pointed at one of the badger cubs as it gobbled down a common worm. 'Look,' she whispered. 'It's Survivor. She has made her way back home.'

Edward smiled and shared her joy. Jennie raised her gun at them, looked through the thermal sight and fired the tranquiliser darts one by one. The badgers slumped to the ground. She clambered down, switched on her torch and examined their prone bodies. From her rucksack, she lifted out five vaccine kits and gave two of them to Edward. It only took a few seconds to inject the vaccine into the badgers' shoulders. The used syringes and needles were stashed securely away.

'Right that's done,' she said with a look of relief on her face. 'We have to wait for fifteen minutes to make sure there are no adverse effects.'

They climbed back up into the tree. An owl tooted, the darkness deepened and the raindrops grew larger but soon the badgers were back on their feet. Jennie waited until they had wandered off into the undergrowth before descending.

In a minute Edward was at her side. He hugged her. 'You are so clever,' he said.

At that moment the heavens opened and the rain started to pour.

'Come on,' said Jennie urgently, 'let's get back.'

*

8th March

Jennie leapt down the stairs to the kitchen for breakfast. Her father was sitting at the table eating a plate of bacon and eggs. She filled the kettle and switched it on. The pips on the radio heralded the seven o'clock news. The headlines were read. One particular story captured Jennie's attention. She stood still and listened carefully.

'In England, the badger cull has been suspended with immediate effect,' read the broadcaster.

'The animal health minister made the announcement yesterday in the House of Commons. She said that the decision had been taken on the basis of recent findings from the Independent Scientific Group. They found that killing badgers has led to an increase in the disease rather than the hoped for decrease. Government scientists are instead recommending the use of animal vaccines.'

Giles huffed. 'So the cull hasn't worked?'

'It's those super spreader badgers,' replied Jennie. Her phone rang. It was Joe Friend.

'There's a team meeting tonight. Can you and Giles come?'

Jennie regarded her father. He nodded.

'We'll be there,' she said.

Later, Giles drove himself and Jennie to the shooting school. The training room was set out as usual with rows of wooden chairs facing the front. At the door Joe gave them a warm welcome and over his shoulder Jennie noticed Tony sitting in the front row. It was the first time that she had seen him since the Boxing Day Hunt. Memories of him, lying unconscious on the frozen ground, came flooding back. Although thinner and paler than before, he appeared fully recovered. At his side was a slim and attractive Freya. She was regarding him with a caring expression.

'Hi,' said Jennie as she took a seat behind them. They turned around and exchanged a few words.

A dishevelled Edward rushed in. 'Sorry I'm late,' he said, 'another emergency.'

Joe started to speak. 'Over the last few months, together we have been fighting bovine TB which has wreaked havoc in the countryside. As you have probably heard today, the government has bowed to public pressure and has suspended the cull – nationally, not just in the West Country.'

'Fools,' said Giles.

'But culling is a hit and miss method,' protested Freya. 'We had so many wasted evenings.'

Joe grimaced. 'I warned you right at the start that badgers could be very elusive.'

'Perhaps less humane methods would have been better,' said Ibrahim. 'I know that in some countries they use dogs or poison.'

'We could never do that in the UK,' said Joe. 'We need a vaccine and soon.'

Jennie's lips remained firmly closed. Edward shot her an encouraging glance but she resisted the temptation to disclose her work on the vaccine.

Joe continued. 'Anyway I would like to thank you all for the professionalism you displayed throughout the cull sometimes in the face of considerable opposition.' A ripple of applause broke out. 'Finally as we are winding up our operations, can you return any equipment you have borrowed and I hope you can join me now for some refreshments.' He indicated the bowls of crisps and nuts, and the bottles of Coca-Cola and wine laid out on a table at the side of the room. Everyone stood up and stretched their legs.

Joe dispensed the drinks and a lively chatter broke out. Jennie accepted a glass of white wine from him. She was standing talking to her father and Edward, when Ibrahim came over to them.

'You know you asked me to find out who the clients of Khan Solicitors were? The ones making offers on the farms?' he asked loudly. Jennie nodded. 'Well, after Tony was seriously injured, I quizzed my uncle. He told me that the company was called Freecommon Landmanagement.'

Tony overheard this remark. Interested in the conversation, he and Freya came over. 'Did I hear you mention Freecommon Landmanagement?' he said. 'My parents had an offer from them to buy Beddis Grange. They refused it, of course.'

Ibrahim scowled. 'I should have asked my uncle earlier.'

'I wonder who owns Freecommon Landmanagement,' said Jennie. She put down her glass and retrieved her phone from her bag. She googled Companies House and typed the company name into their search engine.

'Wow,' she said a few seconds later. 'They have a Bristol address and one of their current directors is none other than Mr Jeremy Boyle.'

Tony winced. 'Let me get this right,' he said. 'Boyle is masquerading as an animal activist but is actually a capitalist.'

Edward frowned. 'I wish I had known that Boyle owns Freecommon Landmanagement.'

'But why did he want to buy up land? Surely not to farm?' asked Giles with a puzzled look.

Edward replied. 'So that he could pretend to be protecting the wildlife. They sold square metres of land to gullible members of the public,' he said. 'Purchasers received a certificate saying that they were freeholders and were conserving the land forever. I know because I paid £20 for two square metres of the West Country.'

'Was it genuine?' asked Freya.

Ibrahim scoffed. 'Of course not - it was an elaborate scam,' he said. 'Edward asked me to check out the small print for him. '

'Boyle was keeping the land for himself?' said Jennie. 'A form of power and land grab?'

'I suspect he wanted to become one of the landed gentry,' said Tony.

'Most probably,' said Edward.

'I had feeling that he was faking his love of animals,' said Jennie. 'Sophie came to realise that as well.'

'He had no compunction about killing poor Gladiator,' said Freya. She saw Tony's eyes fill with sadness and she squeezed his hand.

Jennie looked thoughtful. Pieces of the jigsaw were beginning to fit into place. She remembered that on the day of the hunt Boyle had intimated that he had met Tony before.

'How long have you known Boyle?' she asked him.

Tony hesitated before answering. 'We met at uni. In our fresher year he looked and spoke like an outsider. He was full of get-rich-quick stories. He told us that the wealthiest man in his south London neighbourhood was the pastor of an evangelical church. Apparently he conned his congregation into pinning ten and twenty pound notes onto his vestment at Sunday mass. He spent the money on fast cars and visiting the Caribbean twice a year.'

Freya gasped. 'That's daylight robbery.'

Tony continued. 'Another story he told us was about the owner of a donkey sanctuary earning a fortune by raking in small donations every month from thousands of old ladies.'

'Maybe he realised that he could exploit people's fondness for animals,' said Jennie.

Tony nodded. 'He definitely knew how to make people believe him. In our final year, our tutor Dr Lowry gave us the task of running a mini enterprise.'

Jennie's ears pricked up. Dr Lowry? Was it possible that he was now a Professor Lowry?

'Boyle and I were in the same team,' continued Tony. 'We set up a subscription service. In return for a small sum each week our subscribers paid us to do local conservation work such as planting trees. We targeted people who were concerned about the state of the planet but were too busy to do anything about it themselves.'

Edward laughed. 'So he fleeced the affluent guilty who wanted to offset their carbon emissions?'

Tony smiled. 'Right from the start, the money just rolled in. But Boyle got too greedy and lazy. He raised the subscriptions and stopped doing the hard graft. Money went missing. I suspected him. When I confronted him he turned nasty and punched me. Hard.'

'The bastard,' said Giles.

'He should have been charged with common assault and theft, but Dr Lowry just forced him off the course. I never saw him again until that day in the pub,' said Tony.

'By then he had reincarnated himself as the leader of Fauna Protection,' said Jennie drily.

'But why would he set up a cult?' said Ibrahim.

'It must have been very lucrative. Under the guise of animal activism he was actually enriching himself,' said Edward.

'It was pure greed,' said Tony. 'He always wanted to be filthy rich. He was a real social climber.'

'But to go to the lengths of trying to kill you,' said Freya. 'That is wicked.'

'What's happened to him?' asked Giles.

Tony's expression changed to one of contempt. 'He's in custody charged with attempted murder and causing the death of an animal, but no date has been set for his trial.'

'He should be charged with fraud, embezzlement and theft as well,' said Ibrahim with a look of disgust.

'He's such a bastard,' said Tony. 'I've never trusted him.'

'Let's hope he is locked up for a very long time,' said Edward emphatically. A sentiment shared by everyone present.

*

21st March

The Spring Equinox brought a positive change to the weather and a feeling of anticipation to Green Meadow Farm. The switch to longer days, a stronger sun and more frequent showers resulted in the grass growing at an accelerated rate. Yellow celandine pushed through bare damp soil bringing welcome splashes of colour to the hedgerows.

Jennie rose early. She called to Bramble who came running. Outside Giles and Ian were checking the silage stored under plastic that they had made the previous year.

'What's it like, Dad?'

'Just fine,' Giles replied.

Sophie appeared from the back of a large shed.

'May I join you?'

Jennie nodded and they set off across the fields.

'Today's the day.'

'Not before time,' said Jennie looking at her. Gone was the frightened young woman. In her place was someone radiating confidence and contentment.

'Do you miss your former life?' asked Jennie as they walked past the caravan site.

'Fauna Protection gave me a structure, a vocation and a family.'

'Like the Armed Forces.'

Sophie laughed. 'Uniform and discipline were the order of the day but I'm still an animal activist. I always will be.'

'Me too,' said Jennie, 'except that I prefer the research route. What do you think will happen to Fauna Protection now?'

277

'There are some committed people involved. They just need the right leadership.'

'Why not you?

Sophie hesitated. 'I've been thinking about that,' she admitted. 'It all depends on Ian.'

'He would be supportive whatever you do.'

'We want to farm as well. Fauna Protection wouldn't be a full time thing.'

'New beginnings?'

'When's your viva?'

'Tomorrow.'

'And Edward?'

'I haven't seen him for a while.'

'You know that he likes you?'

Jennie averted her gaze and changed the subject. They tramped along in companionable silence and then turned back to the farm. Douglas Sitwell drove in as they arrived. Ian rushed to hose down his car wheels and to hand him a protective coat and boots to change into. Horns tooted and three lorries rolled up the drive. Ian directed them to the parking area and made them comply with all the biosecurity measures.

Giles exchanged words with the drivers. Nancy came out to watch. In turn, the back of each lorry was lowered. One by one the black and white cows stumbled out and made their way across the yard to the field beyond. As their hoofs hit the grass and their nostrils smelt the sweet country air, they ran faster and faster and started to dance, kicking up their heels and tossing their heads with delight. A bright smile spread over Giles's face and he stood up straighter. His new herd had arrived.

'I'll be able to make cheese again,' said Nancy.

Jennie leant on the fence watching the cows explore their new home. 'But your paintings are selling so well, Mum.'

'They are just a side-line,' replied Nancy. 'Cheese is my real passion.'

Giles pointed to a handsome black and white cow with long eyelashes who was leading the way. 'That's the new Zoe Mudmaker over there,' he said.

'I'm returning to Australia,' said Douglas to them all.

'The outback?' said Giles.

'I fancy trying my hand at cattle ranching.'

'Microsoft is using cattle grazing to offset their carbon footprint,' said Jennie.

'What's happening to Hightree?' said Ian curiously.

'My mother and the cat are going to Minehead to live with my aunt. So I am going to let the farm.'

'Really?' said Ian. 'Sophie and I are looking for a farm to rent.'

'Aren't you still at school?' said Douglas.

Ian was affronted. 'I graduated from agricultural college last year.'

'Are you interested in dairy?' asked Douglas.

Sophie scoffed. 'A cow kicked him when he was about seven years old. Cows can sense when someone isn't confident around them – they are intelligent beings.'

Ian looked embarrassed. 'We are thinking about horticulture – growing vegetables or salad crops.'

'What about a mushroom farm?' said Jennie, 'they can be very profitable.'

Nancy laughed but Sophie gave Ian a thoughtful look.

Douglas turned to leave. 'Come with me now to Hightree,' he said.

Ian and Sophie beamed at each other and without hesitating followed him to his car.

'Remember to keep up the biosecurity won't you?' said Douglas over his shoulder.

'You don't need to tell me that,' said Giles. 'I never want to have bovine TB hit my animals again.'

*

25th March

Jennie put on the black suit and white blouse that she had ironed the night before. She brushed her hair and applied her makeup lightly. Satisfied that she looked smart and professional she went downstairs, had tea and toast before borrowing her father's car to drive into the university.

At nine thirty she knocked on Dr Amina Ahmed's door and waited. When summoned she entered. The office had been rearranged. A large conference table stood in the middle of the room with three chairs at one end, and a solitary one at the other. Three people were helping themselves to coffee and biscuits. Jennie recognised the university's internal examiner Dr Roberts, who was tall with piercing eyes. Dr Bates, the external examiner, was also there alongside Amina attending in her capacity as Jennie's PhD supervisor. This was the panel in front of which she was going to have to defend her thesis.

'Welcome, Jennic, would you like a coffee?' asked Amina in a friendly tone.

'Just water, thank you,' Jennie replied, trying to radiate confidence.

Dr Bates pulled out the chair at the head of the table. 'Right, let's make a start.'

Amina sat on his right hand side and Dr Roberts on his left. Jennie took the seat facing them. She put her copy of her thesis down in front of her.

'Well Jennie you know that this viva is to ascertain that you wrote your PhD?' said Dr Bates.

She nodded.

'We will question you and debate your research, so relax and enjoy the experience,' he said.

280

She took a deep breath. In her head she repeated her mantra of stay cool, calm and collected. She had lived and breathed this PhD for three years. Now was her chance to showcase it.

'I will kick off and ask if you could explain what original contribution your thesis has made to this field of study,' said Dr Roberts. He pushed his glasses back up the ridge of his nose.

Jennie smiled. 'When I started out there was no reliable antibody test to detect if badgers had acquired bovine TB or an effective badger vaccine. I have been able to develop both.'

'You say effective, but what evidence do you have?' asked Dr Bates.

'The results of a clinical field trial,' she said, 'see Table 101.'

He flicked through his copy of her manuscript which was three hundred pages long, bound, with an abstract at the beginning and a conclusion at the end. All the tables, graphs, diagrams and pictures were titled and referenced throughout the work. Checked many times for typos and clarity, Jennie was very proud of it.

Amina reassured the other two examiners. 'I have peer reviewed the results.'

'Ah yes Dr Ahmed, as Miss Cliffe's PhD supervisor, I believe that you deserve a lot of the credit,' said Dr Bates.

Amina glowed with pleasure. 'This research started out fairly run of the mill, but I am pleased to say that some genuine breakthroughs with commercial possibilities have been achieved,' she said.

'Miss Cliffe, can you explain the main research question that you were trying to address?' said Dr Roberts.

'I really wanted to find a way for the local badger population to live sustainably alongside dairy farmers. My family's farm and livelihood have been threatened by bovine TB and I wanted to establish the reasons why the disease was endemic,' she replied.

'The main strengths and the weaknesses are?'

Jennie was expecting this question. She didn't want to be too arrogant. The advice she had read emphasized being humble.

'My research involved first hand observations in the field not just in the laboratory.'

'And the weaknesses?

'My sample size. This work needs to be continued on a wider scale. In more locations and with more badgers. Only then will the true efficacy of the tests and the vaccine be determined.'

'So how will you follow up this project?' said Dr Bates.

'I have been offered an opportunity in the private sector to develop my work on the vaccine.'

'Well good luck with that, Miss Cliffe. Are there any questions you would like to ask us?' said Dr Roberts.

'I would just like to thank Dr Ahmed for all her support that she has shown me throughout this,' said Jennie. She took a sip of water.

'Right, thank you,' said Dr Bates. 'We will now confer. You will know our decision by the end of the day.'

Jennie remembered to smile. She put her manuscript back into her bag and left the room. After pausing to turn her phone on, she made her way to the laboratory. She heard a beep.

It was a text from Edward.

Are you free tonight?8pm? Dinner at my place?

She stared at the screen. Edward was asking her on a date. After all his procrastinations.

Her fingers shook as she typed her reply.

Yes I will be there

She opened the door to the lab. Seeing her suit, Sana said, 'You've had your viva?'

'Have you time for a coffee?'

Sana nodded.

The ground floor canteen was busy with staff and postgraduates sitting at the tables laughing, talking, drinking and eating piles of chips doused with tomato sauce. Jennie and Sana holding their cappuccinos found a spare table at the far end and sat down.

'Tell me about it,' said Sana stirring some sugar in.

'I'm glad it's all over.'

'Did they suggest any corrections?'

'None.'

'That's a good sign.'

Jennie relaxed and gazed around. Sitting at an adjacent table was someone she knew.

'Don't look now, but isn't that Prof Lowry?' she whispered to Sana, who immediately turned around and stared.

'You're right,' she said. 'Apparently his suspension is over.'

'He was at Warwick Uni the same time as Jeremy Boyle.'

'And with Tony McKensie. Ibrahim told me that Lowry and Boyle had a bust up over a woman they both fancied. The irony was that the girl then dated Tony,' said Sana.

'Wow,' said Jennie. 'That would explain a lot. Boyle can hold a grudge for England.'

'Rumour has it that Lowry lost some of Oakfield Uni's money in a scheme – something to do with land investment – but the Governors have reinstated him,' said Sana.

'So the department's funding was cut because of a scam masterminded by Boyle,' said Jennie with a laugh.

'That's a leap of the imagination! I daresay we will never know what actually happened. The governors are very good at hushing things up,' said Sana.

'There's just one final mystery that I want to know the answer to.'

Sana widened her eyes.

'Who was the department's anonymous donor?' said Jennie. She stood up and headed for the exit. As she climbed the stairs, her phone pinged again. It was a text from Amina.

Can you pop into my office?

Reaching the first floor, Jennie ran down the long corridor and burst through Amina's open door. Amina was looking out of the window but hearing Jennie enter she turned round and smiled.

'Ah, Jennie good news. Congratulations are in order. The panel was unanimous that you have passed your viva. Well done, you are now Dr Cliffe.'

'Thank you,' said Jennie her face flushed with relief and joy. 'It's been a real journey.'

The phone on Amina's desk rang.

'Dr Ahmed speaking,' she said. 'Yes that's right. One of my postgraduate students has confirmed that the vaccine is in development.' She paused and listened. 'A report? Certainly. When? Next week. Fine. Goodbye.'

Amina put the phone back on the hook. 'That was the Animal Health Agency. They would like an update on the vaccine.'

Jennie was surprised but replied, 'Of course.'

'You might be wondering why they have requested one? Well they have been the anonymous donor of our department. In return for access to our research,' said Amina.

Jennie laughed. 'Is that why you asked me to help train the badger cullers and why you needed regular updates?'

'They wanted their involvement to be confidential to eliminate any bias in your research.'

'At one point I suspected that Fauna Protection was the donor.'

'They offered but Prof Lowry vetoed them. I don't know why,' said Amina.

Jennie looked thoughtful. 'I know,' she said.

Amina refrained from probing. Instead she asked what Jennie had learnt from her studies.

'So much - not just about badgers - but about love, life and death,' she replied.

Amina smiled. 'You know that your dissertation is good enough to win the Luminosity Prize, don't you?'

Jennie nodded. It was satisfying to have Amina's endorsement. 'I will submit it tomorrow,' she said, her hand reaching for the door handle. But she didn't need to win the prize after all. She had dreamt of working for an international wildlife conservation organisation. Instead she had found her dream job in a totally unexpected place – working with Edward on animal vaccines.

In the corridor outside she unexpectedly bumped into David. He was dressed in a pair of white trousers and a cream jumper and was holding a large cardboard box.

'David, what on earth are you doing here?' she exclaimed.

'I'm clearing out my locker,' he said.

'You're not coming back then?'

'Academia was never really my cup of tea,' he said. 'I've caught the exploring bug so I'm off to Asia.'

'With the red haired girl?' asked Jennie. 'Did you meet her on the overnight bus to Buenos Aires by any chance?'

He laughed. 'How did you guess? I was cross with you when you wouldn't fly out to join me for a holiday in Rio.'

Jennie shuffled her feet. It was a fair accusation. She knew that she could have dropped everything and gone. 'I was too busy,' she said.

David smiled softly. 'I know. What are your plans?'

'I have a job lined up.'

'No time for travel then?'

She shook her head. 'Not at the moment but maybe one day.'

'Goodbye Jennie. All the best,' he said continuing on his way.

As her eyes followed him to the lift it occurred to her that he had always been a nomad and probably always would be. She sighed, stood up straight and gazed ahead. Without looking back she made her way out of the building, across the courtyard to the gate.

The taxi whisked her to Oakfield Veterinary Clinic in record time. It was dark when she arrived. The last customer was leaving holding a pet carrier in one hand and the lead of a mischievous looking terrier in the other. The light in reception had been dimmed but Alpa was still at her computer. Seeing Jennie at the door she came over and opened it. After a brief exchange of pleasantries Jennie bounded up the stairs. She met Edward coming down. His handsome face, framed by a mane of brown hair, met her. He was beaming with delight. She followed him up to his rooms on the top floor.

'So this is where you live,' she said as he showed her into the open plan living room which was dominated by a black leather sofa and a large television. Music was playing softly in the background. She gazed up at the high ceiling and at the modern artwork adorning the walls.

He took her coat. His touch made her tingle with electricity and excitement. A wave of well-being like being surrounded by nature welled up inside her.

'How did your viva go?' he asked.

'I passed,' she said with undisguised delight.

He held her hands and pulled her gently towards him.

'Congratulations, Dr Cliffe,' he said. His lips met hers and they kissed. Long and hard. Her heart fluttered.

'Jennie,' he whispered. 'You're lovely. I love you.'

'I love you too,' she said.

He pulled her onto the sofa, smothered her with kisses and caressed her body. After a considerable amount of time, to Jennie's embarrassment her stomach rumbled.

'Hungry?' he asked with a smile.

'I'm starving,' she replied.

She helped him fry steaks and toss the salad. He poured the wine and they ate at the small dining room table in candlelight.

'So out of interest when did you start to love me?' he asked.

Her face softened as sweet memories came to mind.

'I fell in love with you on the first day I met you at Oakfield Clinic – only I didn't realise it at the time,' she said.

He looked directly into her eyes. 'Jennie, can you forgive me? It has taken me so long to decide everything – I just didn't want to make another mistake – not after being taken in by Freya. I was afraid that all Oakfield girls were the same and that if she had misled me then so would you.'

She laughed. 'You mean how she bought a puppy just to be able to see you, and then when Tony came along with a faster car and bigger house, she dumped you?'

He nodded. 'She made all the running. She initiated all our encounters. I succumbed to her flattery. Looking back, with the benefit of hindsight, I realise that her admiration for me and her ingratiating behaviour was the driving force and without her persistence our relationship would never have developed so far or so fast. I have kicked myself so many times for being so foolish. As a result it took me too long to realise that you were the essential component in my life.'

'But it's all worked out for the best. We're together now and Freya and Tony are well suited to each other.'

'And you turned me down,' he said with a slight rebuke in his voice.

She blushed. 'I was being loyal to David. I thought I loved him but as time went on I realised that I didn't miss him at all.'

'You agreed to meet him when he returned.'

'I can't explain why.'

His eyes danced with merriment at her discomfort. 'And then there was Tony?'

'That happened because you were dating Freya,' she protested reaching for her glass of wine.

He had the grace to acknowledge that he had been at fault.

'And the vaccine business? Will you be coming to work with me?' he said reaching across the table and taking her hand.

'Exactly how is it all going to be financed?'

'My father's rich. He has agreed to be the major investor. He's pleased that I'm starting a business.'

'Oh – so that's why you were in London.'

'He knows that there is money to be made in animal vaccines,' he said. He paused. 'So? What about it?'

'Are you only offering me a job?' she teased.

He smiled tenderly. 'Of course not. This is going to be a personal and a professional partnership.'

The soundtrack changed to 'When I ruled the world' by Coldplay. He leant across the table and kissed her again. The candle blew out and they were left in the dark. Edward lit another match and the candle flickered back into life. Jennie now had all the light she needed.

THE END

Acknowledgments

The biggest thanks go to my husband who read the manuscript as it progressed and guided me on my way. Also I appreciate the support and guidance given by Avril Douglas and her late husband Andrew Douglas.

I could not have written this book without the help provided by Jericho Writers. The wonderful Harry Bingham has taught me the basics of creative writing and self-publishing during hours of webinars and tutorials. My super book cover designer Patrick Knowles helped me with sage comments.

Visit www.lizpaice.com for information on my forthcoming publications and to sign up for your free book which follows what Sophie and Ian did next.

About the Author

Liz Paice is a retired teacher living in London with her husband. She was born in Malta, the daughter of an RAF officer. As a child she lived in many places including Cyprus, South Wales and various parts of England. She studied Geography at University College London followed by teacher training at Jesus College Oxford.

Five words that sum up her personality are: capable, organised, thorough, optimistic and strong. She is passionate about the natural world and the environment including landscapes, fauna and fauna, and ecosystems. Her hobbies and pastimes include reading, travelling, the theatre and cinema, gardening, and writing. She is learning Spanish.

Liz's novels blend romance and adventure with an environmental theme. In her novel *The Luminosity Prize* she tackles the divisive issue of badger culling in the UK.